CRACKHEAD II

ALSO BY LISA LENNOX

Crackhead

Played

CRACKHEAD II

A Novel

LISA LENNOX

ATRIA PAPERBACK

New York • London • Toronto • Sydney • New Delhi

ATRIA PAPERBACK

A Division of Simon & Schuster, Inc.
1230 Avenue of the Americas
New York, NY 10020

First Atria Paperback edition March 2012

ATRIA PAPERBACK and colophon are trademarks of Simon & Schuster, Inc.

For information about special discounts for bulk purchases,
please contact Simon & Schuster Special Sales at 1-866-506-1949
or business@simonandschuster.com.

The Simon & Schuster Speakers Bureau can bring authors
to your live event. For more information or to book an event,
contact the Simon & Schuster Speakers Bureau at 1-866-248-3049
or visit our website at www.simonspeakers.com.

Manufactured in the United States of America

10   9   8   7   6   5   4   3   2

Library of Congress Cataloging-in-Publication Data
Lennox, Lisa.
    Crackhead II : a novel / Lisa Lennox. — 1st Atria Books trade paperback ed.
        p.   cm.
1. African American women—Fiction.   2. Drug addicts—Fiction.   3. Young
women—Fiction.   4. Bronx (New York, NY)—Fiction.   5. Urban fiction.
I. Title.   II. Title: Crackhead two.   III. Title: Crackhead 2.
PS3612.E5496C73 2012
813'.6—dc23   2011035096

ISBN: 978-1-4516-6175-0
ISBN: 978-1-4516-6176-7 (ebook)

This book is dedicated to all of the people who battled their cocaine addiction and won.

You are not responsible for other people's actions. You can only change yourself but in order to do so, the change must start with you.

CRACKHEAD II

PROLOGUE

Boston University, Fall 1989

MARK MY WORDS, without knowledge you're all bound for the welfare line or the penitentiary," said Mr. Giencanna, the instructor for the Introduction to Philosophy class. Nobody was trying to hear him and he proceeded with the daily roll call.

"Mr. Jason Abbott?" Mr. Giencanna called out, fixing his glasses on his hawklike nose.

"Here," a young man in the rear spoke up.

"Casey Bernard?"

"Right here," said another male's voice.

"Miss Natalie Farmer?"

This time there was no reply.

"Natalie Farmer?" he repeated.

A young man wearing a blue and gray varsity jacket nudged Natalie, who was sitting at her desk, dozing off.

"What?" she said sleepily, and with an attitude.

He nodded toward the instructor. "Roll call. That's what."

"I'm here, Mr. Giencanna, sir," Natalie said, wiping around her mouth.

"Stay with us, please, Miss Farmer," Mr. Giencanna said. Al-

1

though he phrased it like a request, Natalie knew by his tone and the piercing look in his eyes that it was, without a doubt, an order.

Mr. Giencanna cleared his throat and continued. "Miss Julacia Johnson?"

Once again, there was no reply. The classroom was silent as everyone looked around to see if there was another student nodding off somewhere. Everyone appeared to be wide awake.

"Perhaps we have another sleeping beauty amongst us," Mr. Giencanna said sarcastically. "Is there a Miss Julacia Johnson present?"

Still there was no reply.

The welfare line or the penitentiary, he thought. No sooner than his eye looked to call the next name, the lecture hall door came flying open.

"Present," Laci huffed, as she rushed into the lecture hall with books in hand. The class fell silent to the remarkable presence before them. There, Laci stood, just as beautiful as ever. Her shiny Shirley Temple curls, full of body, fell across the left side of her forehead, tickling her eyebrow. Her moody brown eyes sparked with a hunger for knowledge.

"Sorry I'm late," Laci said, out of breath as she looked down at her Movado watch, the same one her father had given her for her sixteenth birthday. "But I'm here. I made it!"

"And who are you, sir?" Mr. Giencanna looked past her.

"Ah . . . I'm Din—I mean, Daryl . . . Daryl Highsmith. I'm not on the list, sir; I just got accepted last week."

"Highsmith," Mr. Giencanna repeated, and wrote it down on his student roster.

Laci and Dink sat next to each other and smiled, as the instructor continued to check the class attendance.

Over the next hour and fifty minutes, Laci wrote vigorously, making key notes of Mr. Giencanna's lecture. Dink, on the other hand, sat back in his seat stoically, twirling his pencil in between his thumb and forefinger, which distracted Laci momentarily. She looked over at Dink and admired him in his faded denim jacket and jeans, white T-shirt, and dope man Nikes. The faint smell of Obsession tickled her nostrils. Laci's lingering gaze caught Dink's attention and he met her stare. Dink winked, blew a quick kiss at her, and turned his focus back on Mr. Giencanna. Laci never thought she'd see this day and was amazed.

"Let me ask all of you something," Mr. Giencanna spoke seriously, interrupting Laci's thoughts. He leaned against the podium and adjusted his glasses before speaking again. The class became still; the only sound they heard was the second hand ticking on the clock that hung against the wall. "Everybody has heard the terms good and evil, right?"

"Yes," every student confirmed in unison.

"So, what do you consider good? And better yet, what do you equate with the word 'good'?"

"Angels," a female student called out.

"God," another student chimed in, keeping with the same theological subject.

"Okay, let's keep going." The room became silent as everyone awaited his next question. "What is considered bad, or what do you equate with the word 'evil'?"

"Um . . . the devil?" someone blurted out.

"Just plain evilness," another person shouted, "or when someone does something that's not the norm."

"What's considered the norm?" Mr. Giencanna asked with a smile on his face.

After a few seconds of silence, a girl raised her hand. She sat in the same row as Dink and Laci but because the classroom was so large and filled with students, neither could see exactly where she was. "The norm would be what is socially acceptable. Going back to the question you asked earlier about good, bad, and evil, socially speaking, God and angels are good and the devil and evil are bad."

"Why is that?" Mr. Giencanna asked, now with a mischievous grin on his face.

"Because," she spoke, "how else could you justify the world being created? The Bible says God created heaven and earth. If it weren't for Him, none of us would be here."

Everyone turned to look at the girl while she spoke, then they looked back at the instructor.

"Okay," Mr. Giencanna adjusted his posture, "I'm glad you mentioned this. By a show of hands, how many of you believe there is such a thing as a devil?" Most students raised their hands. "Why is the devil perceived as a bad thing?" he quizzed again.

"Because," the same girl answered sharply, this time with an attitude, "that's just how it is. Haven't you read the Bible? Damn."

Students began to whisper amongst themselves, sensing her attitude.

"Well if you read the Bible," Dink countered out loud, "you would know that the devil was an angel, but did you forget that?"

Students' necks turned and all eyes focused on him.

Taken aback by the comment, the female student tried to look in the direction of the voice that just called her out. "I know that! The devil is in a different category than God and angels," she spat back.

"And why do you say that?" Dink continued, leaning forward to look at the girl. "He was the angel of light and was one of the most beautiful angels in heaven." Laci's eyes grew wide. She'd never thought Dink knew anything about the Bible. "Just like everyday people, he got full of himself and was kicked out of heaven and sent to earth. Then, and only then, did he become 'the devil.'" Dink used his index and middle fingers to mimic quotation marks.

"Well, the devil is still evil," the girl barked angrily and turned her lips up in disgust.

"Why? Is it because you were raised to believe that? What proof do you have? The way you're talking, you're acting like you know the devil firsthand."

Some people laughed.

"Well . . ." she stammered, not knowing what to say next.

"Listen to what you're saying: the devil is evil, but he was an angel, but angels are good. Isn't that antithetical?" Dink continued to challenge.

This time, the whispers became more audible and filled the air.

"What are you doing?" Laci whispered harshly, looking at Dink. Her face was flushed and her eyes darted around the lecture hall. Dink looked at her and then around the class to see what she was trying to tell him with her eyes. She shook her head in disbelief.

Before bringing his focus back to the instructor, Dink saw something that was so noticeable that he was surprised he didn't peep it when he walked inside the classroom. The class was predominantly white. Besides him and the girl he challenged, there were only five black students in the class. He could just imagine what the white students were thinking—a black man challenging God's existence—but that wasn't the case.

"Quiet down now," Mr. Giencanna said in an attempt to calm

the class. "Quiet down." His warden-like expression softened when a smile crept across his face. He was glad that he'd chosen a topic that would generate an emotional discussion that would bring him to the point he was about to make. "Now," he said as he began walking back and forth in front of the podium, "by a show of hands, how many of you have seen either?"

Dink glanced at Laci and wondered what she was thinking at that very moment.

Laci wanted to raise her hand to say that she had seen the devil, but she was confused. Was it the devil himself, or did she witness hell on earth?

"So," Mr. Giencanna walked around to the microphone that was attached to the podium. He leaned forward to speak, but was interrupted.

"Dude, you trippin'," a male voice bellowed, irritated with the questioning. The instructor looked in the direction of the voice. "This ain't no damn religion class. This is Philosophy . . . Philosophy 101 to be exact. You know, an introductory course."

There were a few people who laughed at the remark, but they were also wondering where the lecture was headed.

"What is your name, young man?" the instructor asked.

"T.J.," the young man answered as if he should know. Mr. Giencanna's mouth opened to say something, but Dink spoke first.

"Look, you're right, this is not a religion class, but what he's trying to get you to see is this," Dink sighed heavily. T.J. raised his eyebrow and looked at Dink like he was out of his mind. "Why are we so selective with things we want to see or believe? When he asked the initial question, if we've heard of good or evil, you answered with examples that were religion based, which can be very controversial."

Mr. Giencanna's eyes beamed at Dink's revelation. "As a society," Dink continued, "we tend to believe in things that we've been taught to believe, even if we can't prove their existence, as in religion, or we as a society may have opinions about customs that don't fall within what we consider the norm, but is it necessarily right or wrong? No. Questions of how people live, their ethics, and their logic is philosophy."

Chatter filled the air because Dink now had everyone thinking. Mr. Giencanna was smiling so hard, his face looked strained.

"You know, he has a point," someone confirmed.

"I never looked at it that way," another person admitted.

Again, everyone looked at Dink, this time in a more accepting manner, but they sneered at T.J. because he just got told.

"Dang, T.J., I know you wished you didn't open your mouth, huh?" Simone, the girl next to T.J., said.

The class laughed.

"Excellent answer, Mr. Highsmith!" Mr. Giencanna exclaimed enthusiastically, grinning from ear to ear, but ignoring the other student's comment. "You took the words right out of my mouth." All eyes were back on him except for T.J.'s, who continued to stare at Dink. T.J. was more pissed than embarrassed.

Dink leaned back in his chair waiting to hear what else the teacher had to say. Within seconds, he felt someone staring at him. He looked to his left and saw T.J. leaning back in his chair, mean-mugging him. In the hood, that was a silent threat, so Dink raised his arms outward in a man-to-man challenge.

"Wassup," he mouthed. *I know this punk don't wanna fuck with me,* Dink thought to himself. He didn't want to show the straight-up nigga side of him but if he had to, he'd get 'bout it. Wasn't nothing but a thing.

T.J. turned and looked back at the front of the class. "Yeah, I ain't think so," Dink mumbled under his breath.

He didn't know why T.J. was tripping. Dink was merely trying to explain Mr. Giencanna's reasoning in a way that other
students could understand, and it worked. Dink was used to
schooling people in the streets; however, he had to remember
that he was no longer in the streets. Having never once thought
about higher education, even after scoring a 1440 on his SATs
when he was younger, he knew that if he ever had the opportunity to attend college, he had something to contribute to the
class, but he would have to understand that everyone was there
for the same thing—to learn.

Dink thought momentarily and realized his tone might have
been a little harsh, and that he could have embarrassed T.J. That
was not his intention, so he made a mental note to holla at him
after class.

Dink shook his head, then turned his attention back to the
lecture. What he didn't know was that T.J. wasn't staring at him.
He was looking at Laci.

CHAPTER 1

ALTHOUGH CULTURALLY WHITE in appearance, T.J. was that black man trying to fit in. Black people saw him as a white man trying to be black, and white people felt he was ashamed of the shoes he walked in. Hollering at women proved to be an even bigger issue because T.J. preferred the sistas. They shot his advances down because they felt he was trying to be like that new rapper, Vanilla Ice, who was on the scene. The few that gave him some play thought he was cool until they realized he wasn't about shit—he had issues and was a control freak. White women didn't fuck with him because they figured if they wanted a black guy, they'd go get one, instead of getting with what they saw as a perpetrator.

His father, Thomas James, Sr., had worked as an intern for a very prominent corporate attorney, where he met Sonya Mitchell, who cleaned offices at night. Although he was five years older than she, Thomas James was curious about the seventeen-year-old. After watching her for some weeks and engaging in innocent flirtation, her brown skin and firm body was something that he desperately wanted to experience, at least once in his life. That one time turned into sex on a regular basis. When she became pregnant, Thomas James denied any involvement with her. Apparently he had been engaged all along to a white woman.

T.J. couldn't believe how easy it was for his father to reject him. He felt the sting of his abandonment as he grew older, but even though he was hurt, T.J. never showed his emotions. If his father didn't give a fuck, why should he?

After living comfortably in Philly, Sonya left with her son and bounced around from Jersey to Connecticut to Boston, then to New York for the next eight years until she went back to the place she called home before Thomas James turned her life upside down. In the Boyonton Avenue tenements in Southview, a good kid would certainly fall victim to his environment, but Sonya worked three jobs to ensure that T.J. would have an education that would take him out of the projects.

When T.J. was in middle school, he met Simone. Simone was a chocolate cutie who had a mother and father at home. Although an only child, Simone was a well-rounded good girl. She wasn't spoiled. She was just comfortable and had to work for the luxuries her parents provided her. T.J. and Simone were each other's first . . . first kiss, first time in love, and the first to lose their virginity to one another. When they met T.J., her parents weren't too accepting of him. They tolerated him because Simone said she was in love, but they felt T.J. didn't know what his true identity was and that was something he needed to embrace.

When he moved from Boston, her parents were happy, but T.J. and Simone maintained a long-distance relationship. Boston University was not a coincidence. They were going to be together; but as they spent more time with each other, Simone realized that T.J. wasn't the same person she was in love with before. Something was different about him—and she really didn't like it. Simone had fallen prey to his bomb sex game so they continued to fuck, even during their breakups, but she made it perfectly clear to T.J. that she was fair game for anyone else and it would only be a matter of time before she found that person.

T.J., on the other hand, thought she was joshing and didn't trip off of what she said. Only because she was still breaking him off on a regular basis did he let her believe that someone else could pull her; but if someone came between them, he wasn't going to let her go that easily.

T.J. walked around the Registration Office to scope out the incoming freshman females. He enjoyed the array of women—some fly, some not—but when Laci walked into the office and stood in the line, she was all he could focus on.

For some reason, she looked familiar to him, so he walked up to her and attempted a conversation.

"Good morning, beautiful."

With all the chatter, Laci didn't acknowledge him because she couldn't hear him. He repeated himself and she looked at him.

"I'm sorry, are you talking to me?" she asked, innocently. The registration line was exceptionally long and the office was crowded with what seemed like hundreds of people.

This was the first time Laci had been in a crowd since she left the South Bronx. She looked at the young man in front of her and shyly smiled.

"Do I know you from somewhere?" he asked. "You look awfully familiar." Even after all she had been through during her crack addiction, Laci was still fly. She stood 5′4″ with long black good hair. She was light-skinned because of her mixed heritage and had dark, moody eyes. Laci was thick in all the right places, with a slim waist and B-cup breasts. Her body was bangin' and she had a funky fresh style to match.

"No, I'm sorry," she said politely, shaking her head. *Men and their lines,* she thought.

"Seriously, I know you from somewhere," T.J. continued to pry. "I could never forget your face." He lightly pointed toward her.

"I'm sure if you knew me, you would have remembered," Laci snapped, "and so would I, so please don't step to me with that lame-ass pickup line." She thought he was trying to touch her, but he wasn't.

Laci was surprised at her reaction. The thirty days she spent at rehab had strengthened her as an individual. She had learned to love life again but felt that all people were on some bullshit unless they proved otherwise. The guy who stood before her, she felt, was on a whole 'nother level of bullshit because in her eyes, he was a wannabe and she didn't want to be bothered.

"Now please leave before my man comes." Laci began to feel uncomfortable and hoped Dink would join her soon. He was currently meeting with an advisor.

She turned around and faced the direction of the line again.

"So what? I don't care if you got a man; shit, I got a gal. I was just asking where I knew you from and trying to make conversation," the young man retorted. "I can't stand y'all stuck-up bitches."

"Good," she snapped back. "That means leave then."

Just then, Dink coolly strolled up. "Baby, is there a problem?" He looked at T.J., then back to Laci.

"Nothing I couldn't handle," she told him confidently and planted a nice, healthy kiss on his lips to show anyone else who could have been watching that she was taken.

T.J. didn't like how she played him, but he knew that they would eventually cross paths again. Next time, she'd be the one getting played, and that was a promise.

CHAPTER 2

B Y THE END of this class," Mr. Giencanna spoke, "you may or may not think differently about your religious beliefs, but I guarantee you that by the end of this class," he poked his index finger against the podium, "you will be impartial and look at situations that may arise in everyday life objectively." He emphasized the last word.

"So, are you saying that we don't need to believe in God?" asked the same girl who'd answered the first question. The class looked at the girl, and then at T.J., who sat next to her. He remained silent in a noble attempt to not embarrass himself any further. Dink had had a feeling that question would come up. He was just glad that the girl asked it, rather than T.J. running off at the mouth.

"No, I'm not saying that," Mr. Giencanna confirmed. "Religion is a very controversial subject—one of which we will only touch on in this class. Everyone has his or her own beliefs; however, academically examining religion will make you think. There are many religions—Christianity, Judaism, Islam, and Hinduism, to name a few. Each of these is an ancient established religion with its own unique beliefs and doctrines. Who are we to say what is right and what is wrong? Right now, your answers are very subjective . . . meaning, one-sided. Once you look at the big picture," he raised his arms in the air in a fan-like motion, "you will become more objective and be able to express your objectivity with a valid argument."

Dink smiled and nodded his head. *For a white guy, Mr. G. an ole G,* he thought to himself.

Mr. Giencanna then looked up at the clock and saw that he had thirty seconds left.

"Let me leave you with a quote from one of my favorite philosophers, René Descartes. 'Living without philosophizing is exactly like having one's eyes closed without ever trying to open them; and the pleasure of seeing everything which our sight reveals is in no way comparable to the satisfaction accorded by knowledge of the things which philosophy enables us to discover.' " He stood up and walked in front of the podium. "Class dismissed."

Dink got up out of his seat and flung his large backpack over his shoulder. "Let me get that for you," he told Laci as she stuffed her notebook into her backpack.

As people filed out of the lecture hall, a few students walked up to Dink, welcoming him to Boston University. Some patted him on his back, introduced themselves, then headed to their next class. There were those who ignored him, but there was one who actually stopped to talk.

"Yo man, that was some shit you laid out there," a tall, toffee-colored man said.

Dink observed the man's long, slender frame, clean-shaven face, and short hair that looked like it might have been naturally curly instead of the Jheri curls that most folks were rockin' back in the Bronx. He wore a red and white Adidas sweat suit with matching red and white kicks. He also had a large diamond earring in his left ear, along with a herringbone chain that didn't look like a knockoff. *Dude got a lil' grip,* Dink said to himself.

"Hi," he extended his hand, "I'm Steven, but my friends call me Slim." Dink suppressed a grin. The name "Slim" fit Steven to a tee. He had to stand around 6 feet 8 inches tall and couldn't have weighed more than a buck fifty.

Dink reached out to shake his hand. "Nice to meet you. I'm Daryl, and this is my girl, Laci."

Steven smiled at her and shook her hand.

Just then, a voice bellowed, "Slim...what up, nigga, you comin'?"

Dink, Laci, and Slim looked over at where the voice came from. It was T.J., and he was headed toward them.

T.J. stood about six feet tall and had a nice muscular build, with dark hair that he kept cut close to his head. He had amber-colored hypnotic eyes and shapely lips that he got from his mother's side of the family. He got his coloring, strong-angled jawline, and keen nose from his father's side. T.J. was exceptionally handsome. He dressed in the latest trendy clothing but still stuck out like a sore thumb. He was standing firm, as if he had a point to prove. T.J. wasn't going to back down from Dink.

"Aye, yo," Dink called out to T.J. He wrestled with what he was about to do next. Daryl Highsmith wasn't one to apologize, especially when he'd done nothing wrong, but he realized that he had to be the bigger man. "Hey, about what happened earlier," he looked at T.J. and stood in front of him, "I didn't mean to embarrass you. I was just—"

"Embarrass me?" T.J. interrupted in a shocked tone, looking Dink up and down. "If that's all you got, shit...you need to go back where you came from, learn the shit again, then come at me."

"What did you say?" Dink questioned.

Laci looked at Dink and noticed that he instinctively clenched his fists and tightened his jaw. She knew that even approaching T.J. was a big step for him, so she quickly grabbed his hand and kissed it.

From his observation, Dink saw that at twenty-two years old, he was probably the oldest student in class. Although he was trying to rap to T.J. man to man, he'd let him get that one off, but that was the only thing he was gonna let slide. Dink had come too far to get disrespected by a bitch-ass nigga . . . a white one at that.

T.J. played the game right because he was pissed. He was tired of the rejection and disrespect he received. Never in his short college life had anyone challenged him the way Dink had in class and he didn't like that. "Let's get outta Dodge, man." He looked at Slim. "We got some shit to take care of at the frat house." T.J. walked away.

Slim watched T.J. slink away, then looked back at Dink. He knew his boy was embarrassed. As second-year students at Boston University, T.J. and Slim were taking additional bullshit introductory electives just to keep their GPAs up, but they had more nefarious reasons for taking intro courses—the freshman hotties. They knew the incoming female freshmen would be fly, and provide a new breed of bitches to dip up in. Freshmen always loved attention from the upper-classmen, and both T.J. and Slim were more than willing to oblige.

Slim and T.J. were both products of broken homes and found college life an easy way to escape their pasts. They both paid their own way because their families couldn't afford it. Unlike

T.J., Slim did it the hard way—he worked two part-time jobs and took out student loans.

When T.J. had seen Dink that day in the Registration Office, there was something about him that told him he was more than that squirrel trying to stack nuts . . . he was the real deal, and now here this nigga was, in college, checking him.

T.J. never thought he'd encounter anyone with Dink's ability to think in a Philosophy 101 class. Dink was on a whole 'nother level, and although he was a threat to him, that wasn't what bothered T.J.; that was a mere obstacle in his eyes. What really got him was that Dink had the undeniably finest chick on campus, and from what he saw she wasn't going too far.

"Don't trip offa him," Slim said to Dink as he nodded toward T.J. "He just hatin'. Aye, why don't you come down to the frat house later on? You know, have a lil' drink, shoot some pool, you know . . . hang out, see how we do it."

"Frat house? You mean it's more black folks here?" Dink joked.

Slim laughed. "Yeah man, it's—"

"Excuse me," a tall, slim, caramel-colored honey interrupted, as she brushed past Dink, Slim, and Laci. It was the same girl who'd sat next to T.J. during the lecture. She headed toward the stoically posed T.J. She shook out her shoulder-length auburn hair, then said something to him. With little resistance on his part, she led him out of the lecture hall. Just as she and T.J. got to the doorway, she turned and looked at Dink from head to toe. With a raised eyebrow and a half grin on her face, she winked, and then walked out.

"A'ight, I gotta burn out, but the offer still stands," Slim told Dink, ignoring what had just happened.

"A'ight, cool," Dink responded. "I just may do that."

The two dapped, then Slim bounced and dipped out of the lecture hall.

"Let's go," Laci snapped, shoving her backpack into Dink's hands.

"What's wrong, baby?" Dink asked, noticing her attitude change.

"Did you see how that girl was looking at you?"

"Man, I wasn't even paying attention to that chick," Dink said. Actually, he had noticed the girl. She was stunning. Almost a dead ringer for his ex, Crystal. A shadow cast over Dink's face because he still couldn't get over the malicious part she'd played in Laci's tragic summer.

Dink grabbed the backpack, put his hand in the small of Laci's back, and escorted her out into the hallway.

"Looks like you were really into the lecture," Laci told him, changing the subject, as they headed outside.

"Yeah, he said some stuff that was really deep."

"You're right—the whole good, bad, angel, God, and devil thing was something to really think about," Laci admitted. "You and Mr. Giencanna were about to make that T.J. guy mad, though."

They both laughed.

"Well, if you think about it, Laci, he has a point. We were brought up believing in something that we were *told* exists but in actuality, how do we know? I mean, we know that Jesus was a man who walked the earth, but how can we validate God, the devil, or angels? What about the religions that believe in God, but don't believe in Jesus? That is truly subjective reasoning."

Laci chuckled. "Subjective reasoning?" She stopped and faced Dink. "I didn't even see you take notes."

"I have everything right here," Dink pointed to his forehead. "How do you think I made it this far? You can't take notes on the street, sweetheart. I may be a college student now, but I'm a hustler at heart. I bet Giencanna was a hustler back in his day," he joked.

Laci frowned at the thought.

"The greatest lessons learned come from the streets, baby, and you can't trust everybody, so you have to use more than just common sense to peep game." Laci loved to hear him talk with such passion. "On the streets, baby, a hungry nigga would do anything or say anything just to get put on and come up. But for me, I listen to what's being said. When I hear something that don't make sense, my radar goes off and I automatically think someone's try'na fuck me. It doesn't necessarily mean that they are, it's just that with all the shady shit folks do, you can't trust just anybody and those that can be trusted, you keep close to you. I fucked up in the beginning, but as I grew with the streets, I started looking at stuff differently. I became more defensive, on guard, and more aware of what was going on around me. In the game you have to be careful, because one fuck-up, it's over. It all boils down to being able to spot the real from the bullshit," Dink told Laci. "Besides a broke hustler, ain't nothin' worse in the game than a wannabe hustler, because shit bound to go down."

Dink's thoughts went to Marco and Dame. He was still shocked that his boys would try to play him shady, but repercussions in the hood were a muthafucka. Disloyalty was honored by death. "Niggas will try to get at you all the time, but you have to be sophisticated enough to be able to differentiate between the straight shooter and the nigga tryna take you. You have to work on that balance, and that balance is called . . ."

"Objective reasoning," Laci said out loud.

"Exactly," Dink confirmed. "Niggas take kindness for weakness so you still gotta be cool, all the while, ruling with an iron fist. There's a time to be hard and there's a time to finesse shit."

Laci looked at Dink in awe and with respect. She didn't realize that hustling required that type of thought. "Do you miss it, Dink?"

"Do I miss what?" Dink replied.

Laci was studying the look on Dink's face as he talked about his former life. "Do you miss being on the streets?" she asked.

He paused momentarily. Everything was still fresh and new to him. "Nah, not really. That was just something to do for the time being. But things happen for a reason. I'm where I want to be now."

Dink stepped toward Laci and put his arms around her waist.

Laci smiled at him, and then placed a tender kiss on his lips.

"I knew there was more to you all along," she confessed. "You are truly a smart man." She kissed him again. "And guess what?"

"What?"

"You're all mine," she smiled back at him. "But right now," she looked at her watch, then grabbed her backpack from Dink's grasp, "I'm late for my next class, and this isn't the way to start the new school year. I'll see you after class, baby." Laci quickly kissed Dink and ran in search of her second class.

Dink loved Laci's innocence and smiled while he watched her scurry away. He was glad he was a part of Laci's rehab and saw how much it had helped her. After she had disappeared from his sight, Dink glanced at his schedule, then shoved it in his pocket and flung his backpack over his left shoulder. He strolled through the campus with the swagger of a man who owned the world. It was a new day, and Dink saw that there was another life outside of being a dope man. Of course, the game had given him cash and material things, but now he had the opportunity to exercise his mind. Dink realized that he had it all. Money at his disposal, a girl he loved, and now he was legit. Giving the "what up" nod to those who passed him, Dink confidently walked to his next class, now living the white man's American dream.

CHAPTER 3

SMURF SAT INSIDE Dink's apartment on Gun Hill Road contemplating his next move. It had been a couple of weeks since Dink had left the Bronx, and Smurf needed to make sure that he had everything on lock just as Dink had. He wasn't a sentimental cat, but he couldn't believe that Dink had given him his entire empire—the South Bronx. He was no longer Dink's best-kept secret . . . *he* was the dope man now.

He started exploring the apartment. Although Smurf had been to Dink's place before, he'd never really tripped off of all the luxuries he had because he'd been so busy taking in everything Dink taught him. Dink was a street philosopher and in order to learn, Smurf had had to listen. *Maybe he was schooling me on all of this all along so he could get out the game,* Smurf thought to himself, *but does a hustler ever truly get out of the game?* He remembered arriving at the apartment when Dink called, and seeing the huge Louis Vuitton traveling trunk near the front door.

"Where we going?" he remembered asking.

"We're not going anywhere," Dink had said. Smurf was confused. "I'm going. I'm leaving this place. I've done all that I can do for you, Marco, Dame, shit . . . even Crystal. I got to do for me now."

Smurf realized that doing for him meant following his heart, which meant starting a new life with Laci—a crackhead. He remembered how deeply Dink was wrapped up in her and how he'd always had a smile on his face, even when he saw her at her worst. Smurf knew that leaving was the right move for Dink. He only hoped that one day a woman would make him feel that way as well.

Walking slowly around the apartment, Smurf admired the black art that graced the walls and small African figures that were placed strategically throughout. He looked at the picture that hung above the fireplace. It was a close-up of a beautiful black woman's face, and there was something about the picture that he connected with. There was so much sadness in her eyes that he could relate to. Smurf's thoughts traveled back to his mother. He'd always wanted a good life for her and with him being the man now, he would make sure she would have nothing less.

Smurf stood and studied her for what seemed like hours, as if he was staring right into her soul. Then he remembered that behind the picture was a wall safe. He removed the large picture and leaned it up against the wall next to the fireplace. Remembering the combination that Dink gave him, he slowly turned the dial to the right, to the left, then back to the right. He grabbed the handle gently and turned it.

Click.

Smurf's heart beat rapidly as he looked at the perfect rubber-banded stacks of dead presidents that lay before him. He reached his hand inside and took one out.

He fanned through the stack, inhaling the fresh, crisp scent of money, then a smile crept across his childlike face. Smurf took out the remaining stacks just because he could. A brand-new, shiny Beretta .380 that sat just behind the money shocked him. He took the piece out and walked over to the full-length mirror by the front door and posed. First, he stood with his legs apart and the gun pointed at his reflection as if he were the bad guy. Then he turned to the side to check out his profile with the new piece. Smurf liked how he looked, and the new gun made him feel invincible.

"Yo, Dink—" Smurf yelled, only to remember that Dink was truly gone.

He looked at his reflection, and the tear that he had tried to suppress crept down his sepia-colored cheek.

"Don't be mad, Smurf, I'm gonna always take care of you."

"How you fuckin' leaving . . . leaving me here? What am I supposed to do? This is all I know."

"Naw, my lil' man, you know way more. That's why I'm leaving this all to you. You're the man now."

"What? Leaving what to me?"

"The South Bronx, baby."

Smurf roughly wiped the tear away. For the first time since he'd started working for Dink, he was all alone. Smurf never knew his own father, so he looked up to Dink as a father figure. It was Dink who'd taken him under his wing and taught him not only the code of the streets, but also about life, which sharpened his mind. Smurf's mother had tried to do the same but as he got older, she became too busy with men to make sure he stayed on the right path. Truth be told, Dink had lasted longer in his life than the men his mother had running through her.

Dink gave Smurf credit because he was hungry and eager to work, and he actually listened and learned. Smurf was his most loyal comrade; and because of that, they'd formed a tight bond. Even though Smurf had never actually worked with Dink in his business, he ended up being the muscle Dink needed and the eyes to see what he couldn't. Smurf saw a lot and knew that he could hold Dink down if need be. He'd already got rid of the dead weight when he got rid of that snitch Marco and that bitch-ass nigga Dame; now it was time to get the rest of his soldiers together. But who could he trust?

Smurf remembered all he'd brought with him—clothes, cassette tapes, and sneakers. He shook his head pitifully at what little he had, but then remembered he was the man now, and soon he would have more.

Thank you, man, he thought. *How can I ever repay you?* One phone call had changed his life—from rags to riches—and young Smurf vowed never to live in poverty again.

Smurf looked in the mirror and saw his come-up. With the profound confidence he had gained, he turned and happily sauntered toward the stacks of money and put them back into the safe.

"I ain't gotta want nothin' no more. Now I can get a nice ride, get me some hip gear, and take care of my moms. Shit, I can even pull a fine-ass bitch instead of these corner hoes," he said as he stashed away the last stack. Right before he closed the door, he decided to take two stacks for himself. He closed the safe, put the picture back in front of it, and prepared to leave to meet Dirty, Dink's play cousin who was the big man in Harlem, at the corner store.

Just as Smurf was about to leave, he saw the knob on the front door move. He stopped in his tracks and became quiet. He flipped the light switch off and stood to the side of the door with his gun drawn. Smurf hadn't silenced anyone since Marco.

Smurf had cut across a back street in the West Village when he thought he saw a familiar car in the alley. When he looked closely, he confirmed that it was Marco's ride. Wondering why he was in the Ville, Smurf's thoughts were quickly interrupted when he saw an unmarked Lumina pull up. Smurf wasn't dumb. He knew it was a cop car. When the driver of the Lumina flicked the high beams twice and killed the lights, Marco got out of the car holding an envelope, then jumped in the front seat. Smurf knew Marco had to be a snitch, just as he had suspected all along.

It was unfortunate that Smurf would have to put someone asleep in his own apartment, but whoever it was obviously had a death wish. He heard the person fiddling with the door, then heard something slide into the keyhole.

Click.

The door opened cautiously and the light from the hallway illuminated the glass table in the entryway. Smurf saw the large shadow of someone, but couldn't make out who it was. He raised his gun to the edge of the door so when the person tried to shut it, he would be head to head with his gun. The light came on.

"You got three seconds before I smoke you," Smurf spoke. "Three, two . . ."

"Aye, yo cuzzo, it's me," the man said in haste.

"Who is you?" Smurf spoke menacingly.

"Shit, who *you* is?" the man spoke as he turned around. "I'm lookin' for my muthafuckin' play cousin."

"Play cousin?" Smurf repeated. He put the safety on his gun and tucked it away in the small of his back. Smurf had never seen Dirty until now.

Dirty had the reputation of a smooth businessman with

major playa status. He had connections that were hard to come by in the drug world, making him the only distributor for the Bronx. Little did Smurf know that when he killed Marco and had Dame sliced, he'd done Dirty a favor as well.

Smurf looked closely at Dirty. He was a short specimen of a man, standing only a few inches above him. He was also slightly older than the average hustler in the streets, somewhere in his early thirties, brown-skinned, with a noticeable scar on the lower right portion of his chin. Fresh razor cuts outlined the hairline of his low-cut fade. He was dressed nicely in a red and black Troop jogging suit with a pair of Troop sneakers. He wore two gold rope chains, one plain, the other with a cross dangling from it, and on his left hand he wore a gold nugget ring. He had a reputation as a ladies' man, with women all over the South Bronx, Harlem, and Manhattan. He knew that money talked and bullshit walked, and he didn't mind putting a woman in her place, either.

The larger-than-life image that Smurf had of Dirty quickly vanished, but he looked all of a nigga who knew how to take care of business. His body was muscular, as if he'd done time in prison at one point in his life. Regardless, this was the man and the reason he ate.

"What you doing here?" Smurf questioned.

Dirty looked at him quizzically, as if he should know.

"No, I meant here in my apartment."

"*Your* apartment?"

"Yeah."

"I always crash here when I'm in town." That explained why he had a key. Dirty thought for a minute. "Cuzzo told me to meet you here."

"Anyway," Smurf extended his hand. "I'm Dink's right hand. I'm—"

"Smurf," the man said, still cautious but more-so pissed that a gun had been held to his head just seconds ago.

"Right, and I'm the one you'll be dealin' with until further notice," Smurf smarted back, upset that Dirty had cut him off.

Dirty sized Smurf up and wondered if he was as bad as Dink claimed. He didn't look like a ruthless killer, but he knew that looks could be deceiving. Dirty knew that Smurf had got rid of the weak links in Dink's crew, and for that he was glad; but he and Dink had put a key player in their operations in a most unexpected place. Now it was time for it to pay off and to take shit to the next level. Dirty walked over to the wet bar, grabbed a glass, clunked two ice cubes in it, and poured himself a glass of Absolut. Sitting down on the couch, he swirled his drink in the glass and took a sip.

"I know that Dink is away."

"So you know what's up?" Smurf asked. He didn't plan on giving any more information than he already had. Smurf felt that not everyone needed to know what was going on, but in Dirty's case, if he and Dink were that cool, he would have already known what the deal was.

"I know it all," Dirty confirmed, "and you got yo' work cut out for you, but first you gotta check that goddamn attitude and get the fuckin' bass outta yo' voice when you dealin' with me, son." Dirty put his glass down on the coffee table and walked over to Smurf, who was sitting on the edge of the recliner, next to the couch. Catching Smurf off guard, Dirty grabbed him by the collar. "And if you ever point a gun at me again, I'll kill you. Do you understand?"

Smurf didn't answer. He wasn't gonna get punked by Dirty, or no other man for that matter. The last man who'd gotten in his face was Buck, the nigga who fucked and beat his momma, and Smurf blew him to pieces, but he knew he had to control his anger, so it was best he didn't answer and stuck to the business at hand.

For the next thirty minutes, Smurf and Dirty talked about the product, price, and placement.

"You got your crew in order?" Dirty asked Smurf.

"I got some niggas I been watchin' for a while. I don't trust everyone."

"That's good," Dirty told him. "You need to be cautious. But hey, check this out. I got somebody I want you to meet, and—"

"I choose my own people," Smurf told Dirty seriously, cutting him off. "You know I had to clean house on some of Dink's people."

"Look, youngster, we on the same team here," Dirty confirmed, beginning to get irritated with Smurf's stubbornness. "I trust your judgment because my cuzzo trusted you, but if you let me finish, I was gonna say that I'm cool with you steppin' in the way you did." Dirty shook his head in disbelief about Marco and Dame. "Just meet the man and I trust your judgment. If there's something you don't like, just let me know and we can move on from there. Bet?"

After a momentary pause, Smurf said, "Bet."

"Well, lil' nigga, I'll be back later. I been gone for a while, so I wanna see what's up with the hoes. Ya feel me?"

Smurf smiled. Dirty was going to go find some ass and he couldn't hate. "A'ight man," Smurf laughed. "Handle yo' business."

CHAPTER 4

THE SQUAD CARS and spinning red lights, mixed with the blaring summer sun, made it almost impossible to see. The turn of events played out in slow motion in front of Tonette's eyes as if it was happening right in front of her.

She looked at Crystal as the police shouted to them. The fear in Crystal's eyes told Tonette they were both in trouble. Tonette looked back at the police, who yelled again, "Get on the fucking ground!"

This time, the glare of the sun glistened off the chrome-plated Glocks that were ready to drop their asses at any second.

"I said, drop the fucking gun, goddammit!" the cop yelled again.

In an instant, the officer who continued to yell charged like a bull toward Tonette. She tried to reach for Crystal, but was tackled to the ground. The big, heavy officer had all of his weight on her body and she couldn't breathe.

Tonette put up a good fight, but his strength was too much for her. Next, she heard a popping noise, like something crackling. Then the smell hit her. *What the hell,* she thought to herself.

"She's all yours," the cop said in a distorted voice to someone behind her. Tonette tried to look in the direction of the officer but only saw Crystal standing there—her face morphing into something familiar and awful.

"What the hell is going on?" Tonette yelled. The distorted face quickly came into focus. It was one she couldn't forget. Tonette's blood began to boil and she shouted, "I hate you, you bitch! I fuckin' hate you!"

The face radiated a beautiful smile, then Shirley Temple curls spiraled to her shoulders.

"I'ma kill you!" Tonette yelled as she continued to struggle against the cop. She turned her head to look at him. He was now faceless.

In one quick motion, Laci bent down next to Tonette with a crack pipe in her hand, moving it closer to her ... urging her to take that first pull.

An annoying sound rang in Tonette's ears. She wrestled frantically from side to side, and then sat up, gasping for breath, her heart rate going a mile a minute. She repeatedly blinked her eyes slowly until her surroundings came into focus. *It was all a dream,* she said to herself. *Just a goddamn dream. Shit!*

Tonette was so geeked, she quickly rolled a fat blunt and sat cross-legged in her bed, trying to calm down. After a few tokes on the bud, she mellowed, but as she thought about the events that had gone down over the last couple of months, she became pissed again. Not only was her man, Dame, found dead with his dick cut off and his throat slit from one end to the other, her girl Crystal was killed by the police and her other girl, Monique, was wounded as well.

· · ·

TONETTE HAD BEEN shocked as hell when the police arrived at her home to deliver the news about Dame, but the conversation quickly turned into an interrogation about her high-profile drug-dealing boyfriend and weapons. This was when she realized they were just fishing for information because Dink was the man, not Dame.

When the police asked to search the apartment for drugs, Tonette didn't bother to put up a fight. She used her angelic smile and light-gray tear-filled eyes to convince them that she was completely innocent and knew nothing of their accusations. She was merely a young woman grieving the losses of her boyfriend and a chick in her crew.

Dame had another apartment where he kept the real shit, so she knew they wouldn't find drugs where they lived. They searched the obvious places—under the mattress, in shoe boxes, and even in their VHS tape racks—but what little stash was left, Tonette had already smoked up. In a desperate attempt to find something, the police even picked through Dame's jackets and sneakers, but they still came up with nothing.

"Um . . . excuse me, officers?" Tonette asked, her eyes tearing to the brim.

"Yes, Ms. Thomas." They looked at her in anticipation of what she had to say.

"Y'all come in here accusing me of stuff that I don't know nothing about."

"We have a report that you gave Ms. Moore the gun she was carrying when she was shot. We were also told that your boyfriend is a high-profile drug dealer."

Tonette's nose began to flare. "I don't care what report you have. I don't know nothing about no damn gun and my dead boyfriend ain't no damn dealer. Y'all really need to check y'all's sources before y'all start accusing people of shit they don't know anything about." She paused for a moment and spoke. "I knew something like this would happen when that bougie chick wanted to be friends with us."

"What bougie chick?" they asked, repeating her words.

"Laci, but I guess because she don't live in the hood, y'all won't even question her about anything. That's fucked up." Tonette knew that she was pushing the bar with how she was talking to the officers, but she had to do something to get the attention off her. "You accuse me of having a boyfriend who is a drug dealer and question me about guns, but she's with the top dog. Do I look like I live the life of a drug dealer's girl? No. I even let you go through my things, but you're leaving with the same shit you came here with, and I still got questions." She looked at both of the officers. "Did you find who murdered my boyfriend, and why did y'all kill Crystal?" The officers looked at one another. "Y'all can't answer me that, can ya? All I want are answers!"

The officers knew of Tonette's rep. As a matter of fact, they had been watching the South Bronx Bitches for some time for alleged drug sales and theft. The local police department never had anything on them other than anonymous tips that trickled in, but now after the shooting, it was the best time to investigate them all.

Tonette sat down on her bed with a tear-drenched face and red eyes. "This is just too much right now," she cried and rocked back and forth in front of them. "Just too much."

Her innocent look and acting was on point, because the police left not long after her outburst began.

"Thanks for your time, Ms. Thomas," the officer spoke. "If we have any questions, we'll be back, so don't go too far."

"That's fine, but when you come back, please make sure you have answers for me. That's all I'm asking."

"We'll see what we can do, Ms. Thomas. Thank you for your time." They walked out of her apartment and closed the door.

"What you think, man?" one of the officers spoke as they left her apartment building.

"We got this information from an eyewitness, so something isn't adding up. I'm not touching this one. Let's turn this over to Clifton. I'm sure he'll get to the bottom of it."

"I agree."

As soon as the officers left her apartment, Tonette's anger radiated though her body. She was gonna get to the bottom of this bullshit. She really didn't give a fuck about Dame, because a true hustler wouldn't have slipped the way he did. His dick head was obviously so busy thinking about getting up in some raggedy-ass pussy that he couldn't see he was about to get fucked up. "Dumb-ass nigga," she rationalized, "that's what the fuck you get." Tonette got up and trod over to her mirror. "I know whoever that bitch was, she wasn't fly like me, so fuck her ass too."

WHAT SHE MOST wanted to find out was who the fuck told the police that she gave Crystal the gun to deliver in the first place. She had let it rest long enough, and now it was time to find out.

Tonette picked up the receiver of her Minnie Mouse phone and dialed seven digits. After a couple of rings, a voice answered.

"Hello?"

"Hey," Tonette spoke tiredly into the phone, a ploy to make the person on the other end think she was vulnerable. "Where you been?"

Monique paused before she answered cautiously, "How you doin'?" She ignored Tonette's question.

"Why don't you roll through?" Tonette asked, in her most pitiful-sounding voice. She noticed that Monique had ignored her question, so two could play that game, she figured.

"Uh...I don't know." Because she'd told the police that Tonette gave Crystal the gun, Monique thought it was best to stay away from her.

"Why?"

"With everything that went down, I think we need to lay low for a while."

"Girl, please!" Tonette spoke, irritated. "You think they still trippin' off that shit? Them muhfuckas done moved on. They don't care shit about what happens in the South Bronx."

"Well...I don't know, Nette. With Crystal gone, it just don't feel the same."

"Regardless of what happened, we still the SBBs, baby." Tonette gave her a pep speech. "We the baddest bitches out here." She wasn't going to let this shit die until she put it to rest.

Tonette heard a faint sigh. "Alright, I'll run through."

Just for good measure, Tonette called Shaunna, too. "Wassup bitch? What'cha doin?"

"I got yo bitch," Shaunna laughed. "I ain't doin' nothin'. Just waiting for this nigga to come through. I tried to call yo' ass earlier, you know, see what's poppin'."

"Who the hell you got rollin' through?" Tonette asked. She realized that annoying sound she'd heard earlier while she was sleeping was her phone ringing.

"This dude I met at the club the other night. Shit, you know how I do."

"Well, I take 'bitch' back," Tonette laughed, "you a ho."

"Takes one to know one," Shaunna shot back quickly with laughter.

"Girl, I know you ain't gonna fuck him with that big-ass stomach of yours."

"I don't know what kinda fuckin *you* be doin', but my stomach ain't got shit to do with my pussy," Shaunna joked. "Maybe if he hit it right, he'll knock this lil' muthafucka in the head and tell him to get his ass outta there."

Both girls giggled.

"Well when you done, why don't you head over this way? Monique rollin' through too."

"A'ight, cool. Hang on for a minute." Shaunna put the phone down and within seconds, Tonette heard a faint male voice. "Hey, I'm about to take care of something, but I'll be through later."

"A'ight, cool." Tonette hung up.

CHAPTER 5

WEEKS AFTER THE shooting, Detective Rodney Clifton sat looking at the report of Crystal Moore that he was given by two of his colleagues. It would have been closed as an accidental shooting; however, after questioning the other shooting victim and the alleged suspect, there was more to the case than met the eye.

Rodney Clifton was a thirty-seven-year-old, fifteen-year-veteran of the NYPD. He was a light-skinned black man, tall and slender, with short, sandy-colored hair and freckles. He didn't look like he was capable of being a cop because of his wimpy appearance, and many underestimated him; but those who encountered him knew differently. Detective Clifton had started out like every other officer, as a rookie on the beat, but his commitment to the streets and uncanny way of getting information quickly moved him up the ranks.

He saw the growing number of hustlers on the streets, but unlike most hotheaded cops, Detective Clifton didn't go after them immediately. He watched them long enough to see their weaknesses, their strengths, and their habits. He also noticed that they were hustling strictly in the South Bronx so he figured as long as they stayed in their community, poisoning their own kind, it really didn't matter.

He didn't like black folks who tried to come up without working for it. *Niggas always wanna hustle,* he thought. As a cop, he knew that the corner hustlers couldn't provide anything so he had to go after the big dog, but he also knew that by jumping too hastily, he could fuck up something bigger. As a man, he watched and waited for the right time to make his move.

ON A LATE-NIGHT stroll through the South Bronx, Detective Clifton had seen a young man who caught his eye. He was a light-skinned fellow, a little rough around the edges, standing about 5 feet 8 inches with weight that was too much for his build. Watching him for a couple of weeks, the detective knew that he hustled dope. He could tell because he was always fresh and had his jewelry game tight. The young man also had a flat-top fade with a blond stripe in the front, so he was easy to spot.

Cruising through the same neighborhood a week later, Detective Clifton saw his mark, then activated his patrol car lights and siren. The few skeezers and what looked like bums who surrounded him scattered like roaches, but the young man didn't budge. He just looked at the officer.

With a cocky attitude, Detective Clifton got out of his car with his hands on his department-issued belt, which held his handcuffs, mace, night stick, and gun.

"What'cha doing out here, Marco?" he asked, looking at the young man's belt buckle, which displayed MARCO in gold letters.

Marco looked down at his belt buckle, then answered with a major irritated and condescending tone in his voice, "Conductin' Bible study, man, and you just dismissed my flock. What the fuck you think I'm doin' out here?"

"Watch yo' smart-ass mouth, boy!" the detective grunted through tightly clenched teeth.

"What da hell you want, man? I got bidness to finish."

Detective Clifton noticed the attitude. "Get yo' hands on the hood and spread 'em!"

"For what? I didn't do nothing," Marco protested angrily.

Reluctantly, Marco did as he was told, mumbling under his breath while the officer frisked him. Marco was confident that the small package he'd picked up earlier wouldn't be found.

"Turn around," the detective ordered when he didn't feel anything on the initial pat-down.

When Marco did as he was told, the officer did something that caught him off guard. After patting him down again, the detective stuck his hands inside the front of Marco's pants.

"What the fuck . . . man, get yo' hands . . . what you try'na do!" He tried to wrestle the cop away, but it was useless.

The detective felt around Marco's dick and balls and pulled out a small baggie. Taking a deep sniff of the bag, he smiled and spoke in a teasing tone, "I see you got a large," he pointed toward Marco's hardening dick, "and small package." He waved the baggie in the air. "This looks like an ounce or two to me. Do you know how long this will get you?"

"Man . . . please . . ." Marco began to cry like a true bitch. "That's my boy's shit, man, I'm just . . ."

"Under arrest for the possession of narcotics and intent to distribute," Detective Clifton told Marco as he slapped the handcuffs on his wrists and led him to his patrol car.

Instead of sitting him in the back of the squad car, the detective shoved Marco in the front passenger's side, then he got in on the driver's side and began to drive. Not knowing where he was going, Marco tried to explain himself, only to stop moments later when they pulled up in an empty alley. The detective left his car running.

"What the fuck we doin' here?" Marco asked.

"This a shortcut to the precinct. I gotta book you."

"Please man, no," Marco begged.

"Well." Detective Clifton looked at Marco with a glimmer in his eye. "If you give me a reason not to book you, I may forget about this."

"Please don't arrest me. I can't do no jail time. Please." The wannabe hustler left Marco with a quickness.

"Aw, now you beggin'. You ain't flappin' off at the lips no more like you were before," the officer teased. "I got something for you to do with those lips, man."

"Anything, I'll do anything," Marco pleaded.

"Anything?"

"Yes, anything."

The detective smiled at Marco and removed the handcuffs. He then unbuckled his belt, unzipped his pants, and pulled out his scrawny dick. For a black man, he was a disgrace to the race.

"I can forget all about that sack I got from you, but first . . ." He motioned toward his dick.

Marco knew what time it was and he had to do something to save his ass.

For the next two years, Marco's asshole became a hiding place for the detective's dick. Sucking and fucking was no big deal to Marco because he was already a down-low faggot. Molested as a child and raped repeatedly, Marco held his feelings for men at bay until he was able to unleash them.

Detective Rodney Clifton's sly investigative skills were once again on point. Not only did he find a weak link in the South Bronx's biggest drug ring who was willing to do anything to keep his hot ass out of jail, but the same person provided him with sexual pleasure. What more could a man want?

DETECTIVE CLIFTON PUSHED to the side a file that he was reviewing earlier in the day and looked once again at the statements of Tonette Thomas, Shaunna Parker, and Monique Daniels. He noticed that Crystal and Tonette had records but Monique and Shaunna didn't.

"So these are the so-called infamous South Bronx Bitches," he said to himself, rocking back and forth in his wobbly desk chair, looking at their pictures.

"Hey, Jones," Detective Clifton called out. Officer Terrance Jones was a rookie, fresh out of the academy, and was assigned to a veteran for street patrol. He stood about 6 feet 2 inches, with his weight proportionate to his height. Officer Jones had caramel-brown skin and sported a fade. He had sharp features, a strong jawline, thin but shapely lips, dark brown eyes, and long, dark lashes. He wore an earring in his left ear and most of all, looked good in and out of his uniform.

"Yeah, Clifton," the rookie answered, "what's up?" He walked over to the detective and sat on the side of his desk.

Detective Clifton looked at him closely, then handed him the report. "Take a look at this and tell me what you think." He was hoping the rookie could shed a light on what he thought he was missing, because his own mind was elsewhere.

Officer Jones read the statement given by Monique as well as those of the other girls; then he looked at the picture.

"Where's this girl right here?" He pointed to Laci. "Where's her statement? She looks out of place."

"That's exactly what I thought," the detective told Officer Jones. He looked at his officer, trying not to be obvious, scanning his body.

Officer Jones handed the picture to the detective to validate his point. "Look at her, then look at the other girls." The two looked over the picture again. "It's two different breeds here." Detective Clifton watched Jones's masculine finger point to each girl. "The other girls look like they're from the street." He shuffled through the mug shots of Crystal and Tonette, then the picture one of their undercover officers took of them on the streets. "Look at the clothes, the jewelry, but this girl right here, she really stands out. Actually, she looks like she got her shit together. Nothing like these girls."

"Okay . . . yeah, I see what you're saying, but remember, youngster, just because she doesn't look like she'd fit in with them doesn't mean shit. We busted some wannabe hustlers who used a white boy to transport for them a few years back. In the game, all sorts of people are used for opportunity."

"Yeah, you're right," the rookie confirmed with a head nod.

"We need to find out more about this girl, though. It looks like when the other officers questioned Ms. Thomas, she mentioned this girl. Actually, I put a big drug case on hold because of this one, but something is telling me that they both have something to do with the other," he held up a thick brown file and put it on the corner of his desk, "so I'm not closing this one until I talk to her."

"Why you think they're related?" Officer Jones got up from

the corner of the detective's desk and walked to the chair that sat in front of his own. Detective Clifton watched as he sat down in front of him.

"All of my years in Narcotics," Detective Clifton spoke to his rookie.

"Wait a minute. How did you get a hold of it when you're in Narcs?"

"Because these girls are known to dabble in some type of drug activity. That's why I think both cases have something to do with each other. But the weird thing was the initial call. I have never once heard of a man reporting a woman being crazy without saying why. If a man calls reporting a crazy woman, she's normally going after him for some shit he did to her. From the report, he was also very descriptive." The detective looked in Crystal's file. "He said she was a crazy girl in a red tank top, green Damage jeans, and red Reebok Classics shooting a gun outside. When street patrol got on the scene, the gun was in a brown paper bag, but after it all went down and tests were done, the gun hadn't been fired from the time the person called in until we apprehended the suspect."

"What's so odd about that?" the rookie asked the seasoned veteran. "That shit happens all the time in the hood."

"You're right, but a description that clear with no type of follow-up with us means that someone was trying to set that girl up. Remember, in the report, Ms. Daniels stated that Ms. Thomas gave Crystal the gun, but it was a male who called in and reported her being armed and dangerous. Now, Ms. Thomas is telling us that someone else is involved. Something smells shitty in the Bronx, man." The detective got up from his desk. "A'ight rookie, you ready for a stroll through the hood and see what we can find out?"

After watching Officer Jones, Detective Clifton was was anxious to get back to the hood. He thought back to the last time he had seen Marco—the day he gave him the dossier—but he hadn't seen him since. Marco was known for playing cat-and-mouse with him, but it was time for some booty, so he had to go get it.

"Why don't you sit tight and let me handle this," Officer Jones suggested to his colleague with confidence.

"Handle what?"

"I can go to the South Bronx myself."

"Naw, fuck that," the detective said, shaking his head. "You ain't going down there by yourself, man." *Cock-blocking bastard,* he thought to himself.

"Why not? You think it's dangerous or something?" Officer Jones joked.

"For a rookie, it can be."

"Look, with you having two cases, if you go down there asking questions and shit, ain't nobody gonna say a damn thing to you."

"And you think they're gonna talk to you?" the detective questioned.

"I fit in more than you do," the officer spoke honestly. The swagger that Terrance had, along with his age and versatile looks, did have their advantages in the hood. "Let me do this."

Detective Clifton stared at his young trainee and grinned. His enthusiasm and eagerness reminded him of himself when he first joined the force. After thinking over what Officer Jones had just said, Detective Clifton agreed.

"Well," he said apprehensively, "but just so you know, if you end up with a cap in yo' ass, you went down there without my knowledge. I don't know nothing, I don't see nothing." The detective wanted to cover his ass. "And I ain't going on desk duty because you got a wild hair up your ass."

"Got it," Officer Jones winked, then grinned at his cohort and left. He knew exactly where to go.

Detective Clifton was glad that the rookie had left the office. The longer he watched him, the more agitated he became. Detective Clifton grabbed his keys and left the precinct, headed to Westville.

CHAPTER 6

Smurf went on a mission after he had seen Dirty, and hand-picked three niggas that could hold shit down and lead the army that he had chosen. He had kept an eye on Drake and Chunky when he was the muscle for Dink, and he knew that they could get real gutta with it if need be. Stoney, Dink's boy, was also a part of the crew. Smurf had lieutenants in every borough and their soldiers were in place. He had everything on lock and was ready to get his grind on.

Little did Smurf know, he was a living legend, and many cats wanted to be like him. He knew he wouldn't have a problem with his chosen three because under his watch, Smurf wasn't going to put up with any unnecessary bullshit.

Smurf paged Drake prior to hitting the streets. Waiting for a return call, he decided to go see his mother, whom he hadn't seen since Dink left. He had a surprise for her. With the stash he had accumulated by being Dink's right-hand man, along with the money in the safe, Smurf now had the means to help his moms. She could now live the way she'd always wanted. Nothing was too good for her in his eyes. He figured she wouldn't want to stay at his place, so he furnished another apartment just for her in his building. He couldn't wait to tell her and see the expression on her face.

Smurf drove back to his old neighborhood, and the cats on the streets acknowledged him. The same kids who'd taken advantage of young Smurf's small size as a kid now respected him. He had a commanding sense of power and now truly felt like the man.

When he reached his mother's apartment building, Smurf contemplated going up the back like he used to, but he looked down at his fly clothes and decided against it. Smurf had on a Fila jogging suit with matching Fila tennis shoes. He didn't want to scuff his clean shoes by pulling some Spiderman shit climbing up the fire escape. Besides, he was the dope man now and he had a reputation to uphold. He'd heard that his mother stopped tricking months ago, so it was safe to enter through the front door.

Smurf walked into his mother's apartment and couldn't close the door all the way before his mother came out from the bedroom and walked toward the bathroom.

"Momma!" Smurf shrieked, quickly putting his hands up to shield his eyes. His mother was butt naked and her hair was sticking out all over her head. Smurf knew what that meant— she had just got through fucking.

For years, Smurf had seen his mother used and abused by men. It was a never-ending cycle. No matter how much he told her how he felt, Gloria always dismissed her son's feelings and often took his dignity away by forcing him to bow down to the busters she had running through her. When the relationships were over, Gloria always apologized . . . until the next man.

"Wayne! Baby!" Gloria screamed in shock. She covered up her

private areas and dashed back into the bedroom. She returned with a sheet wrapped around her. "What you doing here?"

Instantly, anger rose in his chest. Smurf tried to push his way past her and rush into the bedroom, but his mother stopped him with a fixed hand on his chest.

"No, Wayne, stop it!" she said firmly.

"Momma, you don't have to do this anymore." He pointed toward her, then to the bedroom. "Move in with me, Momma. I got a nice apartment for you. Fixed up just the way you like it. I got enough money for the both of us." He pulled out a wad of money, ten thousand dollars to be exact, and fanned it in front of her face. "Momma, it's more where this came from." The hard-core killer that the streets knew was now gone and the child that she'd raised was in front of her.

Her eyes bucked momentarily, but the wad of cash didn't faze Gloria.

"Wayne, I can't move in with you," she told him seriously.

"Why, Momma? I can give you everything you want and more."

She looked back at her bedroom, then at her son. "It's not about you anymore. It's about me." She lowered her voice and spoke again with authority. "I've done the best I could with you, but I can't teach you to become a man. I know what you're doing on the streets."

"But that's for us, Momma. I'm only doing this shit to take care of you!" Wayne shouted defensively.

"Watch your mouth, boy, I'm still your momma!" He calmed down and allowed her to finish talking. "That's your way of life, Wayne, and this is mine. Let me live my life," she said, pointing to herself. "Your momma will be just fine."

Gloria's eyes filled with tears. Wayne was her only child, but she'd made a decision about her life: she'd rather be with any man than be alone. She began walking to the door, and Wayne followed her. He got the distinct feeling that she was trying to get rid of him . . . and she was.

Gloria opened the front door and a male voice called out from her bedroom, followed by three hand claps.

"Gloria! Bitch, get back in here now!" he yelled.

Gloria jumped at the startling request. "Bye, baby," she told her son as she once again put her hand on his chest, forcing him to walk backward out the door. She took one last look at Wayne and closed the door.

Not only was Smurf furious, he was hurt. He had seen his mother get dogged out by men for as long as he could remember. Now, he was giving her the opportunity to live the life she wanted without a man fucking her and leaving her or beating her ass. Instinctively, Smurf reached toward his gun and thought about kicking the door in and killing the nigga who was in there calling her like she was some loyal dog. Then he remembered something she'd just told him: "Let me live my life." Those words brought Smurf back to reality. She was right. He now understood that no amount of money that he gave her or his ability to provide for her would be good enough. His mother chose to be a whore and just like with him, her method of survival was her choice.

To take his mind off his mother, Smurf decided to go to the Jackson Projects and round up his soldiers. As he rested at a stoplight, he thought about all that had happened over the last couple of months. Right before the light turned green, a police car sped by him and Smurf's radar went up. There was a familiar face riding shotgun, and if it was who he thought it was, there would be hell to pay.

CHAPTER 7

TWO HOURS LATER, like old times, the three remaining South Bronx Bitches were sitting on the floor around Tonette's dark cherrywood coffee table eating fried bologna sandwiches with mustard and drinking grape Kool-Aid. They were smoking bud and reminiscing about Crystal's crazy ass, filling the air with laughter. That gave Tonette the opening she needed.

"Crystal . . . damn!" she said, somberly. "I still can't believe this shit."

Quietness surrounded them and Monique put her hands up to her face to block out the painful memory that clouded her mind.

"It's been almost two months and the shit still all over the streets," Shaunna confirmed, rubbing her big belly. "What the fuck she doing carrying a gun around like it's nothin', anyway?"

Both Tonette and Shaunna looked at Monique.

"I don't know what y'all looking at me for." She smacked her lips, rolled her neck, and looked back at them with bucked eyes as big as saucers.

"Weren't you with her?" Shaunna asked, trying to get up off the floor to sit on the couch.

"Yeah, but shit, I ain't know what was up. We was goin' to the show," Monique said truthfully. "Dink's ass called her, wanting her to make a run for him."

"A run?"

"Yeah. Wanted her to take something to that nigga, Stoney."

"Stoney?"

"Yeah."

"What the fuck he give her?"

"Girl, I don't know. Shit. What's with all the questions?" Monique raised her voice.

Tonette was getting pissed that Monique was getting loud. Everyone in the crew knew that Tonette had the last word, and when she was onto something it was best to be seen and not heard. Most people would be fooled by Tonette. She had a small frame, a toffee-colored complexion, and the soft smile of an angel, with white teeth that rivaled her light-gray eyes. Even though she looked like Vanessa Williams when she wore her long, relaxed hair parted down the middle, her girls knew what was up. She could be a straight-up bitch—the devil's liveliest advocate—and she didn't hesitate to spew her venom on anyone who crossed her.

"What you mean you ain't know?" Tonette challenged, looking Monique dead in the eye.

"Like I said, I ain't know," Monique retorted sharply. She was now pissed.

"If you ain't know shit, why you tell the police I gave her that gun?"

"Aw shit," Shaunna said under her breath as she looked at Monique, who stood up just in case something kicked off.

"I—I ain't say shit!" Monique stuttered.

"You a goddamn liar!" Tonette's herringbone chains, door-knocker earrings, and gold bangles made a symphony of noise when she quickly hopped up from the floor. "Why you tell them muthafuckas I did that? They came to my crib, searched it, and then told me not to go too far," she yelled. Tonette was ready to kick off in Monique's ass. This would be the test. She knew if Monique didn't fight back, she was guilty. If she did fight back, she'd have to find out who else could have dropped the dime on her and they'd get dealt with. She knew it wasn't Shaunna, because she had been down with her ever since the shit happened.

Tonette didn't give Monique a chance to answer before she clocked her like a nigga, knocking her down on the floor. The two began to tumble, scream, scratch, and bite—a true catfight at its best.

"Goddammit!" Shaunna screamed when she saw that Tonette was getting the better of Monique, who was trying to fight back. Shaunna figured that Monique couldn't defend herself the way she normally would have, considering she was still fucked up from being shot.

Shaunna maneuvered her way up off the couch and attempted to break the two girls up, all the while protecting her unborn baby. "Break this shit up, y'all!" She got in the best position she could to pull Tonette off Monique. "Damn girl, stop!" Shaunna yelled at the top of her voice. Monique took the opportunity to get off the floor when Tonette stopped trying to claw her eyes out.

"Fuck that heifer," Tonette growled. "You wanna run your fuckin' mouth, I'ma give you something to run it for." She lunged at Monique again, but this time Shaunna stopped her, becoming disgusted. They all used to be so tight and never made a move without each other, but now she saw the breakdown of their friendship right before her eyes. She didn't like what they had become.

"You trippin', Nette!" She looked at Monique. "And what about you, Monique? I know you ain't runnin' yo' damn mouth, and for what? Hell, we done worse shit before and they ain't fuck with us." There was an uncomfortable silence that filled the air. "Look . . . we the South Bronx Bitches and nothing can come between that. I ain't tellin' y'all to kiss and make up, but damn, one of us is already dead. We gotta stick together. Y'all need to squash this shit before somebody else get hurt!"

Tonette and Monique were still breathing heavily, like pit bulls after a dogfight, and glared at each other with evil looks.

"Let me go!" Tonette broke free of Shaunna's grasp and started pacing the room. Her mind ran a mile a minute. Everything that could go wrong in her life had. Then suddenly, the smile that she saw in her dream came back into focus.

"It's all that bitch's fault!" Tonette snarled.

"Who?" Both girls asked, startled by her sudden outburst. "Crystal?"

"Naw!" She looked at them in bewilderment, and then shook her head. "That bitch, Laci!"

"How you figure that?" Monique questioned.

"If it wasn't for her stuck-up ass, none of this shit woulda happened." Tonette paced again. "We gon' find her ass and when we do—"

"Hey . . . hol' up Tonette, you trippin'," Monique finally spoke up. She'd already been tired of Tonette blaming everything on Laci before, but now this was over the edge. She looked at Shaunna, but Shaunna looked indifferent.

"What?" Shaunna questioned Monique.

"You don't feel bad for what happened to that girl?"

"Um . . ." Shaunna hummed, "no." She rubbed her belly. "We had to have something to do in the summer." Shaunna laughed like she had just told a funny joke.

"You got that right," Tonette cosigned.

"We ain't make her do anything. Now, if that bitch layin' up in a crack house on her own funky mattress tweakin, shoo' . . . that's on her." She gave Tonette a high-five. "Mo, seriously though, you need to get over it and move on," Shaunna said.

"I can't believe you!" Monique yelled to both of the girls. "That shit was foul, y'all."

"Girl, get the fuck on!" Tonette said, attempting to dismiss Monique. "This about that bitch Laci."

"It's not just about Laci, Nette. My life been fucked up because of drugs, man. My mother was fuckin' with a goddamn addict, got HIV and died." Monique wiped her now wet face with the back of her hand. "And you, Shaunna, you keep on getting knocked up by these niggas out here who slangin' that shit and ain't benefiting from it, damn!" She turned to look at Tonette. "Nette, too many people got hurt behind your little game. Not only is Crystal dead, but shit, Laci could be too."

"Look, I'm sorry about yo' moms and all, but I ain't have nothing to do with that shit. Everybody know not to fuck an addict," she said without emotion, "because they fuck anything, but what the hell you care about Laci for? She thought she was better than all of us, and that includes you too."

"Damn, Tonette! She was, so what?"

"What the hell you mean, so what? She ain't have no right judging us or what we do!"

"And you had no right turning that girl into a goddamn crackhead!"

"Me?" Tonette huffed. "Bitch, you knew it was Crystal's idea, but I guess because it was her idea, you were cool with it, huh? You knew what was happening just like the rest of us and you ain't do shit to stop it, so you just as much to blame."

Monique got tired of hearing Tonette's mouth. She shook her head in disgust and limped over to the couch. Instinctively, she rubbed her still-wounded leg as she gathered her things.

"That's right, get the fuck out, you fat-ass bitch," Tonette taunted as Monique walked toward the door.

Weight was always a sore spot with Monique. Although she was pretty and brown-skinned, Monique was ghetto-girl thick and designer clothing rarely fit her, but she squeezed her ass into what she could. The girls always joked that she was gonna have recurring yeast infections because of how tight her shit was hemmed up. Monique didn't care, though. With her clothes and good looks, nobody could have told her she wasn't fly. Her signature hairstyle, huge, gold, shoulder-length box-braid extensions that she wore in a high ponytail, just topped off her package. She even carried a lighter to get rid of any fly-aways and she always kept the ends burnt.

There had always been a friendly competition between Crystal and Tonette because they were both slim, trim, and fly. They always rolled with the niggas that had bank, but Monique made up her niggas.

Monique could take certain things off of Crystal, though, because they were the closest. More like sisters. Crystal had always told her she was going to say something to Tonette about the way she talked about Monique, but that time never came. Now she was dead and Monique was left to fend for herself.

Monique stopped momentarily. She couldn't believe that Tonette had talked to her like that, but then again, she could.

Ever since the SBBs were formed, Tonette had the final say-so on everything, including real talk. Monique was surprised that Shaunna had her head so far up Tonette's ass, because she talked about her like a dog.

"Bitch, if my leg wasn't fucked up, I swear, I'd kick your ass."

"Come on, I'm right here," Tonette confirmed with her hands raised upward. "Yo' leg ain't got shit to do with you not being able to kick my ass. Yo ass just fat and can't keep up with this right here."

Tonette ran her hands up and down the sides of her trim, lean body.

"I'm not gonna argue with you, Tonette." She looked at Shaunna. "You comin'?" she asked, ignoring Tonette's challenge. Monique looked at Shaunna, then back at Tonette.

"Monique, quit trippin'. All this shit ain't necessary. It's over and done with. Just forget about it."

She couldn't believe that Shaunna would stay.

"We the SBBs, baby. Me, you, Tonette, and Crystal. Even though she dead, but that's the way shit goes."

Monique shook her head sadly, in disbelief. "Be careful," she said to Shaunna, "you know what she capable of." She nodded toward Tonette.

"She a SBB heifer. We got each other's back. But I know one thing: if you walk out that door, you gonna be worse off than that stupid bitch Laci ever was," Tonette warned.

"Fuck you, Tonette, and everything that you stand for!" Monique yelled, slamming the door behind her.

CHAPTER 8

IT HAD BEEN days since Smurf had seen Gloria. Although upset with how she'd decided to live her life, Smurf couldn't turn his back on his mother. He was the only one that she had, and he didn't want to abandon her.

Pulling up to her building, Smurf looked at the front window of his mother's apartment. "I wonder what she's doing in there," he said to himself. He had a feeling she had a man in there, but he didn't want to believe it.

After sitting in his car for twenty minutes, Smurf got out and decided to go see his mother.

"I wish she would have moved with me," he said to himself as he walked up the stairs. The apartment building was so worn down, he wondered if it was a safety hazard.

Reaching the third floor, he walked slowly toward her apartment, 311. Smurf's heart began racing, not knowing what to expect. Out of common courtesy, he raised his hand to knock on the door.

Knock knock knock. A few seconds passed and nobody answered. He knocked again. Still, nobody answered.

Smurf then reached toward the doorknob and turned it. Surprisingly, it turned and allowed him access to the apartment. It was completely dark, but he heard the television playing. Walking through the apartment toward the sound of the television, Smurf kept his hand on his gun. His mother normally didn't keep the door unlocked, and just in case there was foul play, someone would meet his maker, messing with his mother.

Smurf arrived at his mother's bedroom door and saw that it was open. He saw a figure sprawled across the bed.

"Momma?" Smurf looked around, then back at the figure. "Momma!" Still no response. Smurf ran over to her. "Momma!" he yelled again. Just then, he saw a wet spot on the bedspread and a glass where the spot was. Smurf took a deep breath in and exhaled.

His mother had been drinking. Smurf knew that a lot of his mother's problems stemmed from alcohol, but he had never seen her in such a stupor before.

Just as Smurf began to clean up the mess, his mother startled.

"Demond," she said softly, but groggily. "Why did you leave me?" Smurf stopped and listened. "Baby, I tried to make it without you, but you didn't come back. You didn't want me anymore. I gotta find a way to live, baby."

Smurf looked into his mother's face and saw that alcohol was taking a toll on her looks. She had a tear that wanted to escape her closed eyelids, so he touched it with his finger and let it free. This was the first time in Smurf's young life that he had seen his mother so vulnerable. He didn't know who she was talking about and couldn't make out everything she said, but he knew she was talking about someone important to her. But who was he? And better yet, where was he?

CHAPTER 9

LACI STILL SUFFERED from the withdrawal effects of her addiction, but they were lessening day by day. The rehab center's doctors and counselors told her that she might suffer some permanent side effects from the crack cocaine, but Laci said she'd take it one day at a time. Some days were better than others. While she was in her comfort zone during the day at school with other people like her, Laci refused to be in one-on-one or small group situations. She felt that people would take advantage of her, so she rarely hung out.

She often woke up at night from bad dreams, tremors, night sweats, and extreme paranoia, so she napped as much as she could during the day. Laci's body writhed forcefully in her slumber. Dink walked into their bedroom when he came home to check on her. He sat down on the side of the bed and put his hand on her shoulder. "Laci. Baby, wake up."

Laci opened her eyes and blinked to bring her surroundings into focus. Without saying a word, she tore off the covers and frantically jumped out of bed and peered out the bedroom window, then ran to the front window in the living room.

"Baby, who are you lookin' for?" Dink asked.

"Those trifling bitches," Laci grunted through tight teeth. "I know they're here." She ran to the closet and thrashed clothes around, mumbling how she hated them. She tried to leave the room, but Dink grabbed her and held her tightly. He'd known that in time this would come, and he was glad he was there for her. The comfort that Laci felt instantly brought her to tears. "They're everywhere. When I close my eyes, when I'm awake," she cried, running all of her words together. She tried to break free, but Dink held her close to him. "Tonette and them followed me here. Everywhere I go, they're there!" She was on the verge of hyperventilating.

Dink felt lost, because he couldn't imagine how she was feeling inside. Counseling didn't prepare him for this. "Baby, nobody's here but me and you," Dink told Laci softly. She looked into his eyes, searching for the truth, as he walked her to the couch and sat her down. "Just me and you, baby."

Dink went to the kitchen for a glass of water and brought it back to her. Laci drank it quickly and handed him the empty glass. With a blotchy red face and tear-drenched eyes, she ran her fingers through her wild and tangled hair, then looked up at him.

"I'm sorry, baby," she apologized. "I can't believe I'm still having these flashbacks and nightmares." She broke down again. "There must be something wrong with me."

"It's okay, baby, let it out. Let it all out." Dink sat down on the couch next to her, pulled her into his arms, and caressed her hair while he held her. "And there's nothing wrong with you. You've gone through a lot in the last six weeks, more than the average person goes through in their life. It's gonna take some time, Laci."

Laci wiped her wet face with the back of her hand and looked at Dink.

"Thank you." She hugged him tightly. "I'm glad you're here."

"This is where my heart is baby, with you, and I'm not going anywhere." Dink lay back on the couch and pulled her gently against him. He rubbed her back until he dozed off, but Laci thought back to her thirty days in rehab, and the memories of the past summer.

AFTER A DAY *of chillin' with her girls, Laci realized it was getting late and it was time for her to jet. Each of her friends turned on her, expressing how they felt about her.*

"While we're passing blunts and bottles, you're on some chill shit. Like you're propped up on a pedestal. You even act like being around weed smoke is gonna kill you," Tonette spoke.

"But you know I don't do drugs," Laci explained.

"That's some sad shit," Shaunna said. "Weed ain't even a fuckin' drug. It's a natural herb from the ground, baby—like fuckin' goldenseal or some shit."

"If anything, I would say alcohol is more of a drug than weed," Crystal added. "Who you know smokes a joint, jumps in a car, and takes out a family of five on the expressway?"

"You know?" Shaunna said, giving Crystal some dap.

"I know you don't drink, Laci," Tonette said. "And I can totally dig that. But why you frontin' on the weed? A lil' smoke ain't gon' hurt you."

After more ridicule from her friends, Laci thought about it. One pull couldn't hurt. It was just marijuana. Maybe this would stop the girls from always riding her. If one puff of the magic dragon was all it was going to take to show the girls she could get down, it was worth it.

"You got some?" Laci asked Crystal.

"Some what?" Crystal asked.

"Some weed, a joint," Laci said. "I was thinking that I might need a little something to make my rest just that much better."

Laci smiled a mischievous smile and the girls returned one.

"As a matter of fact, I just happen to have some," Tonette said. "It's in my purse in the living room. Hold on. I'll go get it."

Once Tonette had returned with the blunt, Laci examined it with curiosity.

"What are you waiting for?" Crystal asked. "Spark up."

"Why don't one of you guys light it and then pass it to me?" Laci said nervously. The last thing she wanted to do was burn off her bangs trying to light a joint on the stove. "Shaunna, you're good at this, here." Laci stuck the joint in Shaunna's face.

"Now you know I got a Wave Nouveau. If my hair catches fire, we're all blowin' up."

After laughter, Monique egged Laci on. "Come on, Laci, quit playing with the weed. Either light the shit or pass it off. See, Crystal, I told you."

Seeing the smug look on Monique's face made Laci angry. Laci was sick of all of them doubting her and was now more determined than ever to show them that she could hang. Cautiously, she leaned over the flames and lit the blunt.

"That's a girl," Crystal said with a smile. "Now come on in the living room."

Once they'd followed Crystal into the living room, Laci looked at the girls, who were now staring at her, and without hesitation, she took two baby pulls.

"Give me a fuckin' break," Crystal laughed. The other girls stood watching in amazement. They were impressed. They didn't think

Laci had the balls. "Did you see those sucker-ass pulls? Look, Laci, that's some good shit and I don't want to see it go to waste. If you gon' do it, do it. Don't be wastin' the shit."

This was the Crystal that Laci was used to, but it was also the Crystal she no longer wanted to doubt her. Laci took two more pulls, only deeper. Her throat immediately constricted, causing her to cough and begin to feel light-headed. Laci took two more pulls to shut the girls up after they started laughing. Only this time, she didn't cough out the smoke. When the smell hit the air, Laci realized it was something different. It didn't smell like what the girls had smoked before.

AT THE REHAB center, all the other addicts knew the consequences of their choice. There was even a patient with incurable cancer who'd turned to street drugs because her prescription medications weren't helping her anymore, but did that make it right?

Many talked about how they became addicted. Their addiction was so strong that they no longer cared about the basic necessities of life, and some would have welcomed death to end their pain. There were some who were close to starvation, and Laci could relate to that. She was disgusted when she heard other people's stories about what they did while they were on drugs.

Nobody deserved to be turned out. Besides the embarrassment Laci felt, she grew extremely angry. During the treatment, most of her memories of what she did while high were slowly and surely fading, but now they started resurfacing more and more each day.

Laci thought back to the girls and how easy it was for her to get played . . . all because she wanted to fit in. She was furious not only at them but at herself as well for falling for the okie-doke.

All of the fury and resentment that was building up in Laci was turning into something that she couldn't control. It would be only a matter of time before her anger turned into something she couldn't help but want—revenge.

CHAPTER 10

I T WAS AN abnormally warm mid-September day, and Smurf and some of his boys were playing a physical game of three-on-three ball on an outdoor court in the hood. He needed something to take his mind off what happened with his mother.

With every basket that was sunk, the shooter talked shit, and their growing audience high-fived one another and talked shit back, placing bets on who was gonna whoop who. True male bonding at its best. Most of the kids who watched wanted to get noticed by Smurf and found any reason they could to hang around because they wanted to get put on.

There were a couple of kids leaning against Smurf's old-school Cutlass Supreme, another gift from Dink, keeping an eye on things. Smurf broke them off a couple of dollars just to be an extra set of eyes and ears for him because they were in the streets more often and heard more. Not only did he give them money, but just as Dink had with him, he gave the kids books to read to expand their minds. Smurf had a fucked-up childhood and little education, and even though the kids looked up to him, he felt there was no need for them to follow in his footsteps. He kept it real with them, and they appreciated that and watched out for him. Just another way to secure a position in the hood.

Smurf heard the big engine of a souped-up el Camino approaching right behind him. It was his boy Rob from Harlem. Rob revved the engine and maneuvered the large racehorse behind Smurf's Cutlass and got out. Smurf called a quick time-out and slowly walked to him, with a little lean in his swagger. He and Rob held out their fists for some dap once they got close enough.

"Yo, wassup man?" Smurf acknowledged.

Lil' Rob looked at Smurf's young company and bellowed, "Why ain't y'all lil' asses in school? Get on!" He shooed them away like little flies. Both Smurf and Rob laughed as they watched the youngsters scurry away.

"Man, you really fucked up," Smurf said, shaking his head at his boy.

"Yeah, I know," he confirmed, still with laughter. "But yo, boss," Rob said seriously, leaning against Smurf's car, "this red-bone cop been down here askin' about Dink and Dame." Smurf looked at Rob but remained quiet. "Skinny lil' muthafucka with short hair in a white unmarked Lumina." Rob got comfortable on the car. "And man, when you gonna take me out of the goddamn West Village?" he asked angrily, getting off the subject.

Smurf looked at him and cracked a crooked grin. He knew what he was getting at.

"Niggas told us it was some fly-ass females down there, but ain't nothing but some fuckin' faggots holding hands with tight-ass pants on and kissing!" Rob had a crazy look on his face. "Then get this, I'm at my post and shit and the lil' ass-packer in the Lumina wanted to suck my dick." Smurf began to laugh. "Man, fuck you! That shit ain't funny. You know I don't roll like that."

Rob had to make that clear. "Man, I wanted to fuck him in the ass with the barrel of my gun and blow his heart out." He motioned with his hand. "So, if I see 'em again, can I smoke 'em?" he asked with a look on his face that said all he needed was a nod and it was done.

"Naw, nigga," Smurf replied, still trippin' off his boy. "You need to be cool with that fucked-up temper of yours, too." He paused for a moment, getting back to the seriousness of their conversation, carefully contemplating his next move. He knew it was that gay bastard that Marco had been fuckin' with and that was the main reason he had one of his boys posted there. He knew that because Marco was no longer a part of the equation, the faggot cop would sooner or later come back around. Because of that, he couldn't do anything too rash. "Anything else?" Smurf asked him.

"I'on know, man, something don't feel right. Something 'bout to go down."

Smurf looked around at his immediate territory and got up off the car. "Round up the crew and meet me at the joint in thirty minutes," Smurf ordered.

"Got it, boss."

Thirty minutes later, Smurf's key players were at the joint. Drake, one of Smurf's corner distributors, was a smart kid from the hood. He was the pretty boy of the crew, light-skinned and with good hair. Because of that, he always had woman drama. Smurf appreciated his passion for hustling, though. Drake often hipped Smurf on several different ways to push their stash. He was practically an extension of Smurf—next in charge if something were to go down.

Chunky was just that, an abnormally big dude with big features. Smurf couldn't understand a word he said because he had a stuttering problem, but he liked Chunky despite his flaws.

He was sincere and the most confident nigga Smurf had ever known, because Chunky never backed down from anybody. Because of his large size, he often intimidated many, but cops would never think that a big, fat stuttering cat would be in the game. It was all good because Chunky wasn't no punk, and that worked for Smurf.

The third player, Lil' Rob, was the weight that Dirty sent from Harlem. Smurf needed someone just as hard as him, or harder, to keep him secure. Keeping true to the Harlem style, Rob wore nothing but track suits with T-shirts and a large gold-link chain that complemented his open-faced gold tooth. His long Jheri curl was always topped off with a Kangol, and he wore only Adidas, Converse, and Fila sneakers.

He was attractive to many of the hood rats who tried to jock him, but Lil' Rob was arrogant and refused to fuck with South Bronx hoes, because he felt they were skeezers. Smurf called him the enforcer. Lil' Rob didn't have any problem forcing bullets in any muthafucka that crossed the line.

It was a Friday night, and Smurf knew the arcade down in The Hub was jumpin'. Fordham Road, also known as The Hub, was the busiest strip mall in New York, so there was always something going on. Smurf often met with his key players at the arcade because it would be the last place cops would think they would be conducting business.

It was crowded, hot, and noisy from the sounds of the arcade games that filled the air, along with the loud laughter and hollering from the teenage crowd. Smurf and his lieutenants huddled around their favorite game, Commando, and Smurf began his meeting.

"It's been brought to my attention that Five-0 been canvassing the turf. Y'all seen 'em around your way?" Smurf asked as he played the game.

"N . . . n . . . no," Chunky forced himself to say.

"You seen 'em?" Smurf asked Drake.

"Naw."

All four of the guys were concentrating on the game and whoopin' and hollerin' when Smurf started shooting and blowing shit up.

"Them muthafuckas been comin' around West Ville askin' questions about Dink, Marco, and Dame," Lil' Rob confirmed.

"What the ffffuck you ddddoin' in West Ville, mmman?" Chunky asked, looking at Lil' Rob suspiciously.

"Man, fuck yo' fat ass!" Lil' Rob shouted, glaring at Chunky, knowing what he was getting at. Everybody laughed.

"It's only gonna be a minute before they come down here asking that same shit, that is, if they haven't already."

"Okay, well, what you want us to do?" Drake asked seriously, getting back to the meeting. He knew Lil' Rob was a hothead and someone had to think rationally.

"Nothin' right now," Smurf told his boy, coolly. "Just fall back, keep your eyes and ears open. Let me know if you see or hear anything that don't seem right."

"Well, now that you mention it," Drake spoke, "ain't nobody seen them niggas. What's up?"

Smurf looked at his boy, who made him lose a turn.

"Dink had some business to tend to, Marco had loyalty issues. Dame had loyalty issues too, but he got cut up slippin' in some bitch pussy." Smurf shook his head. "That's a damn shame."

The crew became quiet and looked at Smurf. They knew what that meant. "I know you handled that shit, boss," Drake told Smurf with a slight chuckle. He'd known of Smurf when Dink was around. "I thought there was something shady with that bitch Marco, but Dame...I thought he was on top of his game."

The real reason Dame was gone was because he was a cocky, ego-trippin' nigga. Dink had been good to all of his boys and made everyone family, but when Dame threatened him, he realized that the nigga was on some bullshit and had to be dealt with. Dame wanted to shine more than he wanted to grind, but his crew didn't need to know that. Dame went down the best way he could, at the hands of a ho. "Yeah, but we all know all pussy ain't good pussy." Everyone dapped. "But yo, speaking loyalty, let me holla at you for a second," Smurf told Drake.

Instantly, Drake's pager went off. He looked at it and a frown spread across his face as he stuck it back on his hip. The two went off to a secluded area in the back of the arcade. Smurf noticed the other two guys went to scoop up some honeys.

"Wassup, boss?" Drake spoke. He knew when he and Smurf spoke one-on-one, it was serious, and he was glad that it was him that Smurf trusted.

"I been meanin' to ask you...is there something up with your pager?"

"Why you ask that?" Drake asked Smurf, with a perplexed look on his face.

"I paged you earlier and you never returned my call. Let me see it." Smurf grabbed it out of its holder and ran through the numbers. "See, it's right here," he told Drake, trying to jar his memory. Smurf handed the pager back to Drake.

"Shit, I don't know. Probably chillin'."

"Wrong answer," Smurf said. "I'ma ask you one last time. Where were you?"

Drake remembered exactly what Smurf was talking about. He was with his older brother who'd graduated from the academy. The two went riding in his new squad car and his brother gave him some information about a chick he was asking about. Drake knew he had to confess, because he knew that Smurf wouldn't hesitate putting a cap in his ass. Homeboy or not.

"Look, man, I was with my brother, so what?"

"So what? Your brotha is a fuckin' cop," Smurf said calmly.

"Rookie," Drake emphasized.

"It don't matter."

"Look, man, what he do and what I do ain't got shit to do with the other," Drake said forcefully. "That nigga be in the streets as much as we do. So what he got a legal hustle now? I been down with you for a while, man, and you think I'ma fuck that shit up?"

Smurf said nothing.

"Look, man, we got an inside man that can let us know what's going down and when," Drake said honestly. "As a matter of fact, when you saw us, he was asking me about that fly-ass junkie everybody was bangin' over the summer."

"Which one?"

"The light-skinned one. The ho Dink was ridin' dirty with."

"What about her?" Smurf's eyebrows raised. He knew Drake was talking about Laci.

"They looking at Tonette and them because of Crystal being knocked, but his partner thinks they're behind more shit too. Actually, he said his partner put a big drug case on hold to deal with these chicks."

Smurf thought back to the dossier that Marco had on Dame and Dink.

"You know, man, my moms wanted me to go to the academy

too, but I wasn't feeling that shit. Fuckin' PD ain't payin' shit. I got two baby mamas and a gal. Shit . . . a nigga gotta eat."

Smurf shook his head and had a crooked grin on his face. "Y'all pretty muthafuckas can sho' get yourself into some shit, can't you?" Drake frowned. "Well, just as long as it won't mess up our operation, then we cool. Make sure you handle yo' shit, but check it, I need you to do something for me."

"You got it . . . what's up?"

"CLIFTON," OFFICER JONES called out, startling his partner upon his return. Detective Clifton was reviewing the file he had buried in paperwork on his desk. "I got a positive ID on the girl in the photo." The detective looked at the clock, then turned around and looked at his trainee waiting for him to talk. "Her name is Julacia. Julacia Johnson, and get this—she lives in Riverdale."

"Riverdale?" Detective Clifton interjected with raised eyebrows. He noticed his trainee glancing at the file that was on his desk and he shuffled papers to conceal it. "What the fuck she doing bummin' around in the South Bronx? That's actually a very odd combination." Detective Clifton sat back in his chair with his arms behind his head. He stared at Officer Jones and noticed how handsome he was. He thought back to the case at hand to get his mind off his trainee. "The question is how she got involved with those girls. She doesn't look like she'd be mixed up with them."

"Well, I'm one step ahead of you on that," the rookie answered, not giving up how he knew of the girl. Even though he'd learned her name by going to the South Bronx, Officer Jones was just as familiar with her as every other nigga in that neighborhood. He, too, had a copy of the tape of Dame fucking the shit out of her. It was the hottest thing on the streets.

"Well damn, Jones, I'm glad you got your ass outta there without getting shot at. It's a jungle out there."

"Nah it ain't," Officer Jones reassured his partner. "They're nothing but pussycats in the South Bronx," he joked.

The detective looked at him strangely. "Yeah, pussycats."

"But for real, though, it's just everyday life. We just gotta stay on top of what's going on down there, that's it."

"I'm one step ahead of you on that, youngin'," Clifton spoke, "but this makes more sense. Ms. Thomas alluded that someone else may be involved. You gotta give it to Ms. Johnson, though. She's a smart one."

"Why you say that?"

"Whatever this girl is doing, you can damn sure bet she ain't bringing it back to Riverdale. I'm sure once it starts getting dark, she gets the hell outta the South Bronx, hops her little ass in mommy and daddy's car, and hits the Henry Hudson Parkway back home." The detective laughed at his own humor. "Well, what's up with her, rookie, what else did you find out?"

"Nothing much," Officer Jones sighed. "I'm afraid we may not find her."

"Why not?"

"Word on the street is she's out there bad on the pipe and when they've got that itch, trying to find that one crackhead is almost next to impossible."

"A crackhead?" Detective Clifton picked up the picture and looked closely at Laci, then shook his head in disbelief. "This girl right here?" Officer Jones nodded his head. Clifton looked back at the picture and shook his head. "Just doesn't seem right," he mumbled under his breath.

"No telling what this girl looks like now." They both looked at Laci's picture.

They both knew that there was no specific look for a druggie, as they came from all walks of life, but most of the people they arrested were dirty, toothless, and homeless. Scrungy-looking at best, but even on her worst day, Laci didn't fall into this category.

"Look, I don't care what kinda itch she got. We got to find her. I think she could have some information on why or who would report Ms. Moore as being armed and dangerous."

Once the rookie had analyzed the situation as his partner did, he nodded his head in agreement. "You're right, but let me keep working on this. I should have more answers for you by to-morrow."

"Nuh huh, you're not going back down there alone this time," the detective told him. "It's almost night and the area's too bad. They see you in your uniform and all hell will break loose. Rule number one, you always need a backup, and rule number two, don't be a fuckin' wise-ass." The detective got up in Jones's face and pointed a finger. He saw how smooth Terrance Jones's skin was, and he even caught a faint whiff of Eternity for Men. Rodney Clifton was incensed now. "Y'all come in here, straight out the academy like y'all on some robo-cop shit try'na make us look bad. Fuck that shit! I told you I put a big case on hold that could have promoted me to the head of the drug task force, but now, I gotta investigate this shit because a fuckin' cop was involved in the shooting. IA is breathing down our necks. There is a link here with these two cases that I'm try'na work out. I worked too long and hard, man. Ain't no fuckin' rookie gonna take what's right-fully mine."

"Man, I ain't try'na take none of your cases from you," Officer Jones confirmed, moving out of the way of his partner's stank coffee breath and getting his personal space back. "I could care less about that! I'm just trying to help. I know my way around the streets more than you do as an officer."

"I don't care if you were a goddamn blind mouse working your way around a fuckin' maze," Clifton spat, "I can't let you do that. You're fresh out of the academy. You ain't been trained for the streets yet. Especially the Bronx."

"I know more than you think I do," Officer Jones told him honestly.

"Is that so? And how you figure that? You got an insider on the girl or something?"

"No, I just know how the streets work. You go down there demanding answers and shit, try'na bum-rush those kids, you don't know what's gonna kick off. Just sit back at yo' desk, eat some donuts, move some papers and look busy. Let me do this."

"Man, fuck you," the detective retorted. Officer Jones winked at him, signaling that he'd won this round with his comrade, and walked out of the office.

"Hotheaded rookie," Detective Clifton mumbled under his breath. He was glad his trainee was out of his face. He had him so worked up, he needed to go back to the West Village to find some stress relief.

CHAPTER 11

Sonny opened the door to Margaret's house when he heard the doorbell ring. He had been staying with Margaret since Laci went to rehab. Margaret welcomed the company. She had always liked Sonny. He'd developed a dope habit in 1965 and had lost everything, including his relationship with his mother and his brother, Jay. When he was confronted, he took the coward's way out and burned out. He wasn't there for his mother's funeral or Jay's college graduation, marriage, or death. Margaret was big on family because she had a small one, and so she'd searched the streets for her husband's only brother. Once she found him, she vowed to help him and never turn her back on him.

Margaret put Sonny through rehab, visited him, and helped him turn his life around. She even helped him get a job at the local supermarket, but after being clean for a year, he woke up with a jones he couldn't shake. Margaret was brokenhearted that he wanted to go back to his habit, but if he hadn't run into Laci that day at the crack house, who knows what could have happened.

"Hi, can I help you?" he asked the officer who stood in front of him.

"Good evening, I'm Officer Terrance Jones," he displayed his badge, "and I'm looking for Julacia Johnson."

"Why are you looking for her?" Sonny asked in a harsh tone, followed by a worried look on his face. He noticed the officer had an envelope in his hand.

"Is she here?" the officer asked again, in an attempt to look past Sonny.

"Look, officer, no disrespect," Sonny said, "but I'm not going to let you see her or talk to her until you tell me what you want." Sonny knew it was pointless to argue with the officer, so he tried his best to cooperate without coming across as defensive.

"I'll come back later," the rookie officer said, despondent. He knew something was up and hoped that getting answers wouldn't be a problem. It was Friday evening, and he was afraid this would be the start of a long-ass night.

"Officer," Sonny spoke before the officer got to the second step on the porch, "my niece has gone through a lot in the last few months. If something is wrong, I'd like to know." He extended his hand in a formal introduction. "I'm Sonny Johnson and whatever's happening, I'd want to be the one to tell her instead of you. She doesn't need any stress added to her life."

Officer Jones stopped and looked at Sonny. He handed him the envelope he was carrying. Sonny stepped outside on the porch and closed the door slightly in case Margaret came looking for him. He would rather he handle this than his sister-in-law. Sonny opened the envelope and looked inside. He saw pictures of five girls, one of whom was Laci.

"Do you know these girls?" the officer asked.

"Just my niece," Sonny spoke after looking at the picture, "but these have to be those little bitches who—" Sonny stopped talking, realizing his anger was getting the best of him.

"Who what?" the officer asked.

Sonny looked at the officer. "Nothing. What do you want to know about my niece?"

"I'm curious how she knew these girls and if she knew anything about who may have set up Crystal Moore. That's the girl right here." He pointed to Crystal's picture.

"What happened to her?"

"I really can't go into details because I'd like to question your niece, sir. But if you would," he reached into the breast pocket of his uniform shirt and pulled out a business card, "could you have her call me? My number's right there."

Sonny took the card. "Is my niece in any type of trouble?" he asked.

"Honestly sir, it's too soon to tell. Her name came up and we need to question her about her involvement with these girls and see if she can tell us anything about the incident involving Crystal Moore."

"I'll see what I can do," Sonny told the cop, "but I can't promise you anything."

"Well, as long as you try, that's all I can ask; but if you can't, then we'll have to put a search warrant out on her."

"A search warrant?"

"I'm sorry, but yes. It'd be so much easier if she came to us." The officer was truthful but respectful. He didn't want to cause any trouble. He had a feeling that the sex tape, Crystal's death, and Laci's connection with the South Bronx Bitches had to be related in some way. But how?

CHAPTER 12

AFTER THEIR TALK, Drake and Smurf returned to the other guys, who now had the full attention of some skeezers. Drake and Smurf's eyes widened in shock at the skanky girls. Obviously, Lil' Rob and Chunky had awful taste in women.

"I thought that was you," a girl whined to Drake. It was his first baby mama, Tanisha.

"Oh, hey . . . wassup, T."

"Wassup?" she said in true ghetto-girl fashion. "That's all you gotta say to me, 'wassup'?" She stood in front of him, put her hands on her hips, and cocked her head to the side.

"It's kinda late," he told her. "Why ain't you at home with my son?" Drake couldn't stand Tanisha and didn't have much to say to her. She was a neighborhood ho and the word on the street was she'd trapped him with a baby because she wanted one with good hair.

"Shit, nigga, why ain't you home with me and yo' son?" she shot back. "Knock a bitch up, then you move on to the next dumb bitch." She rolled her eyes and looked at Drake as if to say *now what, nigga?*

Smurf and Drake exchanged glances.

"I'ma let you handle yo' family business." Smurf patted him on the back, shook his head, smirked, and walked away.

Just as Smurf began to play a game of Donkey Kong, a sweet voice startled him.

"Hey, Smurf."

The smell of PRIMO caught Smurf's senses, and before he could turn around, he knew who it was. LaQuan. She stood about 5′5″, had dark, smooth skin, and wore a short, tapered haircut. She wore a pair of l.e.i. jeans with leather on the front, with black leather riding boots and a red silk blouse. She also wore multiple dolphin earrings that dangled from her ears. She shifted from foot to foot because this was her first time approaching Smurf and she was nervous, even though she'd heard he wanted to get up on her.

Smurf had wanted to get at her for a while, but business came first. "Hey Quannie, what you up to?"

She smiled at Smurf, glad to hear that he called her Quannie. She'd heard that he referred to her like that from around the way but wanted to hear it for herself.

"Just hangin' out with my homegirls." She looked around, spotted her clique, and pointed to them. "I was hopin' to run into you."

"Yeah, me too," he told her, looking up and down at her body.

LaQuan looked at Smurf innocently and smiled. Along with Smurf's reputation of being a ruthless killer, he was also known as someone who could lay some good pipe. Many chicks chased him and some got what they wanted. Even though young Smurf was only seventeen, he went from not being able to get pussy to having to choose carefully which ho to get it from. If a ho came to him wanting to give him some, he figured something was up, and that could mean the beginning of the end for him, just like in Dame's case.

Smurf pulled nothing but top-notch hoes. They looked good on his arm, but these were the same women who had their hands extended, and always wanted something.

Smurf didn't mind doing shit for females he liked, but he started getting tired of them always saying "gimme" followed by an expectation. The only bitch he would trick for would be his momma and with the way she was rolling, those times were few and far between.

LaQuan stuck close by Smurf for the rest of the night, cheering him on and bumping into him at the most convenient times, brushing her small, firm breasts against him or pushing her pussy against his hip. LaQuan looked innocent, but Smurf knew many niggas who slid up in her. It was his turn now.

An announcement came over the loudspeakers that the arcade would close in five minutes. Smurf looked at his watch. It was one o'clock in the morning. He finished up his game and turned to LaQuan.

"Wassup for tonight? You burnin' out with your girls?" Smurf asked.

"I'm try'na see what you 'bout to get into," she told him. "I really liked how you handled that joystick," she flirted.

It was late, and Smurf had something else on his mind. "You think you can handle my joystick?" he countered.

LaQuan smiled. "Take me home and you'll see how I play the game." She got closer to him and he placed his hands on her small waist. "Let's see how well you take the curves."

Smurf half grinned and pushed up against her so she could feel what he was working with.

LaQuan's eyes sparked with delight when she felt his thick dick press against her thigh. "Let's go."

Smurf drove LaQuan back to her house. After they got out of the car, he walked directly behind her, not once taking his hands off her hips as they walked up onto her front porch. LaQuan paused before unlocking her door.

"Hey, go over there," she whispered and pointed to the gang-way. "My room is the last window. I'll let you in."

Smurf looked at her as if she were crazy, but then he remembered she was just fifteen and probably couldn't have dudes walking through the house in the middle of the night. Only because he had to get his nut out, he agreed to do the Spiderman crawl.

Within a few minutes, LaQuan slowly and quietly raised her bedroom window and Smurf expertly climbed in. He looked around and saw posters of LL Cool J and UTFO.

"Instead of looking at those," she pointed to her wall, "why don't you look at these," she teased, modeling her simple white cotton panties and bra. Smurf pulled LaQuan toward him and roughly kissed her on the lips. LaQuan let him kiss her like that for a minute, and then she backed away. She turned on a small strobe light on her dresser, then flicked off her bedroom light. The rapidly flashing colorful lights flickered while she lay on her bed and watched him.

Quickly, Smurf pulled his shirt over his head and retrieved his gun before he got out of his pants. LaQuan smiled when she saw the erection that filled his underwear.

"Shh . . ." she said when she heard his car keys jingle in his pocket. He quietly draped his pants over her chair.

Just as the rumor around town had it, Smurf didn't lay his gun down when he fucked. Although that turned a lot of girls on, it was a promise that he made to himself when he got his first piece—never get caught without it.

Grabbing his piece, Smurf got into LaQuan's squeaky twin bed next to her.

"Don't make too much noise," she told him, "because my grandmama might wake up."

This was the reason Smurf messed with older girls. Most of them had their own places, so their moms or grandmoms wouldn't be home babysitting them.

LaQuan pulled off her bra and slipped out of her panties. "I wanna see your thang," she told Smurf.

"That all you wanna do is see it?" he whispered in a teasing tone. "I want you to do more than that."

He took his underwear off and held the length of his dick in his hand.

"You like what you see?"

"Oh yeah," LaQuan told him, "that thang is thick. Let's get this shit started."

She lay back and Smurf rolled on top of her. He put his lips on hers, tasting her warm kisses, teasing her with his tongue. He tilted his head down to her neck. He gently traced an "O" and lightly sucked, exciting them both at the same time.

Smurf's hands found LaQuan's breasts and he began to softly squeeze. He then replaced his hands with his mouth, sucking on her firm nipples. LaQuan let out a suppressed grunt as she groped the back of Smurf's head while he sucked on every inch of her breasts.

Smurf then slipped his hand down to LaQuan's pussy, and caressed it.

"That feels so good," she whispered in Smurf's ear. His lips found his way to the side of her neck. LaQuan began grinding her pussy against Smurf's touch. "Put yo' thang in," she ordered.

Smurf took his hand away from her pussy and got on his knees in between her legs. In his left hand, he held his gun and placed it on her chest. With his right, he grabbed his rock-hard dick and began sliding it up and down LaQuan's slippery slit. He found the small opening he had been waiting to get up in.

Slowly, Smurf attempted to ease his way inside LaQuan's tight pussy. He removed his left hand from her chest and placed it, with the gun, to the side of her. He leaned forward. "Relax for me baby," he whispered into her ear when he felt her tighten up. "Don't fight it. Just let me put it in."

LaQuan followed Smurf's instruction, opening her legs a little wider and relaxing. Even though Quannie wasn't a virgin, most of the guys who ran up in her were average at best, and Smurf's dick was bigger than what she was used to.

He inched his way, bit by bit, into her tight pussy.

"Ooh shit girl . . . umpf . . ." Smurf grunted once he was all the way in. "Wrap your legs around my back," he told her.

After LaQuan had Smurf locked in between her legs, he slowly began to stroke her insides.

In . . . out . . . in . . . out . . . in, deep stroke . . . around and around. He stirred her pussy like he was mixing sugar and cream in coffee. Careful not to make too much noise, Smurf reached under LaQuan's ass to dig deeper in her pussy.

She sucked in a deep breath, more in ecstasy than in pain, when he hit bottom. "Oooh shit!" was all she managed to whisper between gritted teeth.

Smurf had her pussy full and at the angle he needed. Her teenage juices let him slide deeper, continuing to hit bottom with each stroke. Teasing her with the head of his dick at the entrance of her pussy was out of the question. The noise the bed would make would certainly wake her grandmother. The groove they had going on was fine for young Smurf. Quannie's pussy gripped him like a vacuum and he really didn't want to get out of her.

Smurf began to pick up his pace as he was near a nut. To keep him from making too much noise, LaQuan grabbed his ass, pulling him deeper inside, and met Smurf's thrusts with a grind of her own. Smurf absentmindedly sucked hard on her neck until he busted a nut.

Staying on the deep stroke until his orgasm subsided, Smurf eased up out of LaQuan's vaginal grip and sat on the bed.

"Go get me something," he told her.

LaQuan quietly opened her bedroom door and tiptoed to the bathroom. She returned with a warm, soapy washcloth.

After Smurf wiped his dick off, he quietly dressed.

Right before he left, he looked back at her and reached in his pocket and peeled off two bills.

"What's this?" she asked, looking at the money.

"Here, take it."

"I ain't no ho, boy," she whispered angrily, not knowing that Smurf knew of her reputation.

That took Smurf by surprise. "Never let no nigga dig up in shit that good without giving you something," he told her. "Call me."

He dropped the dough on the nightstand and scurried out the same way he came. Just another night in the hood.

CHAPTER 13

WHEN SMURF ARRIVED back at his apartment, he found Dirty in the dark, drinking a glass of bourbon. Not saying a word, Smurf noticed that Dirty's eyes followed him wherever he went.

"What the fuck you looking at me like that fo'?" Smurf asked. "I ain't on that homo shit, man."

"Man, why the fuck you think everything about you? Don't nobody wanna fuck with yo' lil' bitty ass!" Dirty shouted.

Smurf sensed that something was wrong with Dirty. He went to the refrigerator, grabbed the pitcher of fruit punch Kool-Aid, walked back to the living room, and sat across from Dirty while drinking out of the pitcher.

After thinking about what to say, Smurf finally spoke.

"Yo, Dirty, look man, we got off to a fucked-up start when you first came here."

"Why you so goddamn cocky, man? I'm here to help you."

"I don't know, man," Smurf answered honestly. "My momma always had these niggas running in and out the house for as long as I could remember. I had to be cocky 'cuz them niggas would put they hands on my moms and I wasn't havin' that shit."

"You know yo' daddy?"

"Naw, I don't know his ass. I don't know whether or not to hate him because my momma ain't never talk about him until recently."

"Well lil' nigga, I ain't have no son either. Dink talked highly about you so when I met you, I thought we could take this shit on the streets to the next level. You a good student, Smurf, you just need to know when to back it down and when to step it up. Why don't you just let me teach you instead of you trying to fight me on shit, man?"

Smurf sat back and listened. He appreciated Dirty's openness.

"So what's up with you tonight?" Smurf asked. "You look like shit."

Dirty twisted his lips. He knew he looked like shit. "Nothing, man." He wiped his forehead with his hand as if he were trying to wipe away a memory. "Just got a lot of shit goin' on these days."

Smurf thought back to his mother and their growing distance. "Me too, man, me too."

CHAPTER 14

DEMOND HAD FINALLY tracked Gloria down. He'd heard word on the streets that she was back in the old neighborhood but hadn't had the nerve to find out for himself, until now. "Glo," he called out when he saw her emerge from her building. He had been sitting outside for hours, and he knew she had to leave sooner or later.

She turned to see who was calling her name.

The car Demond was driving was a magnet to her. She knew the person had money just by the newer-model BMW, but the look of hope on her face vanished when the window rolled down.

"Baby, can I talk to you?"

"I don't have anything to say to you." She continued to walk.

"I know why you feel that way, but just hear me out. After we talk, if you still want me to go, then I will."

Gloria could do nothing but comply. "Come back in two days. Five o'clock in the afternoon. If you're not here, then there's nothing to say."

Gloria knew she needed that time to prepare herself emotionally to hear what Demond had to say. He'd left her high and dry, and she had questions she was determined to get answers to.

Two days later, at five o'clock, Demond was at Gloria's door, knocking. He knocked again in anticipation of seeing her.

"Hi, beautiful," he said when she opened the door. He handed her a bouquet of gas station flowers.

She grabbed the flowers out of his hand. "You got two minutes to talk. So talk."

"Gloria, I don't know where to begin."

"How 'bout from the beginning? Why you push me away?"

"Baby, when I went down, I knew cops would come looking for anyone who was affiliated with me. You were only seventeen. You didn't need to throw your life away because of me."

"Demond, you should have let me decide that. You burned rubber on me and didn't think to look back. I wrote you, you returned the letters. I tried to visit you, you refused to see me. My life has been nothing but shit since you've been gone. I've been waitin' for you all these years and you could have had the common courtesy to tell me what you wanted me to do, instead of pushing me away." Gloria was in tears. "My heart hurts, Demond. I couldn't let you go."

"Do you think it was easy for me to do what I did?" Gloria's words had cut into Demond like a knife. "No, but because I loved you more than myself, I gave you a chance at another life. Not a life of always looking over your shoulder with a nigga like me."

"You shouldn't have decided that for me. That was my decision. I'm tired of all the men in my life try'na tell me what's best for me."

Demond saw the hurt in Gloria's eyes. "You're right, baby. But I'm back. I have seventeen years to make up to you. The decision is yours—let me make it up to you or send me back to where I came from."

CHAPTER 15

AS THE DAYS went on, Laci felt more comfortable at school and with that, she began to trust others and gain more confidence in herself. Even though she had access to the cool million that her father left her, Laci continued to live as a regular college student, and unlike the South Bronx Bitches, the people around her didn't feel threatened by her presence.

Laci's Algebra class let out and she gathered her belongings to leave the room. Just as she began to walk out, someone called her name.

"Laci! Wait up!"

She turned around and saw two white girls and one biracial girl walking toward her. Instinctively, Laci's heart began to race. *What do they want with me?* She continued to distract herself by gathering her books.

"Hi, Laci!" the tallest of the three spoke. "I'm Meranda, this is Gabrielle," she pointed to the biracial girl, "and this is Samantha."

"Hi!" Gabrielle and Samantha said enthusiastically, in unison.

"Hi," Laci replied, although apprehensive. "It's nice to meet you." She noticed that each of the girls was dressed nicely. Meranda's baby-blue and white Gucci track suit with the GG monogram matched her blue and white custom Gucci sneakers, and the black Gucci purse she carried set off her style. Gabrielle wore a Liz Claiborne acid-wash miniskirt, with a red leotard and black Liz Claiborne riding boots. Samantha's tight-fitting acid-wash Guess jeans and a white-collared long-sleeved shirt made her look immaculate, and a black belt showed off her small waist. She had on black Aigner riding boots and a black bag to match. Each of the girls wore diamonds in her ears.

"Hey, aren't you in my Oral Communications class?" Laci asked Gabrielle.

"Yes I am," Gabrielle exclaimed, glad that Laci recognized her. "Girl, the paper you read about self-reflections was the bomb!"

"Thanks." Laci smiled, flung her backpack over her shoulder, and began walking.

"We've been trying to get at you for a few weeks," Meranda confessed.

Laci looked up at her. "Why?"

"No reason, you just look cool. Not fake like most of these chicks around here." The other girls nodded their heads. "So where are you headed?" Meranda asked. All of the girls began following Laci.

"Um, I was going to grab something to eat at the cafeteria. What were you all doing?"

"We were headed to the cafeteria too," Samantha confirmed. "Do you mind if we go with you?" Each of the girls smiled at Laci, waiting for her answer.

They're not the same kind of girls, Laci. It's okay. Go 'head. Her inner self spoke and she had to trust her judgment. "No. I'd love the company and I'm starving!"

The girls chatted about what most eighteen-year-old girls talk about on their short walk to the cafeteria—shopping. It was a far cry from what Tonette and her crew would talk about. Sensing that the girls had no ulterior motive, Laci began to let her guard down.

As they walked to the cafeteria, Laci saw Dink walking toward her.

"Hey baby," she said as they met up. The girls looked on, wondering who Laci was talking to.

"Where you going, babe?" He looked at Laci and the girls that were with her.

"Lunch, but hey," she looked at the girls then back at Dink, "let me introduce you to my friends. This is Meranda, Gabrielle, and Samantha." She looked at the girls. "Ladies, this is my boyfriend, Daryl."

"Hi Daryl!" they all said in unison, grinning from ear to ear, looking at him.

"Wassup." He acknowledged them with a nod.

"You wanna join us?" Laci asked.

Looking at the girls, Dink thought against it. "Naw baby, I'll just see you later." He bent down and kissed Laci on her lips and walked away.

The cafeteria looked different to Laci—bright, clean, and not overwhelming. She and Dink often ate together and she sat while he got their food, but today, Laci was able to get her own and it felt good.

Once all of the girls had paid for their food, they bumbled their way through the crowded cafeteria to find a place to sit.

"So Laci, where are you from?" Meranda asked after settling into her seat, as she cut into her tuna sandwich with a plastic fork.

"I'm from the South Bronx." Laci put her spoon into her chicken-and-rice soup, stirred, and tested the warmth with her tongue.

"The South Bronx?" Meranda asked, taking a bite of the sandwich. They all looked at her in amazement but with concern. "Isn't that kinda rough?"

"Yeah, it is, but I lived in Riverdale to be exact. Most people don't know about Riverdale, so I just said the South Bronx. Everybody knows about that."

"Oh yeah, Riverdale. I heard of that," Samantha said, putting dressing on her chef salad. "That's a nice community."

"Yeah, it's cool." Laci looked among the girls. "So where are y'all from?"

"I'm from Boston," Meranda said, opening up the bag of chips she'd bought with her sandwich. "We live in the South End."

"I'm from California," Samantha chimed in, "Orange County specifically."

"And I'm from Upper West in Jersey," Gabrielle said as she dug into her cheeseburger like it was the last meal she'd ever have.

Laci knew that she would fit in with her new friends. They were a lot like her—they were privileged to have more than the average person. Even though Laci thought it would be easier to not be around people like her, the summer proved differently and she welcomed them.

"Did you ever go to the heart of the South Bronx, where all the stuff was going on, Laci?" Gabrielle asked. "The news always reports stuff going on there. It's just horrible!" She frowned.

"You're right, but that's why I'm here," Laci told her, ignoring her initial question, "to get away from it all and start my life over again."

"Well, we're glad you're here," Meranda said.

Gabrielle and Samantha agreed.

Laci smiled and realized that she finally fit in with people who liked her. She was able to enjoy life.

CHAPTER 16

Dirty and smurf began spending a lot of time together. They had been traveling more often between the South Bronx and Harlem. Unbeknownst to Smurf, Dirty was training him for the next level in the operation.

A couple of days later, at Dirty's suggestion, Smurf called an emergency meeting at the corner store. Both men sat inside the office and waited for the crew to show up. Smurf normally held their meetings on Monday, but a lot of shit had popped off since their last meeting.

"It's important to keep your workers on their toes and not be too predictable," Dirty told Smurf. "Although they're your boys, you have to know their whereabouts at all times. This is where Dink fell short."

The sound of feet stomping down the stairs alerted the men that the crew had arrived. "Boss man," Drake acknowledged Smurf, interrupting his thoughts, as he entered the office before the rest of the troops showed up.

Smurf looked up. "Whoa...," he exclaimed when he saw

Drake's brother in tow, in his uniform. "What the fuck?" Smurf reached for his gun.

"Hey man," Dirty grabbed Smurf's wrist, "everything's cool," he assured him as he looked among the three men. "Come on," he nodded for Drake and his brother to enter the office, "it's time for the meeting to begin."

"Everyone's not here yet, man," Smurf reminded Dirty.

"Yes they are." Once they were all inside the back room, Smurf closed the door.

Smurf was glad that Lil' Rob wasn't around, because the dude would have gotten smoked with a quickness.

Dirty looked at his young protégé. "The rest of your crew ain't coming. That was an exercise to see how quickly they would respond to you, and it looks like you got the crew you need to back you up, man."

Smurf was getting angry. He felt like he'd been tricked. He looked at Dirty, at the cop, and then at Drake.

"Make this good," Smurf demanded. "You know this ain't good for business."

"Look, man, just calm down for a second," the officer said seriously. He was older than Smurf, and more logical, but he also knew of Smurf's rep. "I'm one of y'all. I was working for Dink over on Tremont."

"I knew most of the people he dealt with," Smurf told him seriously, not recalling his face.

"That's nice and all that you think that," the officer said in a serious tone. "But you didn't know all of us. You were his heat, but Dink had a long reach and had corners everywhere. Actually, you gave my brother my corner, yo. I was around way before you came along."

"I don't give a damn if you were around before me," Smurf said defiantly. "It's not even the fact that you a fuckin' pig. Right now, it's the fact that you up in my spot, with yo' fuckin uniform on, man."

The officer rested up against the wall of Smurf's office and looked at Dirty.

"It's all part of the game and it was carefully planned out."

"What you mean?" Smurf looked at the officer, then at Dirty.

"What we doin' right now is just child's play. Crack is just the beginning," Dirty told Smurf. "We 'bout to take this shit to another level and we decided we needed someone on the inside who could help us."

"What you mean, 'we'?" Smurf questioned.

"We, meaning me and Dink."

"He knows about this?"

"Oh yeah, we handpicked this nigga right here," Dirty said, looking at the officer.

"Yep, they did," he confirmed. "Dink wanted an inside man on the force; that's why he got me off the streets. Nigga had me in school and everything. Made sure I made good grades and stayed out of trouble. I couldn't be a part of the fuckin' academy and hang out here slangin' rock. The NYPD investigates all of their wannabe cops and their families. How would it look with me out there with a fuckin' record, saying I wanna be a cop?" He watched Smurf closely and was glad to see him take his hand off his gun. He knew that Smurf was hotheaded and had a trigger finger.

Smurf looked closely at him and calmed down as he tucked his gun away.

"Yeah, so you know we cool like that. I'm Terrance, Drake's

brother." Smurf didn't respond. "But I believe you wanted this." Terrance handed him copies of the information that Drake had asked him to get.

Smurf sat down on the old rickety desk and quickly thumbed through it, grunting at the contents. "What you gonna do if someone asks about this?" Smurf inquired with raised eyebrows.

"Man . . . that's the problem. That in your hand is a copy. The dossier is at the station."

"What the fuck am I gonna do with a goddamn copy!" Smurf yelled. Even Drake looked at his brother like he was crazy.

"I wanted to get that to you so you could start makin' moves. From the looks of it, my partner was working with someone on the streets to get this shit."

"Yeah, I know," Smurf said. "Yo, is yo' partner a skinny lil' light-skinned black dude with that dirty sandy-colored hair and freckles?"

"Yeah man, that's him. Why?"

Smurf laughed for a minute. "You know he a faggot, right?"

Terrance looked at him with a quizzical expression on his face. "Clifton? A *what*?"

"A fuckin' faggot. He likes dick, man."

"How the hell you know that?" Terrance asked, beginning to feel uncomfortable.

"You remember Marco, right?"

"Yeah," Terrance confirmed. "Him and Dink went back a ways; I couldn't stand his bitch ass."

"Me neither, but he exchanged info with your boy and gave him head, too. I saw that shit, man." Smurf's face tightened in a grimace, trying to block out the memory.

"Marco was his contact? Damn!" Terrance ran his hand over his face in amazement. "He was bragging about working on a big drug case before Crystal got blasted. But nobody took his ass seriously because he always talkin' 'bout shit that don't matter."

"Just like a lil' bitch," Smurf said and shook his head.

"The only reason he workin' on the case now and put the other one on hold is because it involved a cop, and it's taking up a lot of his time because nobody is cooperating. I was helping him with it, but when Drake asked about the dossier," he pointed to the folder in Smurf's hands, "I looked in it and had to keep him focused on the girls. I been out there doing some half-ass shit and bringing him back some bullshit information piece by piece. You know, doing this shit rookie style." They all laughed. "Knowing him, he's gonna try to tie the loose ends of the shooting to the stuff in there, and this the kinda nigga that won't let shit die." Terrance had a serious look on his face. "What we need to do is concentrate on the information in there and make sure nothing comes back to the family. The good thing is, Marco and Dame's bitch asses are dead, but we gotta get you, Dink, and Dirty out of it."

Smurf held the manila file gingerly, as if it contained an atomic bomb that could detonate any minute. He sat down behind the desk and opened the envelope again.

He kept a cool demeanor when he saw names and aliases of key people who worked for Dink. It also detailed their lives from the time they were born, their family members, and their particular hustle. There was also a list of stash houses. He even saw some information on himself and a picture of him when he first met Dink, and even a picture of Dink giving him his first piece.

Looking deeper into the file, he saw names and pictures of his local connects and even pictures of the women they all fucked with, but there was no picture of Laci. *That's good,* Smurf thought. The dossier ended with Dirty's name and photograph, where he resided in Harlem, and how often he came to the South Bronx. What he found most interesting was that Dirty had been in prison for a long time, ten years to be exact, but once he got out, he got back into the drug game as if he'd never left. *That's a true hustler,* Smurf said to himself.

"Goddamn!" Smurf sighed and wiped his hand across his face. "This is a lotta shit, man. Actually, we lucky to be out here!" He fanned through the dossier again. "I'm glad I blasted that dick-suckin' muthafucka when I did. So do you think you can make this shit disappear?"

"I'm the police, man," Terrance chuckled. "I can do what the fuck I want. This is my beat, so I'll do what I can to keep everyone away. As long as I'm out here patrolling, y'all good, and if I know anything, this lil' nigga right here," he pointed to his little brother, "he'll holla at y'all."

Smurf nodded and peeled off five crisp Ben Franklins. "Thanks, man." He handed the money to Terrance. "And for that, you good too."

CHAPTER 17

THE NEXT DAY, Smurf decided to call Dink early to let him know what he'd learned in the meeting with Dirty, Drake, and Terrance. He'd called Dink's car phone repeatedly last night but didn't get an answer. Smurf never left messages—too traceable—but he had to talk to his boy. Even though Dink was officially out of the game, he still needed to know, because old shit was now coming up.

"Yo, speak to Dink?" Smurf asked when Laci answered the phone.

"Who is this?" she asked in a sweet voice. She was in the kitchen, making breakfast for them before Dink jetted off to class. It was a Friday and he had a full day of classes, but she was free. Laci planned to make a day out of it and chill.

"Yo, Laci, it's Smurf. What's up wit'cha? How's college life?"

Laci had never met him personally but knew of him because Dink spoke very highly of his young protégé, and they spoke occasionally when he called.

"Oh, hey, Smurf," she acknowledged. "I'm getting better day by day, and college life is just that ... college life."

Smurf gave a slight chuckle. He knew of her only as a crack-head, but by talking to her every so often he came to think that she was cool.

"Hold on for a minute." She put the phone down and walked into their bedroom. Dink came out of the bathroom wrapped in a white towel, and walked to the nightstand on his side of the bed in search of the baby oil.

"Baby, you have a phone call," she told him.

"Who is it?" he asked.

"Smurf."

Quickly, he reached for the phone and sat down on the bed. "Yeah," he said into the receiver. A smile crept across his face when he heard his boy's voice. "My nigga, what's up!"

Laci returned to the kitchen. Just as she was going to hang up the phone, she heard the two men already engaged in conversation and couldn't help but listen.

"Yo, but check this, muthafuckas been down here askin' 'bout yo' girl."

"What about Laci?"

"Naw man, the other chick." Dink knew he meant Crystal. "They also askin' bout that nigga Dame. And remember the shit that happened in The Village?"

"Yeah."

"They talkin' 'bout that too."

Dink paused for a moment. "What you doin' about it?"

"I got my people on it, seeing what he can get. It's cool though, boss. I plan on getting this shit squashed, 'cuz I'll be damned if it blows up in our faces."

"That's my lil' nigga right there," Dink said. "I know you got me, man."

"Oh, and just so you know, a couple of those chicks been 'round here asking about yo' gal."

"Really? Who?"

"The fly one. You know, the one with the gray eyes, and then the thick bitch."

"The pregnant one?"

"Naw, the other one. The kinda cute one." He meant Monique.

"A'ight man, keep an eye on them hoes."

"You got it," Smurf said to Dink. He didn't ask any questions. "Anything else?"

"Naw, man, just holla at me when you make moves."

They hung up the phone.

Laci quietly put the receiver back on the hook. She'd heard what she needed to hear and was pissed that any of the South Bronx Bitches were even asking about her. *For what?* she asked herself. Laci replayed the conversation in her head. She was glad that Dink was going to head out soon. Her plans to chill quickly changed. Like a magnet, Laci was drawn to her former friends. She had a run to make and it was only three hours away.

MONIQUE LEFT HER grandmother's Bailey Avenue West apartment in University Heights with a wide smile on her face. She had gotten the call she'd been waiting for. She was officially a post office worker now and ready to begin her new life.

Good-bye to the scandalous South Bronx Bitches, she said to herself as she happily bounced down the street. She missed the opportunity to buy a Fourth of July outfit because she didn't have any money, but she'd scraped up enough to put the leather Gucci jacket that she had her eye on over the summer on layaway.

In the past she would have gone to Hip Hop Fashions over

in The Hub and boosted it, but now she'd be able to buy it with her own money from her own paycheck. For that, Monique was thankful.

Monique felt she was given another opportunity and she was going to make the most of it. She thought about Laci and felt remorseful. Monique made a mental list to go over to Laci's and see what was up, but as she walked to her destination, she wasn't going to let anything steal her joy.

FOUR HOURS LATER, Laci sat in the familiar surroundings of her home in Riverdale talking to her Uncle Sonny. She was disappointed that her mother wasn't at home, but she hadn't told her she was coming.

After they'd caught up on school, classes, and how she had been doing, Sonny's tone turned serious.

"Sweetpea," he told her, "I have something to talk to you about. I think with everything going on, you have to know."

"What's wrong? It sounds serious." Concern shadowed Laci's face.

"An officer was here asking questions about you."

"Me?"

"Yes. And he was specifically asking about somebody named Crystal."

"Crystal? What about her?" Laci's heart began racing.

"I'm not sure, but the officer said your name came up, somehow."

Laci got quiet and thought back to the conversation she'd overheard between Dink and Smurf. Something was going on and nobody was telling her. Laci wiped her hand over her face and tried to imagine what could have been happening.

"Anyway, they want to talk to you about her and the other girls."

"Uncle Sonny, I don't want to. I just want to put all of that behind me," Laci said truthfully.

"I understand," he said. "I told him that I would give you the message and that it was up to you if you would contact him or not." An awkward moment of silence passed until Sonny spoke again. "Laci, I really think you should talk to them."

"Why?"

"Whatever happened with that Crystal girl, it sounds like those girls are pointing a finger at you. With everything you've gone through, it wouldn't surprise me if they tried to tie you into what happened somehow. Honey, you've started over and you don't need to get pulled into something you don't know anything about. Here's the officer's number." Sonny handed her Officer Jones's card. "What you do with it is your decision."

"Thanks, Uncle Sonny. I'll think about it. I promise." She looked at the clock and saw it was now two in the afternoon. Laci wanted to get home before Dink got out of school. "I need to get back to Boston, but tell Mom I'll call her tomorrow." She got up and hugged her uncle. "Thanks again, and I love you."

Laci got in her car and drove. Her intent was to confront the girls, but now, knowing the police were looking for her, Laci had to be careful about how she devised her plan. *They wanna drag me into shit,* she said to herself, *I'ma flip the script on them.*

Instead of hitting the main highway back to Boston, she took the "scenic" route through Tremont, Soundview, and University Heights. The neighborhood looked different in the daytime than at night, the time she was accustomed to being there. It was more run down than she remembered. She drove past the streets that she and her girls used to stand around on and saw a young man and some other dudes who looked vaguely familiar to her. As Laci continued to drive, she came across St. Nicholas Street in the Jackson Projects. Then she saw the corner store where she'd first tried to cop some smoke. The place looked dirty and dilapidated. In the alley between the store and a run-down building was the spot where many ballers exchanged drugs and junkies shot up. Laci saw what looked like a young girl, about fourteen years old, on her knees. Surrounding her were three dudes—the one in front of her rammed his dick inside her mouth while the other two stood there watching and waiting their turn. It was no shame in the game of a crackhead.

Laci could imagine what they were saying to the girl. She remembered what she was told and the names she was called when she enrolled in Head Doctor 101. It was nothing good. Laci wanted to jump out of the car and help the girl, but the emotion of the situation wouldn't allow her.

She drove on and saw a well-dressed man searching frantically for something in a Dumpster. The man then got on his knees and scoured the ground. Laci slowed down to almost a crawl to see what he was looking for. Almost instantly, the man took off the belt to his pants, quickly wrapped it around his arm, and shoved the needle into his vein.

It wasn't uncommon to find used needles in the area, and people with a serious addiction wouldn't care if the needles were used. HIV and AIDS were the last things on their minds. As long as they could get the last out of the syringe, a little hit was better than none and best of all, it didn't cost them anything.

Laci remembered seeing many fiends offering their dealers jewelry and TVs as payment for their habit. She remembered that Angel, a crackhead she used to light up with, tried to pawn her two-year-old daughter off on her dealer as payment.

"What the fuck I'm gonna do with a muthafuckin' kid?" he yelled at her. "I ain't no damn day care!"

"Come on!" Angel told him frantically, scratching her arms uncontrollably, giving him a snaggle-toothed smile. "Just watch her for a minute while I go do this." She reached her hand out for a rock.

Laci couldn't move to help Angel because she was already on cloud nine. "Where's my money, you stupid bitch?" the dealer yelled at her, "and take this goddamn baby!" He pushed the little girl back into her arms.

"Well, er . . . uh . . . look," Angel said softly, like she didn't want anyone to hear her, and looked around, but she was desperate. "I ain't got no money but see, you know . . . I'm er . . . well, I'll let her tell you." She put her daughter down, relieving her eighty-pound feeble body of the stress of carrying a two-year-old. "Go 'head, baby, tell the nice man what I taught you to say."

The little girl looked up at her mother with a look that only a two-year-old could give. "It's okay . . . go ahead," Angel assured her.

The little girl looked at the man and said, "I'll suck yo' dick," in the innocent voice of a child.

The man was totally incensed. Not only because Angel would exchange her daughter for dope, but also because she'd taught the little girl such a demeaning phrase.

He called one of his boys to come get the little girl while he commenced kicking Angel's ass real good. One thing this hustler had a heart for was little kids, especially little girls. He didn't give a damn about their parents, but little kids he wouldn't fuck with. They drove the little girl to the closest hospital and dropped her off before anyone could see them.

In disgust, Laci was turning the corner to make her way out of the Bronx when she saw a car that looked familiar. Leaning on the car were two girls she recognized immediately. They were Tonette and Shaunna. Both of the girls looked at the expensive sharp-red Mercedes Benz as it drove by, but Laci made no eye contact. She was glad she didn't. She just wanted to get out of Dodge, and fast.

"GIRL . . ." TONETTE SAID, still looking in the direction the car disappeared. "Didn't that look like Laci?"

"Where?"

"In that red Benz that just passed us."

"Girl, please . . . you really buggin' now," Shaunna said. "You saw how bad she was out there." Shaunna smacked her lips. "Once a crackhead always a crackhead."

"Yeah," Tonette agreed quietly. "You're right."

CHAPTER 18

Two DAYS LATER, Tonette and Shaunna sat back in Dame's old-school Camaro and watched anxiously as Tonette's plan unfolded, while eating a bag of Red Hot Riplets and drinking a Pepsi. After they were finished with their snack, Tonette rolled a fresh blunt and took a long toke from it just as her mind went back to the red Benz she'd seen a couple of days ago. *Damn, was that Laci?* she kept asking herself. Shaunna's insistence on getting some smoke brought her back to what she had to focus on. Tonette was still pissed that Monique walked out on her, but getting even was only a thing. *She'll be back,* she told herself.

Within moments, she saw the personal moving crew she'd hired scurry away from Monique's first-floor apartment with all sorts of goods. Both girls began to laugh. One woman was pushing a floor-model color TV down the street in an armchair. Someone else had an armful of clothing, and others came out wearing some of the shit. Tonette chuckled to herself when she saw the two skinniest women struggle to carry the microwave that was on Monique's grandmother's kitchen counter.

They took everything to the nearest thrift store and pawnshop for cash, which they agreed to give to Tonette and in turn, she would hook them up. The thrift store was only three blocks away and the pawnshop was right across the street from the store, so after they were through, they came back for more. Plants, pictures, a telephone, even the toilet seat was worth something to a basehead. If they thought that scratching the paint off the walls would have gotten them another hit, it would have been done.

Once Tonette was satisfied with their deed, she made good on her promise but reminded them that they had to finish their job later that evening to get final payment. They agreed as she gave them their packets of poison and watched as they scrambled away.

A few hours later, after she took Shaunna to pick up her two-year-old son and dropped them off at their place, Tonette went back to where she was earlier and waited. About forty minutes later, Monique's grandmother ambled up the street as the sun began to set. It looked like her feet hurt.

"Hi, Ms. Daniels," Tonette said sweetly as the older woman walked by her. It wasn't uncommon for Tonette to be hanging out in the area. Monique's grandmother figured she was waiting for Monique.

"Hello, Tonette," she said and continued walking. Tonette knew that Monique's grandmother didn't care for her but she was always cordial.

Mrs. Daniels had feared that once Monique moved in with her after her mother's death she'd take up with the wrong crowd. She prayed that she wouldn't. Mrs. Daniels tried to do any and everything for her granddaughter to give her a decent life, but it was too little too late. Monique was a part of the South Bronx Bitches; but Mrs. Daniels prayed to the Lord every day that no matter what, her granddaughter would make the right choices and would eventually get back on the right path.

Since the police had been back and forth asking questions about Crystal and the rest of the crew, Monique's decision to try to get her shit together was the best thing she could do. Her grandmother was proud of Monique's most recent decision to get her GED. Although she had her high school certificate of completion, Monique had thought about college for a hot minute. She sailed through high school with D-minuses and refused to sit through two years of college on the same bullshit. She decided that once she got her GED, she would take the test for a job at the post office. It seemed like she was really trying to do something with her life and her grandmother's prayers were answered.

As promised, the two rat-assed crackheads came tripping over each other out of Monique's grandmother's apartment. One was wearing Monique's Members Only beige polyester jacket that Mrs. Daniels had bought her.

"What the hell you doing here?" She looked between the two females. "And who are you?" Mrs. Daniels raised her purse and was ready to beat them with it. The woman was loud and Tonette started laughing. "And what the hell you doing wearing my granddaughter's clothes?" Mrs. Daniels raised her hand and jerked the skinniest girl by her collar.

"We waiting for Monique to come back," the skinniest one said while trying to avoid the older woman's grasp. Her eyes darted around in front of her looking for a place to run to in case Mrs. Daniels started bugging out.

"She said she was going to the corner store to get some more blow," the other one said, comfortably putting her hands into the pockets of the jacket she was wearing. She was so fucked up, she didn't see that the old woman was capable of kicking some ass and taking names later.

"Get some more *what*?" Mrs. Daniels roughly pushed the two fiends out of her way and stormed inside of her house.

Seconds later, Tonette heard the loudest screech come out of Mrs. Daniels's mouth, then saw her run outside. The screams and the old woman running out of the house scared the two crackheads and they ran away fast, like the 5-0 was on their tails. Tonette's deed was done; now she just had to sit back and wait.

FOUR HOURS LATER, about eleven o'clock at night, Tonette was getting ready to hit her position on the street and was stopped by a knock at her door. She slowly walked over to the door as she was fastening her name chain around her neck, then opened it.

With a nasty scowl on her face, she put her hands on her slender hips and her nostrils flared. "What the fuck you doing here?"

Monique looked like she had been through hell. The dark- and light-blue uniform she wore was wrinkled and unkempt. Her face was blotchy and her eyes were red. Monique's braids were all over her head and it looked as if she had been slapped repeatedly.

"Um . . . my grandmother," Monique said. "She kicked me out."

"So what the fuck you want me to do?" Tonette asked seriously. "That's fam shit and we ain't fam no more."

"I was just thinking that—"

"Well, you thought wrong," Tonette said harshly, interrupting Monique.

"I could crash here, you know, like I used to." Monique was determined to finish her sentence.

"Like you used to? Heifer, you ain't a part of the SBBs no more. The SBBs got each other's back. You walked out, remember?"

"I need a place to stay, Tonette, please."

"Take yo' fake ass on down to the shelter or better yet, go find Laci since you were taking up for her ass. Now get the fuck outta my doorway before I turn *you* into a crackhead." Tonette laughed.

Monique had nowhere to go and felt like she was going to lose it.

"I'm still a SBB," Monique said meekly. "What do I need to do to show you?" Monique was desperate and it was written all over her face. Tonette loved it.

"Well . . . ," Tonette said, pondering Monique's question. "When you leave the SBBs there's an initiation you must pass before you get back in, and that's if I let you back in. If you fail the initiation, then I don't know what to tell ya."

"What do I have to do?"

"Do you really want to know, Monique? Do you really want to be a South Bronx Bitch again?"

Without pondering the decision, Monique had to do what she had to do. "Yes. Y'all are my family."

Tonette stepped to the side as Monique walked in and comfortably sat down on the couch. Tonette closed the door and walked into the center of her living room.

"Naw, bitch, you ain't gonna get comfortable right now. Take your clothes off."

"What?"

"I said, take your clothes off."

"Nette, you know I don't get down like that," she reminded Tonette.

Monique was once again talking back and Tonette's nostrils flared like a bull. "You know what . . ."

"Wait a minute!" Monique cried as Tonette grabbed her by the arm and walked her to the door in a rush.

"I got shit to do, so get ta steppin'!" She opened the door. "You came to my house beggin' me to get back into my crew. You can't do what I ask you to? You flunked your initiation. Your case is closed! Get the fuck out!"

Monique looked at Tonette with tears in her eyes. "Okay, okay," she pleaded, trying to keep Tonette from throwing her out. "Close the door, Tonette. I'll do what you want." Monique had never been with a girl before. She knew Shaunna rolled whichever way the wind blew, but Monique never thought Tonette got down like that. *It shouldn't be too bad. I can do this*, Monique willed herself. *It'll be over in a minute.*

Monique walked to the middle of the room where Tonette was now standing. "Strip," Tonette told her. Monique did as she was told. Tonette smirked and shook her head when Monique came out of her too-tight pants.

"You just nasty," she said to Monique with a snarl. Monique opened her mouth to say something. "Uh uh!" Tonette cut her off. "You only speak when you are asked to speak." She paused momentarily. "Do you understand?" Monique wanted to say something, but this time Tonette gritted her teeth and repeated herself angrily, letting Monique know she wasn't playing with her.

"Yes," Monique confirmed quietly as she continued to undress until she stood butt-ass naked in front of Tonette, who looked at every inch of her body.

"Turn around," she ordered.

Monique didn't put up any resistance and did what she was told.

Tonette quickly stepped into her bedroom and came back within seconds.

"You sure you want back in, Monique?"

"Yes. Yes, I'm sure."

"Repeat after me, you fat-ass cow." Tonette swung Dame's thick belt across Monique's back and she yelped. Tonette's words cut through Monique like a knife—more than the sting of the belt. She couldn't help her size. Her momma was thick, her grandmother was thick, and so was she.

"I will," Tonette sang calmly as she hit Monique again with the belt. She enjoyed watching Monique squirm.

Stunned from the shock and pain and unable to comply with Tonette's wishes, Monique whimpered. She couldn't talk through her tears and the pain.

"Say it, bitch!" Tonette yelled and swung the thick piece of cow leather across Monique's back again. "And quit cryin' like a lil' bitch. This shit don't hurt." She unleashed another whip.

"I will," Monique cried out loud through tears.

"Not talk back," Tonette said. *Whip!*

"Not talk back," she repeated.

"I will," Tonette said again. *Whip!*

The pain shot through Monique's body like fire. "I will."

"Do as I'm told." *Whip!*

Welts were now starting to form on Monique's delicate skin.

"Do as I'm told."

Tonette continued to beat the shit out of Monique until she was balled up on the floor, begging through tears for the beating to stop and asking for forgiveness. Tonette felt powerful as she lashed out on Monique, stopping only because it dawned on her that her neighbors might hear the commotion and she didn't need any additional attention drawn to herself. *Damn, I should have turned the TV on*, she thought.

Looking at the red, bloodied, and welted body of Monique, Tonette was satisfied with her punishment. "Now you a SBB again and this time, just like a marriage, you ain't getting out until we parted by death. Now get the fuck up off my goddamn floor and clean yo' nasty ass up. I got shit to do." Tonette calmly walked toward the door. "And don't eat my fuckin' food. You stayin' with me, yo' fat ass on a diet!"

Tonette left and although moving slowly, with an ego as bruised as her body, Monique did as she was told.

CHAPTER 19

LACI AND HER friends had lunch together when their schedules would permit and they often met up in between classes. Planning to meet up with them at the mall later after her last class, Laci happily stepped to the car where Dink waited for her.

"Hey babe," Dink said as Laci approached.

"Hey Dink," Laci replied and kissed him out of habit on the lips.

Dink grabbed Laci's backpack, opened the back door, and threw it on the seat. As they got inside and Dink began driving, he looked over at Laci.

"You look different," he told her, noticing a change in her demeanor.

"Do I?" she asked, pulling down the sun visor, looking into the mirror.

"I don't mean like that. It's just something about you."

Laci covered the mirror, closed the visor, and looked at him. "I hope you mean it in a good way."

"Yeah, it's good. You just look more relaxed now. Happy."

Laci's nightmares and paranoia had become virtually nonexistent; still, he watched her closely for any side effects she might experience, or worse, any relapses.

"I am." Laci smiled at him and put her hands on top of his. "Oh Dink, I forgot to tell you, I'm meeting my girls at the mall later."

"Your girls? What girls?" Dink asked.

"You know, my friends," she told him matter-of-factly. "Gabby, Randi, and Samantha."

"What you need at the mall, Laci?"

"Nothing, really. We're just hanging out." She looked into her purse and pulled out a fresh stick of cotton-candy lip gloss and coated her lips with the wand as he drove.

"Baby, we haven't been to the mall in a while," Dink replied. "Why don't I take you? Afterward, we can go to dinner, hit a movie or something. Anything you want, boo-boo."

Dink did notice that Laci had started hanging with a group of girls that he didn't know, and he felt the need to protect her. Unfortunately, Dink's protection meant not letting her get too far away from him. His doting attention made Laci feel special, but after a while, it got old and she was beginning to feel smothered.

ALMOST TWO MONTHS had passed since he left the Bronx, but for Dink, being in a different environment made it seem like an eternity. He made the best of it. Dink was the more sociable of the two, but he was still on guard because the lessons he learned from the streets never left his blood. He knew that people always wanted something and they would go through extremes to get it.

College was a different life for him. Slightly older than the average Boston University student at twenty-two, many students wanted to know more about this controversial young man who wasn't afraid to speak his mind. But Dink let only a few students get close to him.

Slim quickly proved to be Dink's boy on campus. He wasn't intimidated by his obvious swagger and hood-rich ways. The fact that Dink and Laci had matching Mercedes-Benzes and stayed laced in the latest designer clothes didn't faze Slim either. Slim was a cool, laid-back cat to kick it with and he had a fresh, care-free spirit. Similarly to Dink, he wasn't on no bullshit, wasn't a slug, and spoke what was on his mind, and Dink welcomed that.

Dink had also becomed acquainted with Simone, T.J.'s ex. They shared a class together, and Dink enjoyed her confident demeanor. While her appearance may have resembled Crystal's, her personality was completely different, and she had an ease about her that Dink immediately took to.

"DINK, CAN I talk to you for a minute?" Laci shook him briskly, waking him up from a nap.

"Wha . . . what's wrong baby?" Dink blinked his eyes and tried to stifle a yawn. He realized that he must have dozed off while waiting for Laci to finish her homework. He threw a pillow under his arm, turned toward her, and began to play with a loose ringlet of hair that bounced on her shoulder.

"You," Laci blurted out. Dink looked at her. "No, me," she said. "Us," she finally said.

"What's up, Laci? You sound confused." Dink realized that whatever Laci had to say was difficult.

"I'm not confused. I mean, I'm happy being in college and with us together and all, but I need space, Dink." Laci sighed. "My friends and I want to hang out and do things together."

"We do those things all the time," he reminded her.

"Right, Dink. But outside of class, I don't see my friends at all."

Dink looked incredulously at Laci. He'd never expected to hear her say anything like this. But after giving it a little more thought, he realized he had become as overbearing as she made it sound.

"Baby," Dink sat up in the bed, "the shit you went through this summer—you shouldn't have gone through it," he said seriously. "Man, nobody should ever have to go through that kind of hell. I promised your mother and uncle that I would protect you, and that's all I'm trying to do."

"Dink, baby, you *are* protecting me." Laci leaned over to kiss him. "You just being here makes me feel that nothing bad could ever happen. But this isn't the South Bronx and my friends aren't like Tonette and the girls." Laci's face took on another look, thinking of the SBBs. "My friends are a lot like me and we enjoy spending what little time we do have together."

Dink remembered seeing Laci a few times with the girls she considered her friends. He felt he was a good judge of character, and he'd never got any bad vibes off these girls. They were a little too stuck up for his taste, but considering where they were, it was the norm. Laci had pled her case to the jury; now it was time for the verdict.

"Okay, baby," Dink responded after a brief silence, "I see what you're saying, but I'm not going to apologize for protecting you. That's what a man is supposed to do for his woman; however, I will loosen up some. I didn't realize you felt this way and I wish you would have told me sooner. I don't like seeing you stressed out about shit you don't need to be stressed out about. But if they try some funny shit, they goin' down too."

Laci understood why Dink felt that way, because he had seen her at her lowest point and knew how she got there. She promised him that everything would be just fine and reassured him that the people she chose to hang around with were a lot like her. Some would say bougies, by some standards, but easily embraceable. Laci felt her kind would never treat her like Tonette and her South Bronx Bitches had and for once in her life, she was right.

LACI BEGAN TO take advantage of the extra room Dink gave her, which surprised him. Coming home on a Saturday afternoon, he ran into the girls inside their apartment, waiting for Laci to get ready.

"Hi, Daryl," Randi said as she sat on the couch with Gabby and Sam. They all had wine coolers in their hands, sipping on them while they waited.

"Hey," he said as he closed the door behind him. "What's up with y'all?" he asked cordially.

"Just waiting for Laci," Gabby answered. "We're going to Rich and Charlie's for a quick lunch, then we're going back to the dorm to watch some movies. What did we get?" she asked Sam.

"I think we got *Lethal Weapon 1* and *2*," she answered.

"Yeah, that's it," Gabby answered as she got up and threw her cooler bottle into the trash can. Dink noticed that she was very comfortable in their apartment, which told him that they had been there before.

Laci came out of their bedroom wearing a pink L.A. Gear sweat suit along with pink and white Nikes. The girls smiled and got up when they saw her. They grabbed their purses and headed toward the door.

"Hey babe," Laci said as she hurriedly grabbed her purse and house keys. "I'm hanging out with the girls, but I'll see you later, okay?" Laci didn't give Dink a chance to respond. She kissed him on the lips and left.

Dink watched as she left the apartment. This was the Laci he never knew—one who loved life and was sociable.

In the girls' dorm room, they relaxed on a couple of bean-bag chairs and laid across the small twin beds watching Danny Glover and Mel Gibson as the comical police officers in the *Lethal Weapon* series.

During the first movie, Gabrielle hit the pause button, got up, and went to the bathroom. As she returned, she unpaused the movie and sat cross-legged on her bed. Rustling with something, she distracted Laci, who turned to see what she was doing.

Oh my god! Laci thought to herself as she watched Gabby open up a small baggie and some papers. She saw her reach into the bag, pull out something that was green and brown, and sprinkle it inside the paper. Gabby looked at Laci, reached back into the bag, and added more, like it was no big deal. Once she got the joint the way she wanted, Gabby rolled it and then licked the edge to seal her work of art.

Laci's heart raced and she became clammy. *I need to go,* she thought to herself. *Oh my God, not again!* Her fight-or-flight instinct kicked in but she felt paralyzed. Lighting the joint, Gabby took a few tokes, then passed it to Randi. After she took a few pulls, she looked at Laci. "You want some?"

Laci looked at the girls, then at the joint. "Um . . . no. I don't smoke," she told her friends.

"Oh, okay. That's cool," Samantha said, passing on the joint too.

They turned back and focused on the movie. Laci's heart rate began to return to normal. She couldn't believe how easy it was to say no and not be judged or teased because she didn't smoke, or chose not to.

Just as the first movie went off, Laci looked at her friends and spoke.

"Girls, um . . . I have something to tell you."

They looked at her. "What's up?" Randi asked, putting the first movie in the case and retrieving the second.

"Um . . . I'm a recovering addict."

They all looked at her like she was crazy. "What? An addict?" Sam spoke. "See, girl," she looked at Gabby, "I told you you can get hooked on that shit."

"Yes," Laci said.

They looked at her in amazement. "Damn! You? An addict? You don't strike me as one," Randi commented.

"Right," Laci told her, "but it's not like you think. I had some friends back home and they tricked me into smoking a joint and they laced it with crack."

The girls' eyes got big as saucers. "What? Aw man, that's lower than low!" The girls got a little closer to Laci, and they put their hands on her back and began to rub her. "Damn, I'm sorry, Laci," Gabby said, feeling bad that she'd rolled and fired up a joint in front of Laci.

"Well, we won't smoke around you, Laci," Randi told her.

"Right, we won't," Gabby cosigned.

"Thanks, I appreciate that," Laci told them. "You don't have to stop doing it around me, but I appreciate you offering that. I'm clean now, but I just wanted you all to know."

That night, when she came home smelling of alcohol and the faint hint of marijuana, Dink questioned her about it. "Laci," he called out to her. Dink noticed that she looked a little disheveled. "Are you smoking weed?"

"Why you ask that?" Laci asked, taking off her clothes, about to get into the shower. She put her dirty clothes in the hamper and put her robe on.

"Laci." Dink pulled at her arm, and sniffed her hair and her face. The smell was very faint, but he knew she had to at least have been around it. He looked closely at her. Her eyes weren't bloodshot and she didn't look extremely relaxed.

"What you doing?" she asked, pulling away from him.

"Ever since you started hanging out with your so-called friends, whenever you come home, you smell like shit you shouldn't be doing."

Laci turned to look at him and gave an exasperated sigh.

"Dink, when I go out with my friends, we go to the mall, the art museums, or just other places we have common interest in. But there are other days we just want to sit back and chill. We go back to someone's dorm room with a bottle of expensive wine and yes, some of them would hit the herb."

"Uh-uh," he said defiantly, shaking his head. "You ain't going around them anymore. I told you if some funny shit kicked off I—"

"Dink, listen to me." Laci looked at him seriously. "The first time they lit up, I almost got sick to my stomach. I wanted to run and get the hell out of there, but when I saw that some of them hit it and nobody tweaked, that's when I realized it was just weed."

"You don't need to be around that shit, Laci. I don't think you're ready for that."

"I told them I was a recovering addict." Dink raised his eyebrows in shock. "Yup, I was surprised I admitted it too and took my chances with how they would react, but I knew they were the real deal when they offered not to smoke around me."

"Why did you tell them that, Laci?" He still couldn't believe she would put her shit out there like that. "Did you tell them anything about me? About where the shit came from?"

"Well, because it's my truth, and I have to face my demons. The truth is, Dink, I am a recovering addict and admitting this is a part of my recovery." She looked at him with hurt written on her face. "To answer your other question, no, I didn't say anything about you. I can't believe you would even ask that."

Dink pulled her close and kissed her hair. "I'm sorry, baby. I shouldn't have asked you that."

She looked up at him and smiled slightly, although still surprised at what he had just asked.

"Wow, baby," Dink said. "I'm proud of you."

What Laci liked most about her newfound friends was that nobody tried to get anyone to do anything she wasn't comfortable with. That included her talking about her ordeal if she didn't want to. With the South Bronx Bitches, Laci had felt she never had a choice, and that made her appreciate her new friends even more. Even though Laci was finally able to be where she fit in and she was happy, she still had hatred in her heart for the South Bronx Bitches.

"This is definitely a step in the right direction," Dink told her. "You know, it's gonna take some time, but one day you'll forget about all the shit you went through over the summer."

Yeah right, Laci said to herself. *Most people can forgive but can't forget, but me, I ain't forgivin' shit.*

CHAPTER 20

WHILE LACI BRANCHED out and became her own woman, Dink began to spend more time with people more like him—Slim and Simone. They made him feel more at home in Boston.

"Hey Simone," Dink called out after their Abnormal Psych class. He walked up to her and helped her gather her things.

"Hey Daryl, what's up?" She looked at him. "Wow, you're looking good today." She admired his dark-wash blue jeans, Timbs, and crisp white oversized T-shirt. Dink appreciated the compliment. Laci hadn't complimented him in a while.

"Thanks," he told her. "You're looking pretty fly yourself." He admired the black and gold Sassoon sweat suit that Simone wore. It hit her curves in a way that should make any man who crossed her path take a second look. "What you doing later on?"

"From the looks of it," she said, noticing how he was checking her out, "I'll be working on this assignment."

"Yeah, me too," he said, remembering that they had been given an emormous assignment with a ridiculous deadline. "Hey, he said we could choose a partner. Why don't we partner up?" Dink suggested.

"I'd like that, Daryl," Simone replied.

"Looks like we're gonna be pulling some late nights," he told her. "You up for it?"

"More than you know." Simone grinned.

Besides studying, Simone and Dink began to spend more time together. They often hung out in the student lounge together, grabbing dinner and playing video games.

One Friday evening, Dink got to the apartment early. He had planned to take Laci to a small, quaint diner that he'd overheard a student talking about, only to be greeted by a note on the fridge:

Dink, I'm out with the girls.
Dinner is in the fridge. I'll be home early.—L

Dink sighed, balled up the note, and tossed it into the trash can. He didn't feel like staying inside, so he decided to go back to the student center. Just as he got in his car, his car phone rang.

"Yeah!" he answered.

"Um . . . Daryl?" a female voice spoke.

"Yo, who this?"

"This is Simone."

"Oh yeah, what's up?"

"I was wondering if you wanted to get together and work on our paper tonight."

Dink paused for a moment and his stomach grumbled. "Yeah, that'll be cool."

"Great!" Simone exclaimed.

Dink could hear the smile in her voice. "Why don't we grab a bite to eat?" he suggested.

"I'd like that, Daryl."

"Can you meet me at the Busy Bee, in say," he looked at

the clock, "twenty minutes? It's on Beacon Street, near South Campus."

"Yeah, I know where that is. Make it thirty."

"You got it."

Twenty minutes later, Dink walked into the quaint little diner and grabbed a booth. He looked over the menu and heard giddy female chatter coming his way.

"Dink?" a sweet voice spoke, and the chatter stopped.

He looked up, and it was Laci and her friends.

"Oh hey, babe, what's up?"

"Hi, Daryl," the other three girls said in unison.

"Hi."

"What are you doing here?" Laci asked, surprised to see him. "Did you get my note?"

"Yeah, I got it. I'm meeting a friend here. We're actually working on a project for class."

"Oh, okay," Laci replied, "that's cool. I'll see you back at home later, okay?" She bent down and kissed him, but just as she was about to walk away, her entire expression changed.

Simone was walking toward her with a few books in tow. She had on a pair of too-tight Gloria Vanderbilt blue jeans, quarter-length black boots, and a black Gloria Vanderbilt V-neck shirt that highlighted her cleavage. Laci noticed that she had on more makeup than she typically wore during the day and the fragrant smell of Elizabeth Taylor's Passion filled the air. Laci knew that Dink liked the smell of the perfume, but she had never made time to get it while on one of her shopping sprees with her friends.

"Hi, Laci," Simone said dryly. "Hi, Daryl!" she said with enthusiasm, and sat down. Laci, along with her friends, looked at Simone in shock as she slid into the booth across from Dink. "Sorry I'm late. T.J. was trippin'."

Dink looked up at Laci. "Alright baby," he spoke. "I'll see you back at home tonight. I'll try to be early." He turned his attention back to Simone. Laci walked out with her friends, at a loss for words.

Meanwhile, T.J. sat outside the diner. He'd followed Simone there after she openly turned down his invitation to dinner and to bed later. He was pissed off when he saw that Dink's car was outside. He saw Laci and her friends leaving the diner as well and could tell from the expression on Laci's face that she wasn't too happy about what she'd seen. T.J. positioned his car where he could see inside the window of the diner and saw Simone and Dink laughing. This was not the first time he'd seen them together and noticed how close they had become.

Even though he and Simone weren't a couple anymore, and he'd started to believe she was serious when she kicked him to the curb, he was bound to put salt in Dink's game. That he was certain of.

AS HOMECOMING WAS getting closer, Simone approached Laci as she was leaving the campus.

"Hi, Laci!" Simone said happily. "Where you going?"

Laci looked at Simone with a strange expression on her face. "I'm going home to Dink. Why?"

Simone was kind of taken aback by Laci's reaction, but continued. "Me and some of my sorors are going to the show tonight. You wanna go?"

Laci chuckled to herself, looked Simone up and down, then answered. "For what, Simone? It's not like we're friends."

"I was just extending an invitation to hang out, but if you don't want to—"

"No. I'll pass, and as a matter of fact, don't call Dink either.

He's busy tonight too." Laci walked off, leaving Simone standing alone.

Not only was Simone a dead ringer for Crystal, which made Laci uncomfortable, she was the same girl who'd eyed Dink in class the first day of school. Laci was suspicious of her intentions for wanting to be friends with her and questioned her sincerity.

Laci walked into their apartment twenty minutes later and saw Dink on the couch, relaxing, flicking through the channels on the television. She was glad he was at home.

"Hey, sweetheart," Laci said, and plopped down comfortably next to Dink.

He leaned over and kissed her. "Hey, babe."

"What'cha doing?" Laci asked as she took her shoes off. She tucked her feet up under her as she snuggled up next to him. Dink draped his arm around her and pulled her close to him.

"Nothing right now." He continued to flick through the channels. After a few minutes, Dink looked at Laci. "Babe, why did you play Simone earlier?"

Laci looked at Dink with an irritated expression on her face. "Oh, she couldn't wait to get a hold of you and tell you, huh? That bitch."

"Hey, what's all that for?" Dink removed his arm and looked at Laci.

"Dink, I don't like her."

"Why? What she do to you?"

"Do you remember how she looked at you on the first day of school? She knows we're together but every time I turn around, I see her. What am I gonna say, 'sure, let's hang,' knowing she probably has a motive? I don't trust her. And it doesn't help that she looks like Crystal."

"So what she looks like Crystal, Laci? She's not her. Why are you so stuck on that?" Dink got up off the couch and walked to window. He felt Laci was dead wrong about Simone and had no problem telling her so, but he had to gather his words before he spoke again. "I can see your point," he said, walking back toward Laci, "but you're wrong about her. She's a cool girl. You need to let go of the pain that Crystal caused. If you let go of the past, baby, being cool with Simone would be a huge breakthrough in your continued recovery. Who knows, you all may end up being friends one day."

Laci rolled her eyes. She didn't buy that, but she just let him talk.

Dink didn't realize it, but he'd given up too much information too easily, sparking curiosity.

"How do you know I'm wrong about her, Dink? It sounds like you know more about her than what you're letting on."

"Why do you say that?"

"Because you are straight-up taking up for this chick, all because I said I don't like her because she looks like Crystal, who just happens to be your ex. There's no way you can tell me that hasn't crossed your mind."

To stop Laci's insecurities, Dink made an effort to take her to more places with him again, on and off campus. At the urging of her friends, Laci chose to spend more time with Dink. None of the girls had men but they knew that another woman, no matter how innocent it looked, could be trouble.

CHAPTER 21

THE FIRST WEEKEND in October finally arrived. It was Boston University's homecoming weekend, and all the hype that had built up over the last few weeks was finally about to become a reality. Even though there weren't a lot of black students on campus, homecoming weekend was color-blind. It was a nonstop party for everyone at B.U.

That Friday night, Laci and Dink attended the traditional bonfire ritual, which kicked off by burning football jerseys of B.U.'s rival university, Northwestern. The marching band hyped the crowd even more. When they played their own rendition of "Can't Touch This," everyone went crazy and started emulating MC Hammer's moves. T.J. and Slim stepped along with the Alpha Phi Alphas and Simone stepped with her Delta sorors. *This is just like out of* School Daze, Laci thought as she sipped on her third citrus-flavored California Cooler and bobbed her head to the music.

Laci noticed how relaxed Dink was. Even though she was right by his side, he didn't seem to pay that much attention to her. She noticed that he was smoking weed and sipping on some

Hennessy straight from the bottle that was passed around. She also noticed that regardless of where Dink was that day, Simone was right there up in the mix. Laci heard Dink mention something about the South Bronx and how some of his boys might come up for the game after making a run. This was the first Laci had heard about it and she began to wonder if Dink was truly through with his former lifestyle.

Saturday would be the big football game and afterward, an after-party was rumored to go down that would make spring break look like a church revival.

The night passed quickly and the dawn was soon approaching. The early fall weather forced Laci to wrap herself in Dink's maroon and gray I.O.U. Legendary jacket. She was ready to leave the party. She'd wanted to go hours ago, but Dink was having a good time so she didn't want to make too much of a big deal out of it. The crowd was more his than hers, but she hung as long as she could.

Laci finally excused herself from the festivities and found a spot on the bleachers outside on the football field, where many students were sprawled out. She was unsure how long she was there, but her bobbing head woke her up. Dink saw her across the way and walked toward her.

"Hey, lil' bit, you okay?"

"Yeah, I'm fine," Laci said through a deep yawn.

Dink looked at his watch and realized it was extremely late. "Come on, sweetheart, I'm sorry," he told Laci. "Let's get outta here." He didn't wait for her to respond before he spoke again. "You hungry? I'm starving."

Not waiting for an answer, he held her hand as he led her away.

Laci and Dink walked into the local IHOP for an early breakfast. It was pretty crowded for five-thirty on a Saturday morning.

After a few minutes' wait, a hostess asked, "How many tonight?"

"Two," Dink replied.

He stood behind Laci with his arms wrapped around her waist while they waited for their table.

"Follow me." They followed the hostess to their booth and collapsed, with Dink taking the side of the booth that faced the door.

"Put your feet up here," Dink told Laci as he patted his lap.

She had on a pair of four-inch heels and he knew her feet had to be killing her.

Tiredly, Laci complied and Dink removed her shoes. He playfully wrinkled up his nose and the two laughed. He began to rub her feet, one at a time.

"Ooh, that feels good," Laci sighed, throwing her head back and stretching her neck from left to right.

Their waitress came over and took their order. Just as she left, an overly loud group of people came into the restaurant. It was Slim, T.J., and some of their frat brothers, along with Simone and some of her sorority sisters.

"Ay, yo Dink! My man!" Slim drunkenly yelled across the restaurant and strolled over to him and Laci. Dink stood and gave him the one-arm shoulder hug—the typical greeting among black men. "Wassup, Laci?"

"Hey, Slim."

"Man, you look like you fucked up," Dink observed.

"Yeah, but shit . . . it's homecoming, baby. This a muthafuckin' tradition," he slurred.

"Well, yo' tradition gonna have you on yo' ass, nigga," Dink laughed. "You know you can't drink that hard shit on an empty stomach, clown."

"I knew I was forgettin' something," Slim laughed. "You know ... I say that every year, but it keep slippin' my mind."

"Every year?" Dink laughed. "You only been here one year, nigga."

"Yeah, but I'll forget next year and the year after that. This way, you can't ever say I ain't think about it." They all laughed.

Slim looked up and saw that Simone and T.J. were headed toward them.

"Hi, Daryl," Simone acknowledged happily. "Hey, Laci," she said with an obvious change in her voice. She looked back at Dink, and said with excitement, "I came up with a topic for our Abnormal Psych project. Mental illness: the voice of reason."

"The voice of reason, huh?" Dink pondered. "Yeah ... I like that. That's cool," he confirmed with a smile.

"Laci, I'm surprised you still hangin'," Simone joked as she looked at her. "You normally be passed out by ten." Dink and Simone laughed between themselves, but Laci wasn't very happy. He had to have been sharing stuff about her with Simone and she didn't like it one bit. "You wanna get together soon, Daryl," Simone looked at Laci, "to work on our paper?"

"Yeah, that'll be cool. Just let me know when and where," Dink said.

"Just know, we may have to pull some late nights because we don't have a lot of time left, but I'm sure we'll make everything work." Simone grinned and nodded. She looked at Laci, then back at Dink. "If I don't see you at homecoming or tonight at the party, I'll definitely see you in class." She smiled at Dink and returned to her group.

"You plannin' on sittin' with them or what?" T.J. asked in a condescending tone to Slim, after noticing the exchange between Simone and Dink.

"Hold up, man," Slim replied and resumed talking to Dink. "So y'all rollin through tonight or what?"

"I dunno, man," Dink looked at Laci, "baby girl ain't really into the whole party thing. Besides, she wanted to go downtown to do a little sightseeing. So after we get some rest, that's where we headed. I don't know how long we'll be out."

"Don't mind me," Laci told him curtly. T.J. saw the annoyed look she gave Dink. "I'm sure we'll be done early, then you can just go get yo' party on with Simone," she said sarcastically, in her most proper white-girl voice. "Besides, I may have a little surprise for you. By the time you get back home, it should be all ready."

"Surprise, huh?" Dink looked at Laci, ignoring her tone, then looked back at the guys. "Well, the lady has spoken. I'll roll through, but I'm burnin' out early because I wanna know what this surprise is." Dink smiled at Laci.

"A'ight, homie," Slim said, pounding fists with Dink. He walked toward the table with his group.

T.J. looked at Dink and Laci and walked away; however, he made a mental note in the back of his mind to find out what this surprise was. He had a surprise of his own as well.

"You're awfully comfortable with Simone, Dink," Laci said after an uncomfortable moment of silence. "Abnormal Psych, huh? Why didn't you tell me you had a class with her up front?"

"It's no big deal, Laci. When I told you that you needed to let go of your past, you made it perfectly clear that you wanted nothing to do with her, so I didn't think it was worth mentioning."

"Oh really," Laci said.

"She's cool, Laci, you just gotta get to know her."

Laci was about to speak, but their food arrived and she was starving. Besides, she didn't have too much more to say.

AFTER A COUPLE of hours of solid sleep, Dink and Laci headed downtown to experience the sights and sounds of Boston. It was a beautiful Saturday morning for a tour—slightly cool, but the radiant sun took the briskness out of the air. The sky was blue, with sparse white clouds. A perfect October day.

The two went on a guided tour of the Freedom Trail. Laci enjoyed the history lesson given by their tour guide, who performed as Abigail Adams. At each site they stopped, Dink listened attentively as the guide gave them a brief history of the destination. The Boston Common, King's Chapel, the Old State House, and the Boston Massacre Site were places that Dink had heard about but never thought he'd see in his life.

They also visited the Paul Revere House. Dink only knew of Paul Revere as the cat who ran through the town on his horse, yelling, "The Redcoats are coming!" But after visiting his home and learning of his plight, Dink now understood why this was in history books—his journey made him a legend, a true G.

Their last tour was Boston Harbor's Constitution Cruise. They saw the Old North Church and the Bunker Hill Monument, as well as other historical sites.

Afterward, the two dined at a quiet café, then Dink drove them home. It was now six o'clock in the evening and Laci was curious to see what would happen next.

"Go ahead and start getting ready for the party," she urged sarcastically, hoping Dink would have changed his mind. "I'm sure Simone is waiting for you." She threw her purse on the couch, kicked her shoes off, and retreated to the bedroom to change her clothes.

Dink looked at the clock, then back at Laci. "Babe, it's too early to go to anybody's party. I ain't no square," he laughed.

"Oh, sorry," Laci retorted. She returned wearing a pair of gray sweat pants and a white tee. Dink noticed that when she walked past him, her ass jiggled a little bit and her pants were riding up her crack, which meant she had no underwear on. She also wore no bra and her nipples stood at attention. Laci picked up Dink's jacket off the back of the couch and searched his pockets. Once she'd found the lighter, she lit the delicate paper that surrounded the herb that she held in her hand.

"What the hell are you doing, Laci?" Dink shouted as he grabbed at her wrists, but Laci pulled back, avoiding his grip. She knew he would be pissed.

"What? This right here?" Laci waved the joint in front of her face. "It's no big deal ... Isn't that what you told me earlier at the bonfire?" Without thinking, Laci deeply pulled on the bud. "Here," she suppressed a cough, "want some?" She held the joint out to Dink. Laci hadn't forgotten that laced weed was the beginning of her problem but right now, she didn't care. She was pissed and trying to make a point.

Dink was getting angry because Laci had become defiant over the past couple of weeks, but this was taking it too far.

"What's really going on with you, Laci?" Dink asked as he sat her down on the couch.

"What do you mean what's going on with me? Nothing." Laci was pissed that he was still trying to go to the party instead of staying in with her. "Look, just say what's on your mind."

"Look, I know you consider those girls your friends, but

damn, every time you come home, it's something different. Either you smell like you been drinkin' or smokin' weed but now, it's both. And now you got this shit right here." He held up the joint in his hand.

She hadn't wanted to tell him that she'd been hitting the weed again because she knew that he would get upset, but today, she didn't give a fuck.

"So what if I have? It's only weed." Laci took a defensive stance and continued. "I'm not that same impressionable girl from a few months ago. Besides, I'm surprised that you even noticed or care." The bud had burned out, and Laci fired up the lighter that was in her hand and took another toke. "You want some?"

"No, I don't want any, and where you get it from anyway?" He grabbed her wrist, trying to get the joint out of her hand. "As a matter of fact, why do you think I don't care?" Dink threw a bunch of questions at her. This was not the Laci he knew and loved.

"In there," she pointed toward their bedroom, "but wait a minute, you didn't seem to have a problem when Simone offered it to you, but you don't want it when I offer it to you?" Laci jerked her wrist back.

Dink stopped in his tracks. "Ahh . . . so that's what all the attitude is about, huh? Simone."

Dink realized that Laci was jealous. Under normal circumstances, or with anyone else, he would have put a bitch in her place, but this was Laci and not just any girl. He loved her and had promised he would take care of her.

"Baby, come here." Dink reached out, took the joint out of Laci's grasp, and gently pulled her toward him. "You don't have anything to worry about. And this shit right here," he waved the joint around, "ain't even called for." He kissed her on her forehead and held her tightly. "I love *you*, and no other woman could take your place." Laci turned her head away from him to keep her tears from falling, but Dink took her chin in his fingers to make her look at him. Tiny tears escaped from her brown eyes. "In the time we've been together, have I ever lied to you? Have I given you a reason not to trust me? It's you, Laci . . . all about you. Things I do are for you, because I love you."

Laci looked at Dink and searched his face for sincerity. She saw, once again, the hustler from the South Bronx whom she'd fallen in love with. The man who gave up a life of familiarity for a life of uncertainty, all for her.

"I'm sorry, Dink," she said with tears in her eyes. "Yes, I do trust you, but I just look at Simone and I see Crystal. I know you loved her."

"You're right, but I fell out of love with her the minute I saw you. I had love for her but nothing like what I have for you." When it all came down to it, Dink saw Crystal as not being much different from the rest of her crew. She was okay to look at when dressed up, but she wasn't wifey material. Laci was.

"Then to remember how she played you—"

"What you mean how she played me?" Dink questioned.

"She would talk about stuff she did and tell us stories about it."

"What kind of stories?" He was certain that Crystal didn't run her mouth about shit she wasn't supposed to, but he had to ask just to make sure.

"About other dudes, Dink."

He remained quiet. Dink never thought that Crystal would step out on him because he was holding it down. He knew he didn't fuck her as often as she liked, but he took care of home and home included her pussy, or so he thought. Now the shit was out in the open, confirming the rumors he had heard of her messing around.

Laci was eager to tell Dink what she could remember because she thought that, just maybe, this would work in her favor with Simone.

"What else did she say?" he questioned.

"Um . . ." Laci dug back into her memory, "something about a nigga with deep pockets was worth his weight, but a nigga with a deep stroke was priceless."

"Umpf," Dink huffed. He was glad shit went down with Crystal the way it did. If it hadn't he would have had to go back to the South Bronx and handle her himself. He was throwing bricks to keep her in a lifestyle better than she was accustomed and she'd played him.

"Dink, you may think I don't have a valid reason for my ill feelings toward Crystal, um, I mean Simone, but to me, it's too close to home. Here you have a class with her, y'all are hanging out more, and then I overhear you talking about the Bronx. What else would I think? Crystal's there and I just wonder, if she wanted you back, what would happen with us." Dink's eyebrows raised, but then he remembered that he'd never told her that Crystal was dead. Laci paused momentarily. "Can you understand how I feel?"

"I can see how you could feel a little uncomfortable, baby, but Simone and I are just cool, and getting back with Crystal, nah, that ain't happen," Dink said confidently.

"You don't know that, Dink."

"Yes I do."

"How can you be so sure?"

"Because, I just know," he said abruptly. "Look, baby, stop with the questions. There are just some things you don't need to know, and the less you know, the better off you'll be." Dink knew that eventually his sudden disappearance would be questioned and he didn't need Laci getting caught up in it.

Dink had been keeping tabs with Smurf, and the streets were still abuzz about Crystal's death and how Dink just burned out and disappeared. Most at first thought he was taking it hard, staying in hiding until the funeral, but even at the small grave-side burial, Dink was nowhere to be found and people began speculating.

Better off? That phrase clicked something in Laci's head, then she thought back to what he had just told her, *things I do are for you, because I love you.* She tried to shake it off, but there was something about that comment that bothered her.

"Baby, come here." He pulled her close to him again. "I got you, boo-boo, I got us." This time, Dink kissed Laci, deeply. Her body reacted to his touch and she wrapped her arms tightly around his neck, not wanting to let him go. Their tongues danced in unison with each other as their bodies merged together as one. But within minutes, Laci broke her embrace.

"Go get ready for the party," she told him as she removed his hands from around her waist, taking the joint out of his hand on the sly. "I'm gonna get ready for tonight."

"What's happening tonight?"

"You and I have been together for a while, Dink, and I do love you, very much. I want to take our relationship to the next level. I want us to make love tonight. I want you, Dink." She smiled and kissed him again.

Realizing that was the surprise she had planned, Dink's man-hood began to swell.

"I want you too, baby, but I don't have to go." He ran his hands up and down her back. "I'd rather be here with you anyway."

"Aw . . . thanks, baby, but seriously, I want you to go. I trust you, Dink." She gave him a loving hug.

"Now it looks like you try'na get rid of me."

"No, never. I just want everything to be perfect for tonight."

"Baby, anything you do is perfect. You can never do anything wrong in my eyes," Dink told her as he held her tightly. "Well . . . since you try'na get rid of me . . ."

"I'm not," Laci interrupted in a high-pitched whine followed by a giggle.

"I'ma go ahead and shower, then head out to see if I can catch up with Slim before the party."

Dink headed toward the bathroom. Laci heard the shower turn on, and then heard the sound of the water hitting Dink's body. She went to the bedroom and pulled out her sexiest nightgown. She also had candles and a bottle of Chardonnay she had purchased earlier in the week that was already on their makeshift wet bar. She wanted to set the mood. Laci was ready to take their relationship to the next level. She and Dink had been together for two months and had never made love. There were plenty of times it could have gone there, but Dink said that it was important to him that they were together emotionally rather than physically first. He and Laci fell into a serious relationship very quickly, but he didn't want their sexual relationship to move too fast. He respected her and he wanted their relationship to have a solid foundation.

Dink stepped out of the shower as Laci entered the bathroom. Although she had seen him naked before, something was different now. The beaded water on his smooth brown skin gave him a glow and outlined every taut muscle. She handed him a towel and allowed her eyes to take in his body. Looking at Dink's muscular chest, strong arms, and rippled but thick stomach made Laci's pussy get wet and begin throbbing slightly. She crossed her legs and leaned up against the wall in order to curb the feeling she had.

He had well-toned legs and pretty feet—no corns, bunions, yellow toenails or foot fungus or funk, like most of the men who ran up in her back in the South Bronx. Laci's eyes scanned over his dick. It was thick, a little darker than his skin color, and hung nicely between his legs.

A dick had never given Laci pleasure when she gave the only thing she had to feed her habit—her pussy. Her orgasmic cries came from the almighty glass dick that she sucked on, which was worth more to her than life itself.

The sexual urges that ran through her body while she looked at Dink let her know that tonight was definitely the night.

"Babe, you sure you don't wanna go?" Dink asked Laci, drying off, not paying attention to how she was looking at him.

"I'd love to, but I really want to set the mood for tonight. I want everything to be right."

Laci ran bathwater for herself after Dink left the bathroom. Even though she loved being around her man, she was going to take advantage of some much-needed solitude once Dink left for the party. About fifteen minutes later, he emerged from their bedroom.

"Whooo . . ." Laci whistled. "You lookin' pretty fly there," she beamed. She could see that even Dink's style had changed from when he was in the Bronx. He would often stunt in a Sergio Tacchini sweat suit, a Polo shirt, and wore two gold rope chains with a Batman medallion around his neck, but now he stood before her looking like a black male supermodel. Dink wore a pair of dark denim Karl Kani jeans, a black large hoodie, and black high-topped Adidas sneakers. He even smelled like Obsession—Laci's favorite cologne. Laci knew her man was fine, but most of all she knew he loved her. After talking to him, her uncertainty about the strength of their relationship was gone and she knew that nothing could come between them.

"A'ight, baby," he told her as he grabbed his leather jacket. "I won't be too long." He tugged at Laci gently by her waist and pulled her toward him. "You go ahead and get ready for tonight. I'll be back at a decent time."

CHAPTER 22

DINK COULDN'T MAKE it to the car quick enough before Laci picked up the phone and called her mother.

"Hi, Mommy," she said into the receiver as she plopped down on the couch and tucked her feet up under her.

"Hey, sweetheart, how are you?" Margaret loved hearing from Laci. Even though they talked every day, it wasn't the same as being able to see her daughter face to face.

"I'm fine. I miss you, but I'm fine." There was a pause on the phone. "Mommy, can I talk to you about something?"

"Yes, sweetheart, you can talk to me about anything." Margaret's heart dropped. Laci had been through a lot. She couldn't imagine what else she had to tell her, but she would take it in stride, whatever it was.

"Mom, something is going on with me and Dink."

"Something going on like what, honey?"

"I really don't think he wants to be here."

"What do you mean 'here'? You mean in school, or with you?"

"With me. Actually, he's doing great in school. I was surprised at first. You know, you never think someone like Dink would

151

know anything outside of the streets, but I was shocked. But he's been trippin' off of me having my own friends. Whenever they want to do something, he'll come up with something for us to do, but he's cool when I hang around him and his friends."

"Tell me about these girls, Laci."

"I found a group of girls that I like, that's it."

Margaret's heart began racing. "They're not like those—"

"No, Mom, totally opposite. Randi, Gabby, Sam, and I have a lot in common."

"Like what?" Margaret asked.

"Private school background, travel during the summer, good grades, and shopping."

Margaret and Laci laughed. "But Mom, Dink has a so-called friend named Simone, who I can't stand. He says she's not a threat. He even told me that I should move forward with my life, but how do you know if someone is with you because they want to be or they feel they have to be?"

Margaret understood Laci's concern.

"Baby, I can understand how you feel but remember, Daryl wouldn't be there if he didn't want to be there. He gave up a lot to be with you and I'm sure he wouldn't jeopardize that. But with this Simone girl, if he tells you that there's nothing to worry about, trust him, sweetheart. Daryl doesn't strike me as a man who would say something and not mean it."

"But Mom, what I didn't tell you is that she looks a lot like Crystal, his ex."

Margaret became quiet, but after a few seconds, she spoke again. "Honey, I agree with Dink and think you should move forward. Don't be afraid to face the future because of your past." She got quiet for a minute. "Maybe you should get to know her. Even if you two don't become friends, remember the old saying, keep your friends close and your enemies closer."

Margaret knew this was a tall order; she knew that forgiving wasn't easy and this was something they both had to work on.

"Remember, sweetheart, he wouldn't be there if he didn't want to be there, and try to be nice to Simone. She's not his ex."

"Okay, Mom. Thanks."

Laci got off the phone with her mother and thought back to an earlier conversation with Dink. She realized that he was telling her something indirectly without saying too much. *Things I do are for you, because I love you.* Laci never thought Dink would resort to violence, because she had never seen that side of him; however, she realized that no matter what environment Dink was in, violence was not beneath him.

FORTY-FIVE MINUTES HAD passed and Laci just wanted to clear her mind, get in her bath, relax, and get herself ready for her night with Dink. She went into her bedroom, undressed, and put on her thick white terry-cloth robe and matching slippers, then pinned her hair up. She went back into the bathroom to add more hot water to her now cold bath. After she added Vaseline Intensive Care Moisturizing Bath Beads, she submerged her hand in the warm water and swirled it around. Laci inhaled the fresh scent, wiped her hand on her robe, then walked into the living room and turned on the radio. Flipping through the stations, tired of the rap that Dink listened to, she found some pop music. Laci flopped into the kitchen and poured herself a glass of Boone's Farm and came out, humming along to Culture Club's "Karma Chameleon."

Taking a sip of the wine, Laci fired up the joint she'd had earlier. Her uncle had put a lot on her mind, and she was curious about what could have happened with Crystal. Her mind went a mile a minute, so she needed something to slow it down. Taking a hit off the joint, Laci walked back toward the bathroom, then stopped when she heard a knock on the front door.

Not looking out the peephole, Laci flung the door open.

CHAPTER 23

ONETTE WAS STILL obsessed with finding Laci. Over the last three weeks, she hadn't had shit else to do, so she drove through the streets of the South Bronx. She even made Monique go into various tenements and crack houses looking for the girl.

At Tonette's bark, Monique even followed Angel, a known crackhead that Laci used to base with, but she came up empty-handed.

To avoid getting her regular beat-down by Tonette for by not doing what she was told, Monique promised her that she would find Laci.

It was the first Saturday in October and nobody had seen or heard from Laci since the end of July. Tonette began to wonder if she was dead, even though she could have sworn she saw her weeks ago in the red Benz. It was as if Laci had disappeared, and she didn't like that.

When Tonette arrived back at her apartment after being on the streets all night, she immediately went to Monique, who was on the couch asleep.

"Wake yo' ass up!" She shook Monique hard, then nudged her in the forehead, repeatedly.

Monique immediately sat up and looked at Tonette. Now trained, she was quiet. Tonette hadn't allowed her to talk yet.

"I been try'na find this ho for weeks now," Tonette said, needing to talk, pacing the floor back and forth in front of Monique, "and I can't find her anywhere." Tonette continued to pace. "I'm really beginning to think she's dead. What do you think?"

Monique remembered Tonette mentioning that about a week ago, but she let her talk and remained quiet. Tonette noticed that it looked like Monique had something to say. "Go 'head and talk," she demanded. "Damn!"

"Remember this is the South Bronx. The streets don't care about a bitch getting blazed, but as soon as a muthafucka dies from an overdose or someone kicks they ass for some blow, then there's heat. If there ain't no heat, she ain't dead." Monique knew she was always good on her feet, but Tonette never let her or the other South Bronx Bitches have any say-so in anything. Because of that, most of them kept their opinions to themselves. Even if they were right, if Tonette didn't think of it first, it wouldn't be dealt with.

"You're right," she told Monique. "Damn, I didn't think about it that way." She softened her demeanor, then looked at Monique. "So you think she up and burned out?"

"With the habit she had, I don't think she could have just burned out, but you could be right, Nette." Monique had to correct the wrong she'd just made. To tell Tonette she was wrong, even if her thinking wasn't logical, could have dire consequences, so she had to flip the shit and quick. "Girl, she could have tweaked her lil' ass all the way to Brooklyn, Manhattan, Queens, and Staten Island and back. Just make one big circle,"

Monique confirmed. "Wouldn't it be something if she had different mattresses all over?" she laughed.

"Or if she dragged the one she had all over." Tonette's eyes began to sparkle with laughter at the visual.

Monique chuckled, "Girl, stop it. Well you know, crackheads need love too," Monique sang in true Klymaxx fashion. She and Tonette laughed together like nothing had ever happened between them. "We'll find her, Nette. I promise. We da SBBs, baby. Ain't nothin' we can't do."

"That's right," Tonette confirmed. "We da baddest bitches out here." She looked at the clock on her wall. It was close to seven in the morning and she had had a rough night. It was time to get some sleep.

"Tonette?" Monique called meekly. She wasn't certain if she was still able to talk, but she tried her luck.

"Yes?"

"I'm gonna get ready to go to the post office and I'll hit the streets when I get back home, okay?"

Monique was thankful she had a job when she arrived at Tonette's door. She couldn't imagine being under Tonette's thumb 24/7. She didn't tell her about the job the night she arrived at her house. After the severe beating, Monique just wanted to go to sleep. The next day when she got up to go to work, she ran into Tonette, who was coming in from a hard night's work. After Tonette questioned her about where she was going, fearing an early morning beating, Monique admitted that she had a job. She had to, because she had to get to work and she knew that Tonette would deter her. After a couple of weeks of beatings, Tonette's daily attacks began to cease.

Truth be told, Tonette was getting bored and needed a challenge. She thought about her crew and became angry. She was on the streets hustling, Shaunna was a career baby mama, fucking anything with a dick to get hers, and Crystal was now pushing up daisies. Monique was the only one of the crew doing something legal that could amount to anything. Although jealous, she decided to use it to her advantage. Monique was the only one who didn't have a record, so Tonette made sure that Monique was building her credit, too. She knew that with good credit, and being legal, if things got hot, Monique would be the one to have her back if something were to go down.

Not having heard from Shaunna, Tonette wondered if she was playing her to the left.

"Okay," Tonette yawned. She walked to her bedroom. "Oh, and Monique?"

"Yes?"

"Thanks."

Monique felt relieved. This was the first time in weeks that Tonette had been remotely nice to her, and she would do what she had to do to keep it that way.

CHAPTER 24

AFTER TAKING A much-needed rest, Tonette awoke fresh and ready to go. She checked her stash and saw that she was low. Too low for her to go back out on the streets without re-upping. "Shit!" she said as she checked her pager, which had been blowin' up since she laid her head down.

Tonette realized that she'd had it easy for a minute, hitting the streets with Dame's stash that he kept at the other apartment, but now it was almost gone and she had to get back on a serious grind. In the past, if she'd needed some quick cash, she would skim some blow off Dame, then sex him down real good. But shit, his bitch ass was history, so she had to go through Dink until she found another trick she could cop from. Hustling was cool with her, though, because it gave her something to do to keep her mind off of Laci, but she was still angry and demanded to be in control. Control, anger, and an evil bitch was a deadly combination, and everyone who encountered Tonette knew it.

It was seven o'clock on Saturday night and Tonette was waiting on the corner at her usual spot for Smurf. She knew something was up because she had paged Dink earlier that day, but it was Smurf who called her back.

"Someone page a pager?" Smurf spoke into the nearest pay-phone receiver.

"Who dis?" she questioned.

"Who dis? You paged me." Smurf was beginning to get pissed. He didn't have time to play games.

"Dis Tonette. Where Dink?"

"Oh."

"Oh what?" Tonette snapped, recognizing the voice.

"Girl, you need to check dat attitude."

"Anyway," she huffed, "where Dink?"

"Takin' care of business," Smurf retorted quickly. "I'm returning his pages, so wassup?"

"I need my normal stuff."

"I'm tied up right now," he told her, "but meet me at the spot later on tonight. Around ten." He hung up the phone before she could reply.

He would have sought her out sooner, but his first priority was to get shit on the streets right, getting his troops in place to keep the operation moving.

But when Dink asked that he keep an eye on the girls, and then Laci asked the same thing, Smurf knew something was up. He knew Dink was on top of his business and after what Laci told him, they both had a good reason for keeping tabs on them.

Smurf knew Tonette by her reputation and knew that her crew didn't operate without her. She was a slippery little bitch and he didn't want to get caught slippin' with her.

CHAPTER 25

O H!" LACI GASPED, "it's you."

"Well damn, don't sound so happy to see me."

"What do you want, T.J.?"

"I wanted to rap to ya for a minute." He pushed his way inside the apartment. "How was your little, uh . . . outing?" T.J. said sarcastically.

"It was really nice," Laci told him, ignoring the sarcasm in his voice. "We enjoyed it." Laci noticed a strange look on T.J.'s face, which made her really uncomfortable. "Um . . . look, T.J., I know you didn't come all the way over here to ask me about sightseeing. Daryl isn't here, but—"

"I know he isn't," he responded, and closed the door behind him.

Laci watched him closely.

"Don't worry," T.J. told her when he saw the worry in her face. "I ain't gonna hurt you."

Laci stood in front of him, waiting for him to speak. She wished that she wasn't completely naked under her robe, so she pulled the neck closed in an attempt to conceal herself. "Okay, can you make it quick? I have something I have to do."

"Oh yeah," he remarked slyly, "like get that surprise ready?" T.J. sneered at her. "You know, you're very beautiful." He reached out and touched one of her black curly tendrils of hair and watched as it bounced on her shoulder. "I told you that when I saw you for the first time." He lightly grazed her cheek with his finger.

"You buggin'," Laci said and gently moved his hand away. "You got a girl, remember?"

"Yeah, whatever," he chuckled nonchalantly. "It seems like she's been preoccupied with Daryl lately," T.J. spoke, pronouncing "Daryl" in his most proper dialect.

Laci huffed. "T.J., don't go there. Ain't nothing happening. They're just friends." Absentmindedly she took a long pull off the joint. Even though Dink had put Laci's jealousy to rest, she really wanted to believe what she was saying was true.

"Is that what you really think?" T.J. said, his voice growing higher with every word. "Wake up, girl, are you blind? You know they fuckin'. Ever since that nigga been around, she ain't got time for shit else, including me."

"T.J., just go. I ain't getting in the middle of you and Simone's shit." Laci began to lead him to the door.

"No!" he exclaimed, stopping her in her tracks. "This is something you need to handle."

"And how do you expect me to do that? I ain't Daryl and I definitely ain't Simone. As a matter of fact, you so worried about him, damn, why don't you control that bitch? You such a big man," Laci snarled. She already had her suspicions and his accusations weren't making things better.

"You gonna do what I tell you to do, Laci. I came over here to talk and I'm being nice, but I'm not gonna be this way too long," he threatened. "Keep running your mouth, it's gonna get you in trouble."

"Fuck you, T.J. And if I don't?"

He looked at Laci with a devious smile plastered on his face. T.J. took in Laci's robed body from her head to her feet and back up, then smiled seductively at her. His gaze made Laci uncomfortable. He looked at her like the men who had used her for their sexual pleasure in the past. Laci tried her best to hold it together, standing firmly, to show him that she wasn't afraid of him; then she noticed an erection through his pants. "T.J., you gotta leave," she said forcefully, "now!"

T.J. laughed heartily at Laci. He knew she saw his dick straining through his pants and it turned him on. "I ain't gonna touch you," he reassured her. "You cute and all, but I don't fuck with your type."

"What the hell is that supposed to mean, 'your type'?" Laci became angry at T.J.'s remarks.

"Remember when I told you I knew you from somewhere? Well, I know where now."

"I said go," Laci warned.

"I'll go," he told her, "but before I do, I just wanna show you where I know you from." He walked up closer to her.

Laci held her wine glass tighter, prepared to use it to hit him on the head if necessary.

He opened his letterman's jacket and retrieved a VHS tape from the lower pocket. He then walked over to the VCR that sat on top of the new 27-inch color, popped the tape in, and pushed play.

Laci's mouth dropped. *Oh my God!* She saw herself on the floor on all fours with some girl's head eating out her pussy, while her head was laid against someone's stomach. The video was grainy, so the male body just looked like a gargoyle. Next, the gargoyle began to prep her ass and pussy with some type of oily substance, then he inserted a finger in her asshole. The gargoyle finally came into focus and Laci saw who it was. It was Dame.

She gulped down the remaining wine. "Wha...Where the hell you get this?" she yelled.

"It wasn't that hard," he told her truthfully, grinning as though he had just won the lottery. It was the hottest thing on the black market and it had made its way from the New York City boroughs to the surrounding areas. T.J. jacked off to it when Simone was being stingy with the pussy, and that had become more frequent now that she was smiling up in Dink's face all the time.

She looked at the screen again. "Turn this bullshit off!" Laci yelled and ran toward the VCR.

T.J. grabbed her by the arm. "Naw, watch this." T.J. took hold of her face, forcing her to look at the television.

Laci saw Dame's dick positioned at her glistening pink slit. He was fighting a losing battle in his futile attempt to make his way into her tight pussy. She saw him motion to Quita, who put a crack pipe back into her mouth. Laci saw herself take a deep pull, then Dame eased his way into her.

Dame stole her virginity while she was on a drug binge and that, she could never get back.

Laci saw herself bang her fists on the floor and beg for something. She couldn't decipher what she was trying to say. She tried to turn her head away, but T.J. forced it back to the television.

"Watch this...this the good part right here." T.J. seemed to really be into what he saw on the screen. Laci was forced to watch as Dame brutally beat his meat inside of her and violated her body. She saw herself perform as if her life depended on it, and at that time, it did.

Tears streamed down Laci's red blotched face, reliving the memory she had suppressed. She had no idea that the night she lost her virginity was taped. With every thrust Dame inflicted on her, she sucked on her savior—her glass dick. Laci saw Dame grab her by the hips, stand up over her ass with his dick still in her pussy. Next she saw the base of his dick begin to pulsate. He screamed out in sheer ecstasy, then turned to the camera while he continued to pump and expel his cum inside her virgin walls. What happened next shocked her but made T.J. laugh. Dame stuck his tongue out at the camera. Laci almost threw up.

"Man, that was gangsta! That was some I-don't-give-a-fuck shit right there!" He cheesed hard. "Who was he doing that for? Your man?" T.J. laughed.

Laci was at a total loss for words. If her parents taught her anything at all, it was respect for herself, and more importantly, her body. Being the good girl she was, she listened to their words, but she finally saw what she never wanted to see: degrading herself as a woman and using her body to get what it needed.

"Now, as I asked you nicely earlier, keep yo' man away from Simone. It's a very simple request, Laci. Personally, I don't care what you gotta do, just do it."

"And if they still continue to be around each other?"

"I'll just have a video release party," T.J. said coolly. "People will see you for what you really are, a common ho. It's plenty of dudes around here that wanna holla at you and I'm sure after seeing this, they'd want to make a part two to this tape. You'll be a star," T.J. joked, "Laci Johnson—crackhead." T.J. looked into the atmosphere and waved his arms as if displaying the title on a screen.

"I'm not a crackhead or a ho!" Laci argued.

"Well, this tape says otherwise. It's the tape against your word, Laci. When muthafuckas see it, who or what you think they gonna believe? Now handle yours."

T.J. traced the lapel of Laci's robe with his finger and it draped open a little bit. T.J. saw the small apple-shaped birthmark on the top swell of her left breast. He wanted to see more, to see if her titties were just as firm as they looked on the tape, but just from the little peek he had, he knew that Laci had more than a mouthful and they weren't saggy. Laci slapped his hand away.

"What you tell me earlier?" T.J. said in an attempt to play absentminded. "Fuck me? Naw, you smart-mouthed bitch. Fuck you." T.J. coolly walked out of the apartment and closed the door.

CHAPTER 26

DAMN, BOY, WHAT took you so long?" Tonette spoke hastily once Smurf had driven up in Dink's car. "My pager been blowin' up and shit."

"Look, girl, I ain't got time to deal with your mouth today. Get yo' ass in the car and let's do this."

Tonette didn't appreciate Smurf's attitude, but she got in anyway. They drove to an alley, where Smurf parked the car.

"Here," he handed her one sandwich bag full of marijuana.

"Where my other shit?"

"Be cool. I got some more shit coming in," he told her matter-of-factly.

"New shit? Like what?"

"Ice. You heard of it?"

"Hell yeah!" Tonette sounded hyped. It was that same shit that Dame had, and it had her customers flying off the chains.

She looked at the bag of weed Smurf gave her. "Well, until you get that, what about my rocks?"

"I'ma need you to push the other shit," he told her, ignoring her question.

"What you mean you need me to push the other shit? Nigga, I don't work for you. I do my own thing."

"Do your own thing, huh? I got the boroughs on lock. Where you getting your shit from?" Tonette didn't answer. "Whoever you getting it from gets it from me, but check it, where you get the shit you had?" Tonette became quiet. She knew she'd stolen a lot of her shit from Dame, a little at a time, so he wouldn't notice anything was missing.

"I didn't think you could answer that." Smurf quickly fiddled with his strap, which was on his waist, and laid his Beretta on his lap. "You call me to get yo' shit but you stole from Dame. He got his shit from me, so that means you owe me a little debt," he told her. Again, Tonette remained quiet. "That means, rules have changed."

When he thought about all of the people who worked for him, he figured he was lacking one thing . . . a female. He could use a girl to cater to his female customers, because a nigga would trade some blow for a head job and tax the next man in a heart-beat. Smurf also had plans for her to cater to him as well—his way to keep her close.

"Nigga, where Dink?!" she yelled.

Coolly, Smurf looked at Tonette. "I'm making you an offer, little girl—"

"Little girl?" Tonette snapped. She looked at him with her gray eyes, which once sparkled but now were cold. "Nigga, please, you don't know what I'm capable of."

"Whatever it is, I'm sure it's minor league, but yo, check it. Where is Dame's shit?"

"What you mean where is it? I sold it, nigga."

"Well, where's my money then?"

"Huh?" He'd caught Tonette off guard. She made the *pssst* sound with her lips and quickly tried to get out of the car. Smurf was pissing her off. Before she could open the door all the way, Smurf grabbed her forearm, forcing her to stay in the car.

"This a business meeting, so sit yo' ass down."

Tonette had no choice but to do what he said. Sure, she was the baddest bitch on the block, but she wasn't a match for no nigga. A ruthless killer at that. Smurf's reputation preceded him and she knew he was a crazy-ass nigga.

"You heard me," he repeated, "where's my money? This a business. I supply, you sell, I get my cut. Dame sold, he'd give Dink his cut."

"What that gotta do with me?" Tonette became aggravated.

"Everything," Smurf told her truthfully. "You see, Dame was slippin'. Boss man let him operate by his damn self. Never once did he look over that nigga's shoulder. Unfortunately, Dame wasn't handling his business and he left owing us a debt. That's where you come in."

"I ain't got shit to do with that," Tonette protested.

"That's bullshit and you know it," Smurf said calmly. He looked at his watch. He had things to do and Tonette was now wasting his precious time. "In the dope game it's every nigga for himself. Most niggas would have smoked you by now on the strength of you being that nigga's gal, but you in my crew now so you gotta work that shit off." Tonette rolled her eyes at Smurf.

"You know I got ice and shit about to take off. It shouldn't take you that long," he said seriously. "Work your debt off and the rest is yours, minus my cut. So what it gonna be? You in," he asked, "or you out?" He caressed the shiny chrome that lay in his lap. "I'll give you a minute." Smurf looked at his watch.

"You ain't answer my question," Tonette told him. She'd heard what he had said, but she had questions that needed answers too.

"And what's that?" he sighed.

"Where is Dink?" she said slowly. "Why you drivin' his car and why you answering his pages?"

"Look, things changin' around here. He's the top dog and he still grindin', so quit trippin'." Actually, Smurf was beginning to get pissed by the interrogation. He knew where Dink was, and Laci for that matter, but Smurf's loyalty to Dink ran long. He was asked by Dink earlier to keep an eye on Tonette, and that was what he was going to do.

He put the car in drive and drove in silence to where he had picked her up. Once there, he stopped the car, then reached over and yanked the bag of weed out of Tonette's hands.

"What you doing, boy?" She tried to get it back from him but couldn't.

"Taking my shit back. You want something from me and I want what's rightfully mine. Until you're able to do that, you're cut off. Ain't nobody gonna fuck wit'cha," he said in plain and simple English and glared at Tonette. She knew what that look meant—get the fuck out. Tonette hopped out, but right before she slammed his door shut, Smurf spoke. "When you ready, page me." He smirked at her. "Oh, and don't slam my door. Close it like you got some fuckin' sense."

Tonette couldn't believe he was checking her, but she did what Smurf asked. Actually, his bluntness and demands turned her on. That's what had kept her with Dame. He didn't put up with too much of her shit.

Tonette got into her car and drove in silence back to her crib. Along the way, it hit her suddenly that Dink's disappearance and Laci's absence were too coincidental. Tonette thought long and hard, and realized that Dink didn't have any reason to stick around. Crystal was dead and he was feeling Laci, who had disappeared.

"Wouldn't that be fucked up," she said to herself, "if them two were together?" She continued to drive. "Fuck that shit—if that nigga won't help me find her, I know who will." Tonette got off the elevator and marched toward her apartment. When she walked in, Monique was on the phone. Within seconds, Monique wrapped up her conversation. Tonette was too tired to even care who she was talking to. Something wasn't right and she couldn't keep wasting her time on kicking Monique's ass.

"Hey, Nette," Monique spoke. She was comfortable enough now to speak on her own. "What's wrong with you?" Tonette was obviously focused on something, because she was pacing back and forth in front of her. "Oh, that was Shaunna on the phone. She had her baby. A boy, eight pounds, thirteen ounces. She said she had been in labor for damn near a week."

Tonette didn't say anything. She didn't give a damn. She just kept pacing.

"What's wrong with you?" Monique asked again. She was hoping that she hadn't done anything wrong to piss Tonette off again.

"Shit, that damn Smurf. Nigga done pissed me off."

"Smurf?" Monique questioned.

"Yeah, girl. I paged Dink so I could re-up and Smurf's short ass called me back. Now that nigga drivin' around in his ride, claiming his territory and shit."

"Straight up? Where's Dink?"

"Dunno, but when I asked Smurf about him, he ain't say shit." Monique remained quiet. "But that's cool ... I got what I need right here." She looked at a scrap of paper with Laci's phone number on it. She'd found it in her pink and white satin baseball jacket. She was glad she didn't get rid of it.

"Girl, what you 'bout to do? Shit, I want in!" Monique sounded hyped.

"Just sit back and watch a pro at work," Tonette bragged. She dialed the number she had for Laci.

"Hello?" a crisp, clear voice answered the other end.

"Hello," Tonette spoke back, "is Laci home?"

"Who's calling?"

"I'm a friend of hers, Ton—"

Laci's mother cut Tonette off before she could finish her name. "You aren't a friend of my daughter's. Friends don't hurt each other. You've done some despicable things to Laci, but I'm here to tell you, this is the last time you'll hurt anyone. The police need . . ."

Tonette got pissed at Margaret's constant yakking and hung up on her. This wasn't the first time her mother had run off at the mouth, but Tonette vowed it would be her last. Deep down, Tonette was still jealous of Laci. Her intense envy boiled over into pure hatred. She'd never had anyone in her corner the way Laci's mother was always in hers. Even after turning her out, her mother still cared.

"What happened?" Monique asked, noticing that Tonette was angry.

"That bitch called herself going off on me and hung up."

"Nette, you can't go over there."

"Why not?"

"By going over that girl's house right now, it wouldn't be a good move."

"I don't give a damn!" Tonette yelled. "That bitch had the

nerve to get at me like that? She and her daughter both deserve to get a foot up they ass for that."

Monique noticed that Tonette wasn't mad—her nostrils weren't flaring. She was just pissed that Laci's mother jumped hard at her and she wasn't prepared for that.

"Look," Monique said seriously, "let's give her a few days to cool off, then I'll go over there and see what I can find out."

"You? Why you?" Tonette quizzed. "I'm the leader of this group. And remember, you was feeling bad for that heifer." She looked closely at Monique and squinted her eyes. "You ain't try'na jump on that bitch's side again, are you? Because if that's the case, you goin' down with her too."

"No, Tonette, I'm not feeling bad. I'm just looking out for you."

"Yeah, right." The edges of Tonette's lips turned upward. "How you figure that shit?"

"If you go over there and Laci's mother tries to act like a bitch and call the police, I'ma be bailing yo' ass out of jail. But if I go and she tries that stupid bitch shit, they come and run me ... I'm clean. I have a job and no record. What the fuck can they charge me with?" Monique whined and batted her eyes with a sinister, sly smile on her face. "I'm just looking for my good friend Laci."

Tonette could not do anything but laugh. After a brief moment of silence, she spoke. "Girl, you a crazy ho," she told her.

Although Tonette didn't agree to it with exact words, Monique knew that her reasoning was logical and Tonette understood. To agree with an idea that wasn't initially hers, Tonette played the silent game, but nodded her approval.

CHAPTER 27

LACI STAGGERED SLOWLY toward the couch and plopped down.

She put her head in her hands. She was too mad to cry, but she remembered that her uncle had given her the card of an officer who came by the house looking for her. She dug around in her purse until she found the card, then picked up the phone and started dialing. Within seconds, Laci put the phone down without completing the call. She didn't know what she wanted to do. On one hand, she wanted to call and tell the police what happened to her this past summer. On the other hand, she just wanted to forget the whole thing, but then she remembered that they wanted to talk to her because someone had thrown her name out there. Laci wanted to do what was right, but doing what was right could possibly put Dink behind bars.

Most of all, Laci was disturbed by the fact that T.J. had the tape and by what he wanted her to do because of it. She could have fucked him to keep him from showing the tape, but she wasn't no ho. Any man she would be with from now on would be by choice and not necessity.

Dink already knew that Dame had fucked her. He'd never

brought it up after she told him, but how could she explain a videotape of her having sex not only his boy, but Quita's stankin' ass too?

She figured that Dink wouldn't realize that it was as close to rape as a sexual act could get. Who would think that when it looked like just another addict fucking for crack? It was all on tape for anyone to see, and considering what T.J. said, people liked it. Nobody would ever think it was a total violation of her body.

Laci thought back to her brief conversation with her uncle, and she picked up the phone again and began to dial.

"May I speak to Officer Jones?" she said when someone answered.

After she was put on hold briefly, a man answered the phone. "Detective Clifton," the voice blared into the receiver.

"Um...uh...may I speak with Officer Jones? This is Laci Johnson."

"I'm sorry, Ms. Johnson, but he's off today. May I help you with something?"

"My uncle told me you wanted to, uh...ask me some questions?"

"Johnson," he said, trying to remember the name. "Julacia Johnson?" he asked.

"Yes," Laci confirmed.

"Ms. Johnson, thanks for calling back." Laci remained quiet. "I wanted to talk to you because we're looking into the death of Crystal Moore and Rick Young."

"Death?" Laci screeched. "Rick who?" she asked. She had never heard that name before.

"Oh, I'm sorry," he said. "You probably know him as Dame."

Dame's dead too? she thought to herself.

"Would you be able to come to the station and talk to us about this?"

Laci became quiet. "No, I'm away in college. But Detective, I'm curious, why are you looking for me?"

"You've been named as someone who may know more about this case. We have a picture of you with the group of girls known as the South Bronx Bitches, Ms. Johnson." Laci stayed silent. "Look, you may or may not have the answers we're looking for, but we just need to tie up some loose ends on this case. We questioned the other girls and you're the only one we haven't spoken with. The girl who was with Ms. Moore at the time of the incident is no longer cooperating, and you're the only other one without a record, so we really need your help."

"Help doing what?"

"Finding out why Ms. Moore was set up. We also know that her boyfriend ran a drug ring here in the Bronx and now he's nowhere to be found. Every time their name comes up, yours does too, and it looks like nobody knows much about them or is willing to talk. So we need to get to the bottom of it. Ms. Johnson, this is serious business; if you can't come to us, we'll have to come to you."

Laci's heart started racing and she hung the phone up abruptly.

"God, please," Laci said out loud, "please let this nightmare end."

CHAPTER 28

THE PARTY BEGAN like any other college party scene. The students were celebrating the 42–7 ass-kicking that B.U. gave Northwestern, but it quickly turned into something resembling Atlanta's spring-break Freaknik.

Once the alcohol was flowing freely and the weed had been passed around to everyone, the atmosphere got crazier. The horny girls started to dance wildly with each other and on whatever surface could hold their weight in order to entice any guy that was paying attention. With a ratio of two to one, a man could have his fantasy of more than one girl in a night.

"Jingling Baby" by LL Cool J filled the air and the girls grinded their pussies against the men who were standing around watching. They also teased them by rubbing their breasts against any man who would give them attention. The boys danced along with their freaks of the night, but a few had a hard time hanging out when they couldn't take the sexy grinding any longer without wanting to get up in it.

Dink was busy breaking the grip of three freaks who'd been eyeing him since he walked into the frat house.

"Baby, we offering you an around-the-world proposition," one of the girls told Dink. "Have you ever had three women at the same time?" She looked at Dink and licked her lips. "I'll suck your dick while my girl eats your ass and my other girl sucks your balls. Come on, baby, let's get down."

"Aye, yo, Slim," Dink called out. He followed it up with a two-fingered whistle.

"What's up, yo?" Slim said when he'd made his way over to Dink and the three freaks. The girls looked at Slim and approved by nodding their heads. They whispered to each other about who was gonna do what.

"Ladies, why don't y'all take care of my boy here." Dink quickly told Slim what they wanted to do and he happily obliged. "I've been around the world before. Actually more times than you want to know," Dink told the freaks, "so here you go, have fun."

The girls winked at Dink as Slim put his long arms around them. He gave an upward head nod.

"We'll try to bring him back in one piece," one of the girls told Dink as they walked away in search of a little privacy.

Dink had never thought that the people he encountered at the frat house—honor students and future leaders of America—would have that type of freak shit in them, but sex was a universal language that everyone spoke and understood.

Simone laughed at how many women were coming on to Dink, so she stayed close to him to ward off the skeezers. She knew he didn't want to be bothered and he was truly her boy. Plus, she didn't want any of the other guys there try'na get up in her panties tonight either.

Just as they were finishing a game of pool, T.J. came busting into the party. He was loud and obnoxious. It was obvious that he was drunk. T.J. had been drinking since he left Laci earlier that evening. His conscience was really fucking him up. He knew he wasn't a real thug, but he had an image to uphold.

"Look at this bullshit," Simone said to Dink. She was embarrassed. "That's the reason I don't fuck with his ass." She pursed her lips and shook her head.

"Don't even worry about that," Dink told her. "Go 'head and rack 'em. I'm 'bout to get up in that ass tonight," he joked. Simone laughed, and that was all T.J. needed to hear for him to storm over to the two.

"What the fuck you think you doing? Who's ass you gonna get up in?" T.J. boldly yelled at Dink and swung, connecting his fist with Dink's jaw.

In an instant, Dink instinctively clocked T.J. in the face, knocking him to the floor, then pulled out his piece. Dink never traveled far without his iron. Regardless of being on a college campus, he still had to watch his back and wasn't gonna let nobody punk him. That was his street mentality.

Slim and a few others rushed to Dink to keep him from killing T.J.

"Whoa, what the fuck just happened?" Slim's shirt was off and he stood there looking silly with his scrawny, long legs sticking out of his boxers. The freaks that Dink had passed off to him were making good on their promise, but when he heard the commotion, he was concerned about what was happening to his boys.

T.J. rubbed his jaw and drunkenly got up off the floor.

"Come on, nigga," Dink yelled. "You been fuckin' with me since I got here. I don't fuck with wannabe niggas, but I been wantin' to get at you for a minute. Bring yo' ass!"

"Dude!" Slim said forcefully. "Can y'all tell me what the fuck just happened?" He was becoming disgusted with the constant conflict between T.J. and Dink. He suspected that T.J. had a big issue with Dink, but Slim never thought this kinda shit would kick off.

"That nigga all over my gal. Fuck his punk ass!" T.J. yelled.

Some of the spectators started laughing, because that was a punk move on T.J.'s part.

"T.J., you straight-up buggin'," Simone told him. "What you talking about? We was just playing pool!"

"Bitch, fuck you! When I'm through with this nigga, you next. I told you I wanted you to stay away from this ghetto-ass mutha-fucka, but you act like you ain't hearing shit I'm saying."

"T.J., you trippin'." Simone was pissed off. T.J. had never called her a bitch before, but calling her one in public took the cake. "He got a girl."

"Now you takin' up for his ass. You a ho just like his gal."

Dink had had enough. He broke free from Slim and the other dudes and tackled T.J. to the ground. *Clunk.* Something flew out of T.J.'s jacket. He looked at Dink and laughed, with blood and saliva coming out of his mouth.

LACI GREW FURIOUS at the memory. A flashback of her most de-grading moments, which were even worse than what was on the tape that T.J. had shown her, flooded her mind. The memory of an unlimited amount of men and women using her for sex made Laci's stomach turn.

Oral sex, anal sex, vaginal sex, and the smells of bodily fluid she was constantly sprayed with stuck in her mind. The names she was called—most she had never heard of—rang loud and clear.

At her lowest point, Laci would have fucked a dog right in the middle of the South Bronx during rush-hour traffic if it would have fed her habit. Junkies stole, lied, and would sell their soul to the devil if it would give them the hit that their bodies needed.

At that time Laci knew she looked like shit and she didn't give a fuck, but everyone still wanted a piece of her. Not only because she was fly but also because she had a reputation that anything goes, and best of all, they didn't have to break her off anything more than some dick and a hit.

Many local and nonlocal ballers had had a taste of the ripe young strawberry. Nothing else compared to it. They enjoyed running trains on her just to see how much she could take. One night she had eight guys running through her young body. Oftentimes the men wanted to see just how far she'd go for her high and during group sex, they made her suck the dick or eat the pussy of another druggie who was shooting up. The ballers she fucked didn't want to share her pussy with other druggies because Lord only knew what diseases they carried. They wanted her snatch to themselves.

With tears pouring from her eyes and close to hyperventilating, she picked up her phone and dialed the number again. Upset that she received a machine, Laci left the best message she could in her condition.

An image of her sucking the dick of a homeless junkie played on repeat in her mind. She ran to the bathroom and threw up just as she remembered him nutting off in her mouth. It was the most horrid thing she had ever tasted in her life.

Almost instantly, a large, warm hand grabbed her shoulder.

Laci's heart almost jumped out of her chest. Her mind was all over the place and she prayed it wasn't T.J. again.

"Baby, what's wrong?" Dink asked, picking her up off the floor. "Have too much to drink?" When he walked into the apartment, he'd seen two empty bottles of wine on the floor.

Laci hugged Dink, glad he was home. Dink broke her embrace and looked at her angrily. It was a look she had never seen before.

"What's wrong?" she asked.

"That nigga T.J.," Dink said. Laci's heart dropped to the pit of her stomach.

"T.J.? What he do?" Laci asked anxiously, afraid that he would have shown Dink the tape as well as others.

"I don't wanna talk about it." Dink helped clean Laci up, but the alcohol he'd drunk earlier put him in another mood. As he led Laci to their bedroom, he turned her toward him and gently pushed the white spaghetti straps from her gown off her shoulders, then gently eased the delicate fabric down over her slender but curvy body.

Dink's sultry gaze met Laci's as he undressed. He stepped to her and held her naked body in his arms.

"I need you, baby," Dink whispered in Laci's ear, enjoying the feel of her body next to his. He breathed heavily while he kissed her neck and trailed kisses to her breasts, then back up.

Laci's body reacted to Dink's touch. Her breathing matched his while she allowed her lips to meet his and they exchanged a long, passionate kiss.

Her hands traveled up Dink's strong back, enjoying the feel of his muscular body. The intensity of the moment excited her and she allowed Dink to lay her down on the bed.

Although Laci's pussy was wet and she wanted Dink to make love to her, her mind was elsewhere. She couldn't get the tape off her mind and the lingering feel of T.J.'s touch off her breast.

Just as Dink attempted to enter her, Laci tensed up.

"Dink, no."

"Baby, it won't hurt. I promise I'll be gentle," he told her, putting his mouth on hers with a passionate kiss.

"Dink, please stop." Laci broke the kiss and struggled against the weight of his body. Finally he realized she was serious. "I'm not ready for this. I . . . I can't." Laci got up and ran to the bathroom.

She splashed cold water on her face and looked at her reflection in the mirror. *What's wrong with me?* Everything seemed so surreal. After she'd gathered her composure, Laci walked back into the bedroom and sat down next to Dink, who had put his boxers back on. "Dink, I'm sorry," she said quietly, putting her hand on his shoulder. "I just have a lot on my mind."

"It's okay," he told her, reaching for his T-shirt. He quickly put it on and lay down. Laci got in on her side of the bed and snuggled up next to Dink. Laci put Dink's arm around her. She needed him to hold her before she lost it.

S MURF WAS AN eager student and learned more and more about the mechanics of drug trading. Dirty taught him everything he should know and then some. Smurf now made all the decisions and negotiations about what came into the South Bronx.

Smurf also took a personal approach with Dirty. He learned that Dirty went to jail when he was seventeen years old and took the entire rap to protect someone else.

Because of all the product that Smurf brought into the hood, his crew stepped up their game and did their job, so Smurf rewarded them handsomely. It was a win-win situation. Once he got back in the hood, he linked up with his boys, Drake and Lil' Rob.

"Yo, boss," Lil' Rob called. "I got some freaks from Harlem rollin' through tonight. You know how I do it. You want in?"

"Shit . . . depends," Smurf retorted. "They them hoes from last time?"

"Naw, man, this some new shit."

"Good . . . good, 'cuz old pussy gets dug out," Smurf laughed. "You know how to get a hold of me, man." He thought back to

LaQuan. The pussy was getting better every time he hit it, but Smurf would never turn down a fresh piece of ass. And lucky for him, he had all kinds of women to choose from.

Brenda, a chick he'd met through one of his boys, was money hungry. She was fine, and kept to her motto of whoever had the most bread would be the one to get the head.

Maria was a mixed black and Spanish *mamacita*. Smurf really liked her at first because they could have a real conversation. But that was just her game to get into his psyche, so she could make more demands. Smurf didn't have time to deal with the drama for a piece of booty.

Thinking about using all these women got him thinking about his own mom, who had been used time and time again. Smurf hadn't seen her since their talk, but he always left money under her door.

On his way to Tonette's, he saw a new-model red BMW. He looked at the driver and thought he saw his mother. Smurf followed the car, and true enough, it was her.

He knew that his mother couldn't afford a car like the one she was in, so Smurf surmised that she had to be dealing with a hustler.

His mom had come up and it wasn't because of him. Smurf was angry now. "Man, fuck her. Talking about she gonna try to change. Tellin' me she can't accept my help, but when it's another baller who doesn't give two shits about her it's cool? Fuck that. Guess you can't take the ho out of the woman," Smurf said aloud.

CHAPTER 30

ONETTE SAT IN Dame's 1987 navy-blue Chevy Camaro and blasted "Colors" while she watched her customers rock her spot. It was a busy Saturday night and the dead were walking. She saw the men, women, and children that the crack epidemic affected. *It's a shame,* she told herself, *but it's all about money and somebody got to do it.*

Her spot was poppin' and she decided to go in to service more of her customers. She didn't care where they got her payment from, they'd always come up with it. Many of Tonette's customers were tried-and-true junkies. Because of this, they would come back numerous times a night and each time, with a wad of bills in their hands for their needs.

Tonette was known to her customers, and it was time to show her face again. She walked into the vacant building and immediately felt she was going to pass out from a stench like that of decomposing bodies. Beneath her feet crunched used vials of heroin. To the right, Tonette saw junkies fighting one another over their last hit. To her left, she saw what looked like a man, sucking another man's dick. Her stomach turned at the sight. Then straight ahead lay a basehead on a piss, blood, and cum-stained mattress looking like she was halfway dead. The girl looked familiar.

Tonette walked closer. Most girls would have been afraid to go into a crack house alone, but she wasn't. She had what they needed and because of that, she was protected. Also, Tonette was known to put a foot or two up someone's ass if anyone tried to fuck with her. Her reputation for abuse preceded her and it got worse when she became angry or wanted to prove a point.

The high-yella girl on the mattress had a slim build and her dark hair was matted to her head.

Adrenaline began to pump throughout Tonette's body. *There, that bitch is right there,* she said to herself. *I'ma finish this bitch off for good,* she thought as she approached the girl.

With her foot raised, ready to kick her, she was startled when the girl called her name.

"Yo, bitch, wassup?" The girl cracked a snaggle-toothed smile and struggled to get up off the mattress. Her thin frame seemed to fold with the pudge that stood out in her belly. She looked like a starving African—skin and bones but a bloated stomach. It was Quita. She used to be a part of the SBBs until Tonette kicked her out two weeks after Laci came into the picture. "What you doin' here? Lookin' to score?" She laughed dryly.

Tonette hated Quita because she'd fucked with Dame. Even though she was Dame's main bitch, Quita was right up there on the food chain. One time when she and Tonette went to blows, Quita lay low for a while putting work in for Dame, but it never stopped him from fucking with her. Quita was cut off abruptly after Dame was killed, but she had already bitten the other hands that could have fed her. She'd dissed other hustlers because she was with Dame, but now that he was dead, it was easy for her to get played, laid, and turned out.

"Look at this stupid heifer," Tonette said out loud to Quita. "Looks like you really came up."

"I sure did," Quita said as she pranced around, scratching her arms uncontrollably. Tonette could do nothing but laugh. "Look, girl, can we get over the bullshit? We was friends once," Quita chided. "Besides, we did have something in common."

"Bitch, we ain't neva have anything in common."

Quita smiled, then started laughing. "Dame, bitch, or did you forget? We was both fucking his ass."

Tonette smacked Quita across the face. Quita fell down on her mattress and a rancid odor wafted upward.

Tonette turned up her nose.

"You still jealous, Nette. Always jealous of somebody."

Tonette was about to stomp that bitch's head, but then Quita started crying. "I need a hit. I need it bad. My baby will die if I don't get a hit. Please!" she was on her knees in a praying position, begging Tonette to help her.

"Baby?"

"Yeah, right here." Quita rubbed her belly.

"Who would get yo' stankin' ass pregnant?"

A crooked smile ran across Quita's face. "You didn't know Dame was gonna be a daddy?" Quita didn't know who the father of her baby was. She just wanted to fuck with Tonette. She hated Tonette as much as Tonette hated her, but what happened next, Quita wasn't prepared for.

Tonette's nostrils flared. The bottom of her Reebok sneakers found Quita's body and she stomped her until she was certain she was dead. Tonette hacked up a thick glob of spit and shot it at Quita. She walked away without bothering to look back.

It was just another Saturday night in the hood and time to get back to work.

CHAPTER 31

THE WEEKEND COULDN'T pass quick enough. Laci was ready to get back to the normalcy of college life. The alarm clock went off, waking her. After turning it off, she stretched and reached over toward Dink.

"Dink," she said tiredly, "get up." She patted his side of the bed only to see that he wasn't there.

Getting up, she padded out to the living room and saw Dink zipping his backpack.

"You leavin' already?" Laci said, looking at the clock.

"Yep."

"Did you eat breakfast?"

"Nope."

She looked at the clock again, and back at him. "Hang on for a minute. Let me shower and throw some clothes on. We can grab a bite to eat, then go to class."

Dink picked up his bag and grabbed his keys. "That's alright," he told Laci. "I have a lot to do today. I'll just see you later."

Laci watched as Dink walked out the door. She couldn't believe how quickly their relationship had changed. In three months, they went from being happy to being unable to be in the same room with each other. It was an uncomfortable situation, so Laci spent more time hanging with her friends than staying home and working things out with Dink. Little did she know, he stayed out as well. Neither wanted to approach the subject.

After Laci's class, she met up with her girls. "Y'all wanna go to the Gucci store later on?" Sam asked the other three girls. "I think I need another purse." She held up her newest purchase and inspected it.

"Girl, please. When did you get that one?" Randi laughed.

"Two days ago, but you know I can't live without my Gucci!"

The girls giggled.

"Yeah, I wanna cop that new quarter-length jacket," Laci chimed in. "You know, the white leather one?"

"Ooh girl, that was cute!" Sam acknowledged. "And it would look fabulous on you, dahling." She held her head up in the air and looked down her nose like a prima donna with a fake accent.

Laci laughed, but then her facial expression turned grim. "Oh God," she mumbled under her breath. She saw T.J. walking toward them.

"Ooh, here comes that fine-ass T.J.," Gabby said.

As the girls walked toward him, Laci's stomach began to tighten.

"Yo, wassup, ladies?" he said when the girls were in ear distance. He leaned over to whisper in Laci's ear, "Wassup, superstar?"

Laci rolled her eyes at him and T.J. laughed as he walked away.

"What was that all about?" Randi asked.

"Girl, nothing," Laci told her. "He's just a no-good asshole."

Randi looked at Laci, then back at the girls. "So when we burning up the mall?"

"About four o'clock," Sam told her. "Is that cool with y'all?" She looked at Laci and Gabby.

"Y'all go ahead without me," Laci told her. "My stomach been acting up lately."

"Laci, you okay?" Randi asked. She was the mother hen of the group. "You been kinda sharp-tongued lately."

"I'm sorry. Just a lot going on, you know."

"Well, if you need us, we're here for you."

"Thanks."

Whenever she was on campus, Laci tried to steer clear of T.J., but he always seemed to find her, which added to her almost constant pissed-off mood. Laci hadn't been feeling well for some time now and attributed it to being under a lot of stress. She had been eating and sleeping a lot more because of it. With all the drama of college life, the uncertainty of where she stood with her man, Simone smiling in Dink's face every chance she could, T.J. threatening her, and the NYPD harassing her, Laci felt like she was being pulled apart at the seams and would soon go crazy.

She realized that this feeling was why many people in her group therapy session turned to drugs—to temporarily escape the problems they were having in their lives—but Laci was determined never to go down that path again. Because of that, the only place that she would feel safe was back home and in her mother's arms. She called her mother and couldn't hold back the tears.

"Hi, Mommy," Laci said through sniffles.

"Hi, sweetheart!" Margaret was always glad to hear from her baby. "How've you been? I was thinking about you earlier today when I went to the mall. You know shopping isn't as fun with your uncle as it is with you." Margaret laughed. "Men just don't have the patience."

Laci tried to muster a laugh, but it turned into a cry. "Mommy, I need to see you."

Margaret teared up on her end of the phone, hearing her daughter so distraught. "Baby, what's wrong? Did somebody do something to you? Do I need to come to Boston?" she said with urgency and panic in her voice.

"No, Mommy, you don't need to come here, but I do need to get away for a while. I have midterms coming up, but I can ask my professors if I can take them early. I can tell them I have a family emergency at home, so can I come home?"

"Can you come home?" Margaret asked. "You know you don't have to ask me that." She didn't want her daughter to resort to lying again, but in essence, this *was* a family emergency. Her family. "That's fine, sweetheart. I can't wait to see you."

They made plans for Laci to take the earliest flight from Boston to New York on Thursday, with Margaret picking her up from the airport. She would stay the weekend. Laci was happy.

"WELL, GODDAMN!" MONIQUE said when she reached her destination. Tonette had given her the address she got from 411. Driving, she slowed down and perused the neighborhood. "Look at this shit!"

At no time in her life had Monique seen anything as lavish as what she saw before her eyes. She'd never thought streets like this existed in the South Bronx.

She parked her car, a little hoopty she'd bought after she started working at the post office, a few houses down from the last house on the block and studied it closely. The white brick Colonial-style home exuded elegance and screamed money. Monique thought it resembled the White House, only South Bronx style.

She got out of the car and slowly strolled toward the house. Even though it was late October, the lawn was still green and looked like thick, luxurious carpet. There was someone outside planting fall flowers around the shrubbery. The air even smelled different—cleaner and more fragrant.

As Monique walked up the steps and onto the front porch, she realized why Laci had a rich air about her. She knew no other life and she was definitely a product of her environment.

Melodic chimes rang faintly after Monique pushed the doorbell. She turned around on the front porch and faced the street. The homes on the block were were like the rich white people's homes that she saw on soap operas. Just when she began imagining herself living in a fly crib like the one across the street, the front door opened.

"Yes? May I help you?" the woman questioned.

Monique turned around and gasped. She was caught off guard because she couldn't believe just how similar Laci and her mother looked.

"Hi," Monique said in her most proper voice. "Is Laci home?"

"Who are you?"

"I'm Monique." She extended her hand. "Monique Daniels, a friend of Laci's."

Laci's mother was never formally introduced to Laci's group of friends, so she started going off again, almost worse than she had earlier in the month. Sonny heard the commotion and went to the door to see what was happening. He stopped, not showing himself when he saw Monique. He remembered her face from the photo Officer Jones showed him. She was a little thinner, but her face hadn't changed much.

"You really call yourself a friend of my daughter's?" Margaret barked. "Friends don't hurt one another. If you call yourself a friend, I'd hate to see what you would have done if she were your enemy, young lady." Laci's mother stopped and stared at Monique, then started again. " 'Young Lady' is too good for you. You . . . you are a devil in disguise." It was the same thing she'd said to Tonette, and Monique could see why she was so upset.

Laci had never told her mother exactly who gave her the crack because she was so caught up trying not to hurt her any more than she already had. Besides, Laci realized that she didn't *have* to take that first hit. She had to take some sort of responsibility for her actions as well.

Margaret felt that every black girl who called inquiring about her daughter was the one who'd introduced her to drugs and for that, she was still furious, but she was irate now that someone came by her house looking for her daughter.

Monique was quick on her feet and knew how to get the focus off of herself. She didn't need Margaret to keep going off on her. Actually, she needed her to shut her mouth and listen. Monique knew that she was stuck between a rock and a hard place dealing with Tonette. The only reason she was a part of the SBBs again was to assure that nothing else went wrong around her or those she loved.

Monique was at her wits' end when Tonette pulled that shit at her grandmother's house and she felt she had no other choice but to join the group again. She lied when told Tonette that her grandmother put her out of the house. Her grandmother was one of those older ladies who would fuck somebody up and pray about it later, but it was Monique's choice to leave home because she knew that Tonette was capable of going to extremes and she didn't want to put her grandmother in any more unnecessary danger.

Margaret attempted to close the door in Monique's face, but Monique's quick thinking prevented that. "I can understand how you feel and I would too if I had a daughter, but I *am* Laci's friend," she spoke roughly.

"Were you the one who gave her the drugs? Whose idea was it and where did they come from?"

Monique looked Margaret in the eye. "It was Tonette," she told her truthfully. "Our other friend, Crystal, was killed by something unrelated to what happened to Laci, but it was Tonette who was behind the whole thing."

Monique never thought she'd be a snitch, but she felt that it was time to come clean. She reasoned that by helping Laci, she would help herself in the process by easing her mind before she left the South Bronx.

Although fairly new at the post office, Monique worked hard and was well liked, so her supervisor had agreed to help her transfer to another location, out of state, if a position became available. She wanted to move as far away as she could, and that time was upon her.

Monique told half of the truth when she answered Margaret's third degree. She felt it didn't matter whose idea it was, or where the drugs came from; it was the fact that Tonette handed Laci the first puff of the poison that changed her life.

Typically, Monique wasn't one to run her mouth, but she hated Tonette, and she didn't care what Margaret did with the information she was feeding her. Monique had to really play her cards right because she knew that putting Tonette's name out there could backfire, and if Tonette found out, she might as well dig her own grave next to Crystal's.

Monique was simply hoping to right the wrong she played in Laci's addiction by admitting to everything, and hopefully Margaret would help her save herself. She could really get on with her life then and put the SBBs behind her.

"I tried to stop them. I swear I tried. I even wanted to warn Laci, but it was too late. They all turned against me. Can you at least tell me if she's okay?"

Margaret became silent and her eyes filled with tears. "My daughter was a *crackhead*," she said through a low growl.

Margaret's silence alerted Monique that something was wrong. "*Was?* Oh no … please don't tell me she … she's …." Monique stumbled over her words and feet, falling against the white pillars, hyperventilating. "First Crystal and now Laci?"

Her performance was so powerful that Margaret could do nothing but listen.

"I told the police, I told them about Tonette and—"

"You actually told the police?" Laci's mother quizzed, interrupting Monique's outbursts.

"Yes." Monique wiped the tears from her eyes. "Ms. Johnson, so much has gone on all at once. You heard about the shooting on the news didn't you? The girl with the gun who was shot? That was Crystal. I was with her, too. I actually was shot myself." She motioned toward her leg. "That's when I told them."

"You're the survivor of the shooting?" Margaret remembered the story. "The girl who was killed. Was that the girl who hurt my Laci?"

"Um, not really," Monique again half told the truth.

"What was she doing with a gun?"

"I don't know, ma'am," she answered truthfully, "but Tonette insisted on getting back at Laci. She's blaming her for every-thing." She wanted to get Margaret's focus back on why she was there.

"Look, Ms. Johnson, I'm not perfect like Laci. None of us are. I wasn't raised in your type of world, but I am who I am and I know I've fucked up . . . uh, I mean messed up by dealing with the crew, but that sh—mess that went down wasn't my fault. But I guess I'm guilty by association. It's cool, though. All I wanted to say was I'm sorry about what happened to Laci and if I could change things, I would." Monique turned around to leave. What Laci's mother did next surprised her.

"I appreciate your apology, honey," Laci's mother said and embraced her. Looking at Monique's face and seeing how dis-traught she was, Margaret told her, "Come on in. Let's get you cleaned up." She wanted to talk to her a little more: Sonny hur-riedly left from behind the door and retreated to his room. He didn't want Monique to see him. He knew what the South Bronx Bitches were all about and he didn't trust any of them. He thought it best for him to remain on the low until he could figure out what was really going on.

Monique followed Margaret into her home. She looked around and observed the plush surroundings—white walls, brass and crystal fixtures, light-colored wood, and oversized fur-niture. The floor-to-ceiling windows revealed a backyard like a golf course with an in-ground pool. *Laci's got it made,* she said to herself. *I just hope her mother will forgive me.*

CHAPTER 32

LACI LAY ACROSS the couch, seeing how well her plan was unfolding. Causing conflict between her and Dink was the easiest way to get out of Boston without him wanting to follow her. Unfortunately, Laci felt that the rift she'd caused really unmasked the underlying problems they had. She hated to see that they were drifting apart and she hoped that the trip home would give her the time she needed to analyze the situation.

Laci heard keys jingling at the front door. Dink walked in.

"Hey, Laci," he said as he walked past her and into the bathroom. He returned to the living room and hung up his jacket.

"Dink, can I talk to you for a minute?"

He turned and looked at Laci after he closed the closet. "What's up?" He seemed to be a little on edge.

"Um . . . I been thinkin', um . . . I think we need to have a little break from each other." Laci choked on her words. She'd never thought she would have to tell Dink this.

He looked at her, puzzled. "What do you mean 'a little break'?"

"Just some time apart," she clarified, trying to suppress a tear. "I think I'm going home for the weekend."

"What about studying for your midterms? That's next week, babe."

"I'm going to see if I can take them earlier."

"Why you try'na go back home?"

"With everything that's going on, I need to get away."

"What do you mean 'with everything that's going on'?" Laci looked at him like *nigga, please.* "Does this have anything to do with what happened, or didn't happen, between us that night?"

"A little, but it's other stuff too, Dink. Actually, the police want to talk to me. They actually went to my mom's house looking for me."

"The police? What the fuck for?" Dink thought for a moment. "Naw, you ain't talking to nobody. Fuck that!"

"They want to talk to me about Crystal and Dame." Dink remained silent. "Did you know they were dead, Dink?" He looked at Laci without answering. "Did you kill them?" she asked seriously, looking at him.

"I ain't kill nobody," he told her truthfully, looking back at her.

"Well, did you have anything to do with it, Dink?"

"Don't ask anything you don't want to know the answer to, Laci. For real, though." Dink didn't tell Laci everything because if something were to go down and the authorities questioned her, they couldn't trick her out of any information because she knew none.

"Well, regardless of what you say, I just wanted to let you know that I'm going home and I need you to take me to the airport."

"What you gonna do about the police?" he queried.

"I guess I'm gonna have to talk to them. I don't want to, but I'll just do it and get it over with. Just because stuff ain't right between us don't mean I'm gonna say anything about you, so can I count on you to run me to the airport?"

"Whatever you want, Laci, whatever you want."

THE NIGHT BEFORE she was to leave, a knock awakened Laci from her nap on the couch. She walked over to the door and looked through the peephole.

"Damn," she sighed. *What the hell does he want now?* She didn't want to open the door, but decided it would be best. "What do you want, T.J.?" she said exhaustedly.

"I'm just stopping by." He once again barged his way into the apartment and slammed the door behind him. "Where's Daryl?"

"T.J., I don't know. I just got up from a nap." She ran her fingers through her hair and yawned. "Where's Simone? You ain't keeping up with yo' girl. Oh, but I forgot, she ain't yo' girl anymore, right? And that's because of what again?"

"You know your time is running out, right?" T.J. remarked, ignoring her snide remarks. "And you know where Daryl is, right? He's with Simone."

"Whatever, T.J."

"Actually, I saw his car parked in the parking lot by her dorm." For once in his life, he told the truth.

"T.J., look, you're gonna do what you want with that tape, so have at it." Laci was tired of his threats. She felt he wouldn't carry them through because he was nothing but a bitch-ass nigga, but bitch-ass niggas did desperate things in desperate times.

"You don't care anymore?"

"Not really." She yawned again. She called his bluff.

"Well, if you don't care anymore, that means you won't mind

giving me some of that shit you were throwing around on the tape then, right?"

Laci looked at him disgustedly. "Get the fuck outta my house, T.J.!"

He reached inside his pocket and pulled out something that was near and dear to sweet Laci. He pulled out what looked like a new corn pipe and a nice-sized white rock. "You want this, don't you, Laci?" he said, waving it in front of her face.

"No!" she yelled.

"Your man is fucking my girl, Laci. Don't you realize that? You haven't noticed that he hasn't been at home at night? Shit, Simone hasn't either." He put the rock into the bowl of the pipe and lit it. Laci couldn't move. *Am I really an addict?* she asked herself. *God, please . . . no.*

The stone fizzled and popped, producing a foggy yellow smoke. Laci wanted to run but she couldn't move. The smell that she had forgotten reached Laci's nostrils and burned her nose.

"T.J., please go," Laci cried with her hands over her mouth and nostrils. *I'm doing fine . . . up here on Cloud Nine . . . I'm gonna sail up higher . . . up, up, and away . . .* The monkey started to rear its ugly head. Laci tried to block it out. "God it hurts. Please stop the pain!" She fell to the floor.

"Let me make you feel better," T.J. begged. "I won't show anyone the tape. It will be our own little secret." T.J. began to unbutton his pants.

She looked at him with pleading eyes. "Please, just get out . . ."

CHAPTER 33

Daryl? SIMONE POURED each of them another cup of coffee. "Daryl?" she said again and waved her hand in front of his face.

"Huh?" he responded.

"What's up with you tonight?"

He looked at Simone. "Um, just some stuff with Laci," he admitted. The two were pulling an all-nighter on their Abnormal Psych project at Busy Bee's again.

Simone had never seen Dink so distracted. "I'm not going to pry, but if you want to talk about it, you can talk to me."

Simone poured cream and sugar in her coffee and stirred. She took a sip of it. She wrinkled her nose up when Dink drank his—black, no sugar or cream. Dink laughed at her reaction. Simone turned her attention back to her book until Dink spoke.

"Actually, she's been trippin' lately, smokin' and—"

"Laci? Smokin'? You got to be kidding me!" Simone interrupted him. "She don't look like she'd even smoke a candy cigarette," she joked.

"She is a good girl. She's just reacting because you and I have been hanging out. When she called me out on it, I defended you, and things haven't been the same." Dink didn't feel the need to disclose the botched attempt of making love.

Feeling flattered that he'd defended her, Simone had to defend Laci's actions as a woman.

"Daryl, I can understand how she must feel," she said. "Actually, I feel bad for being part of the reason why Laci feels the way she does."

"Do you?" Dink questioned. He was amazed. Most black women wouldn't have given a damn.

"I owe her an apology."

"How do you figure that?"

"I was blatantly disrespectful to her on the first day of school by flirting with you. I saw the both of you walk into the lecture hall, but I just thought you were late. I didn't think anything of it. I had no reason to think that you two were a couple until later. I don't deny flirting with you but as I got to know you, I wouldn't dare cross that line because I think we've built a nice friendship, don't you think?"

"Yeah, you're pretty cool," he told her.

"And most of all, I respect how loyal you are to Laci. Most men, black men at that, wouldn't be."

Dink nodded. She was right. Most men, black or white, would have taken advantage of the closeness with a woman other than their girlfriend. Dink knew that Simone was telling the truth. Time and opportunity were a muthafucka. He had the opportunity, she had the time, and at one point he used to be a muthafucka, but his love for Laci stopped any desire he may have had.

"Well," Simone said hesitantly, "I think after this project is over, we should cool it for a bit. T.J. has been trippin' as well, making accusations and shit, and I really don't have time to deal with his drama."

"What's really up with y'all?"

"Nothing. I caught him cheating and I broke up with him," Simone said, matter-of-factly. "When I did it before, I always went back, but this time I haven't and he can't handle that."

"I ain't worried about that nigga or whatever he thinks he is, Simone."

"You don't know him, Daryl. When he puts his mind to something, he won't give up on it."

"What kinda accusations he making?"

"That we're fucking."

"Well we both know we're not, so—"

"Right," she cut him off, "but I wouldn't put it past him to put it in Laci's mind that we are. Actually, he told me he saw her and told her that. He tried to insinuate that he had done something with her, but I know he hasn't."

"What did he say?"

"It was some bullshit, man. I really don't want to talk about it."

Dink looked at her, urging her to fess up.

"Something about her being a crackhead. T.J. always be lying about shit, so you can't believe anything he says." Simone shook her head. "Laci a crackhead? See, that's the main reason I ain't with his ass."

"When did he say that to you, Simone? I mean, why did he say it? What were y'all doing?"

"He got mad when I wouldn't give him none. When he starts going off like that, I just tell his ass to go to his dorm or back to the frat house."

Dink's anger was starting to boil. "I'm sure if he came at her like that, she would have told me."

"With the way things are with you right now, I doubt it. If I were in her shoes, I wouldn't say shit. I'd just try to bust yo' ass." She gave a laugh, and he tried to force one. "But for real, Daryl, we put a lot of work into this project tonight and I'm beat. Go home to Laci and make things right before you can't anymore."

"Thanks, Simone," he said and patted her hand. Reaching into his wallet, he threw a one-hundred-dollar bill on the table. "Tell the waitress to keep the change. Oh," he looked into his wallet again and pulled out another hundred-dollar bill and handed it to her.

"What's this for?" she asked before he left their booth.

"For your services, Ms. Psychologist," he joked. "You're going to be damn good once you graduate." He smiled and darted out of the diner and headed home to where his heart was.

IT WAS EARLY Thursday morning and once again, Dink was nowhere to be found. Laci remembered he'd been at home when she went to bed but when she woke up abruptly from the all-too-real nightmare she'd had about T.J., she noticed that he was gone. She paged him a couple of times but he never returned her calls. Becoming furious, instead of waiting for Dink to come home, Laci called the local cab company to take her to the airport. She was ready to go home.

Twenty minutes later, Dink walked into their apartment. All of the lights were on.

"Laci?" Dink called out. "Baby, I need to talk to you. Laci!" He walked into their bedroom and to his shock, he saw her packing an overnight bag. "Where are you going?"

Laci didn't respond. All she could do was visualize him with

Simone. His mouth was saying one thing but his actions were saying something different.

"Laci, don't you hear me talking to you?" he questioned. He was tired and abrupt in his tone, but he needed to talk to her. Laci continued to shove more things into her bag.

"Where you going?"

Again, Laci didn't answer. "Baby!" He grabbed her arm. "Talk to me, now!"

"Okay, you wanna talk? Where the fuck were you all night? Guess you were too busy doing whatever it was you were doing to remember that I'm going home this weekend."

"What? Aw . . . shit." Dink remembered that he was supposed to take her to the airport.

"Now you remember, huh? I paged you a couple times, too. What were you doing where you couldn't call me back?"

"I didn't get any pages, Laci."

"Well, I did."

Dink unclipped his pager and looked at it. His eyebrows raised when he realized it was on silent and saw their home number displayed twice. He thought he'd turned it on vibrate when he was at the diner, but obviously he hadn't.

"I'm sorry, Laci. I turned it—"

"Whatever," she spat angrily. "Where were you last night? When I went to sleep, you were here. When I woke up, you were gone. Actually, I've been noticing a lot of that lately."

"I was with Simone, but—"

"Exactly. Simone!" Laci shouted. "I don't want to hear it anymore, Dink. I know you fuckin' her."

"What? No I'm not."

"Yeah, right. Do you really think I believe that?"

"I'm sorry, baby. I can understand why you may think that, but—"

"It's more than a thought," Laci barked.

"Why? Is it because T.J. told you?" he asked, remembering what Simone had told him.

"It doesn't matter anymore, Dink."

"Yes it does. Here I am trying to tell you that I've been wrong for just leaving the way I have. Trying to explain what's going on, but you wanna listen to that wannabe nigga."

"Whatever, Dink. I don't know what to believe anymore," Laci answered with an exasperated sigh. She gathered her bag and tried to walk past him. He stood in her way.

"When did he tell you that?"

"He's mentioned it plenty of times. Here, at school—shit, wherever he could find me."

"Here? He's been here? In our crib?"

"You been at Simone's crib?" she countered. She tried to get around him but he blocked her again.

Dink's face began to distort. He was mad as hell. He didn't want Laci around T.J., but the fact that he had been in their apartment without his knowledge made him feel threatened.

"Now what the hell you mad about?" she asked Dink, noticing his expression.

"What did you do with him?" Dink's voice was low, almost a type of growl. In typical nigga fashion, he flipped the situation back around on her, with a puzzled expression, sparking more anger in Laci.

"Hold up," she cocked her head to the side and looked at Dink with surprise, "what are you trying to say?"

"He knows about your addiction, Laci."

"Former addiction," she spat back.

"Yeah right, former addiction. You smokin' weed, drinking and shit. I don't know what you doin' no more."

"Oh, so we gonna go there."

"How does he know about it, Laci? The only people who know about it are you and me—oh, and your little bougie friends." He looked at her with menacing eyes. "I know I didn't tell him. Your friends are too stuck-up to talk to him, so that leaves you. Did you tell him or show him what you do when you're under the influence?" Dink shot back at her.

Within seconds, the left side of Dink's face stung from Laci slapping the shit out of him.

"You don't know what the fuck you're talking about. He didn't even touch me!" Laci tried to walk away but Dink grabbed her by the arm. "Let me go!" she yelled and yanked her arm out of his grasp. "Now you try'na accuse me of shit I never did."

"You accusing me of fucking Simone!" he yelled.

"That's because you're around her all the time, Dink!" Laci was in tears now and angrier than she had been in a long time. "A few months ago, I was a crackhead, and if you think you're not a part of the reason, you need to think again."

"Girl, you really trippin' now," Dink said and tried to walk away.

Laci ran in front of him and stopped. With a red and tear-drenched face, she yelled, "Tonette got the shit from Dame. You were the go-to man, so it was yo' shit that got me addicted. You didn't think I knew that, did you, but not once did I blame you! Do you know why, Dink? That's because I love you!" Laci grabbed her purse. "Now you wanna start this shit. You know what, Dink," she huffed, "for you to be so damn street smart, you don't know shit about the heart. Everything I did was for you ... try'na protect yo' ass so you wouldn't get hurt. If a crackhead ho is how you'll truly see me from now on, then crack the code on that, muthafucka—we're through!"

Laci ran toward the front door and slammed it behind her. She prayed her cab was waiting for her.

"Laci, wait!" Dink yelled, but it was too late.

CHAPTER 34

LACI RAN INTO her mother's arms when they met at the airport.

They hugged for what seemed like days. Her face was still blotched from crying earlier, but she was now home and she was safe.

Margaret looked over Laci's shoulder. "Honey, did Dink come with you?"

"No, Mom, he's back in Boston. I needed to come here by myself."

Margaret looked at her daughter. Something was obviously wrong between Laci and Dink but if she didn't want to talk about it, Margaret figured she wouldn't press.

Three hours later, the two women were sitting in the food court in the mall. Laci was finishing the last of her Sbarro's spaghetti and meatballs and garlic breadsticks and Margaret was finishing her chicken Caesar salad. They were gearing up for a day of shopping and pampering.

"Honey, you're looking great," Margaret exclaimed. She was glad to see her daughter looking healthy again and glad she was also eating.

"I'm glad you think so, Mom. I haven't been feeling well." Laci yawned before popping the last of her breadstick in her mouth.

"Why not, sweetheart? You coming down with something?" She felt Laci's head.

"I don't know, Mom. It could be stress. A lot has been going on."

"Honey, I can call Dr. Stevens if you'd like. He'll make a house call."

"That's fine, Mom," Laci said quickly. When Laci was younger and had a sniffle, her mother would call the doctor. She always thought her mother went overboard with things, but at this point in her life, she didn't mind. Laci needed that right now.

"Is this last year's stuff?" Laci's mother teased, pulling at her top. "We can't have that." Both women laughed and headed off for a much-needed mother-daughter shopping spree.

Thursday and Friday, Laci and her mother hung out just like best friends. Just as Margaret had promised, she contacted Dr. Stevens. His schedule was booked, but he told her that he could fit Laci in early Saturday morning.

Laci sat inside Dr. Stevens's office updating her patient information form. While she read over the form, her eyes stopped on the section that indicated listing any drug use. *If he knows about my addiction, I know he won't give me anything,* Laci thought. She wasn't taking that chance, so she checked "no."

As Laci sat and thought about how things were turning out for her, she thought about Dink. Being away from him, she missed him and wanted to talk to him. Hearing his voice every day on her mom's answering machine, wanting to talk to her, let her know that he cared.

"Miss Johnson," a nurse called, snapping Laci out of her thoughts. "Follow me, please."

The nurse led Laci to an exam room. After she took Laci's vitals, she handed her a paper gown. "Please undress, cover your bottom with this and top with this, and the doctor will be with you shortly."

Within fifteen minutes, the doctor arrived.

"Laci," he spoke. He extended his hand for a handshake. "How can I help you today?"

"Hi, Dr. Stevens. I'm not sure what's wrong. I've been under a lot of stress lately. All I want to do is sleep. I also have a lot of mood swings."

Dr. Stevens looked over Laci's history. "Hmm . . . you're a full-time student?"

"Yes."

"How many hours do you take?"

"Eighteen."

The doctor let out a deep sigh. "That's certainly enough to make you feel the way you do, young lady," he confirmed.

Laci nodded.

"Let's see," he said as he read over her medical profile. "Is there any history of heart disease, stroke, or cancer in your family?"

"No."

"Any history of depression?"

"No."

"Have you ever been addicted to any type of narcotics?"

Laci paused momentarily. "No."

"When was the last time you had a physical?"

"Um . . . a couple of months ago, I think," Laci told him.

The doctor finished writing his notes, then took the stethoscope from around his neck and placed the earpieces into his ears. He listened to Laci's heart and lungs.

"Please swallow for me," he told her with his fingers lightly on her throat.

Dr. Stevens made a notation on Laci's chart.

"What did you just do?" Laci inquired.

"I was checking your thyroid. If your thyroid function is off, you could experience irritability or restlessness. Please lie back for me." Dr. Stevens began to feel her abdomen and performed a quick vaginal exam.

"Umm . . . there's a little discharge," he told her as he took the big white Q-tip out of her vagina and slid it across a small, thin lab slide. After he was done with the exam, he helped Laci sit up and called for his nurse, who arrived within seconds.

"I need you to do a full lab workup on Miss Johnson," he told her. "Afterward, can you run everything to the lab and have them rush it through?"

"Sure thing, doc."

The nurse took urine and blood from Laci.

"It'll take about thirty to forty minutes for your results to come back, Miss Johnson," the nurse said. "You can get dressed and wait out in the waiting room."

"Okay, thank you." Laci got dressed and went back out to the waiting room. Rummaging through the latest *Essence* and *Ebony* magazines, fatigue came over her and she dozed off.

"Excuse me . . . Miss Johnson . . . Miss Johnson . . ." The nurse gently nudged her. Laci looked at her watch. She had been asleep for almost an hour. "The doctor will see you now."

Laci got up and rubbed her eyes. She followed the nurse into Dr. Stevens's office.

"Miss Johnson," the doctor spoke, "please have a seat." Laci sat down. "Your lab results are back."

"Okay, and . . ." Laci said with hesitation.

"Looks like you're pregnant. That explains the mood swings and restlessness."

"Pregnant?" Laci yelled. Her heart dropped. "Pregnant? NO way!" Laci had never thought of the obvious, but when she thought back to the night she lost her virginity and all the other times she used her pussy as compensation for crack, pregnancy was certainly a possibility. She was so high most of the time, condom use wasn't even a discussion, and Lord only knew who or what ran up in her.

"I take it that this is not a good thing for you?"

Laci cut her eyes at him and remained silent. The doctor took that as his cue to move on.

"You also have BV."

"BV? What's that?"

"Bacterial vaginosis. It's actually a pretty common vaginal infection that women get. When was your last period, Laci?"

Laci got quiet. She couldn't remember. "I'm . . . I'm not sure," she replied truthfully. "I've had so many things going on."

"That's fine," Dr. Stevens told her. "Here, let me give you the name of another physician in the clinic who deals with pregnancies. I'm an internist, not an OB/GYN." Dr. Stevens wrote down a name on his prescription pad. "Before you leave, schedule a follow-up appointment with her within a week. You need to have an ultrasound to determine just how far along you are and start prenatal care right away."

"Dr. Stevens . . ." Laci said in a soft voice.

"Yes, Laci?"

"What if I don't want the baby?" She stared the doctor in his eye.

"I understand," he told her. "There are several clinics in the city that perform terminations as well as provide support for alternative options. I'll write down the numbers for you too."

Laci left the clinic in a daze. She got in her mother's white 1989 Mercedes-Benz 560 Series and drove. The more she thought about her situation, the more and more pissed she became. Instead of going in the direction of Riverdale, she headed to the South Bronx. It was still daytime, so she felt safe. As Laci drove along the streets people ogled the expensive machinery, and the street hustlers called out for her to pull over. Laci wore her long curly hair down and free-flowing. Along with a pair of women's Ray-Ban shades, she had a nice shade of soft pink Revlon lip gloss on her lips. From what they saw, she was fine and they wanted to get to know her.

"AYE, Y'ALL," DRAKE said to Smurf and Chunky. "Y'all see that chick that just left outta here in that fly-ass 5 Series?"

"Yea . . . yea . . . yeah," Chunky spat out hard, still looking in the direction the car was driving. "She was fly, wasn't she?"

Smurf saw her momentarily but he was preoccupied by LaQuan, who was trying to get him to slide through her grandmother's again so she could get some more dick.

"That looked like that ho that was on that tape."

Smurf's ears caught the conversation. "Who you talkin 'bout, man?"

"That light-skinned chick. You know, the ho that used to hang around Angel and dem."

Damn, that's Dink's gal, Smurf thought to himself. *I wonder what she's back for.*

CHAPTER 35

To GET IT out of the way, Laci made her way to the police department. She was directed to the interrogation room, where Officer Jones and Detective Clifton arrived within minutes.

"Thank you for coming, Ms. Johnson," Officer Jones spoke as he sat across from her. *Wait a minute,* he thought to himself, *that's Dink's girl.* He remembered her from the tape, but he'd also seen Dink sporting her around the hood some months back.

"We wanted to talk to you because we think you may have information on Crystal Moore and the whereabouts of her drug-dealing boyfriend," Detective Clifton said.

"*Alleged* drug-dealing boyfriend," Officer Jones corrected.

"I got a file on both of them," the detective barked at his young protégé.

"I'm sorry, I don't know what you're talking about," Laci told both men.

Detective Clifton glared at Laci in an attempt to intimidate her. "So are you saying you don't know who Crystal Moore is?" He opened up the file that contained all of the SBBs pictures, including hers. He placed the photos in front of her.

"No, I'm not saying that." Laci stayed calm and cool.

"Well, please tell me how you know these girls," he asked, staring at her.

"Wait a minute," Laci said. "I'm coming down here to help answer your questions." She looked at the detective with tears welling up in her eyes. "Why are you talking to me like this? What have they told you about me?" Officer Jones handed her a Kleenex. "I don't have anything to do with them and I shouldn't have gotten to know them in the first place."

"It was pretty ingenious what you did though, Ms. Johnson. Doing your dirt in the South Bronx and not taking it back to Riverdale. Are you their connect?"

Officer Jones looked at his partner in disgust. "Man, chill out," he told him.

"Dirt?" she questioned. "Connect? You think I'm involved in drugs? Do I look like I'd be involved in that mess?" Laci looked between the two cops.

"It takes all kinds," Detective Clifton spoke.

"Well, you know, at one point, I *was* into drugs." Detective Clifton's face lit up like a light bulb. "But not in the way you're thinking. They played the cruelest joke on me. The worst that anyone could play on anybody."

"What's that?" Officer Jones spoke in a calming voice, hoping to diffuse his partner's tone.

"They gave me a joint laced with crack and I ended up an addict." She looked at both officers again.

"Whoa . . . they what?" they both asked.

"They gave me crack," she repeated. "First it was laced weed, but then they gave me more. I had a full-blown addiction."

That explains the tape. Officer Jones thought to himself.

"Ms. Johnson, did Crystal Moore have anything to do with it?"

"I'm not sure how much say-so she had in it, but I'm sure she knew about it. She was one of them too." Laci wiped her eyes and blew her nose.

"Did you give her the gun she was carrying the afternoon she was shot?"

"Did you hear what I just told you?" Laci asked, raising her voice, tired of the questioning about Crystal. "You're questioning me about something I know nothing about, but I tell you that they turned me into a goddamn crackhead and you just sit here and do nothing about it?"

"Honestly," Detective Clifton told Laci truthfully, "there's nothing I can do."

"What do you mean there's nothing you can do? I told you they turned me into a fuckin' crackhead!" she yelled.

With a pointing finger, he continued his assault on her. "You were the one on drugs, Ms. Johnson. They didn't force you to take it."

Laci got up with a quickness. "Ohhh!!!" she yelled as she stormed out of the interrogation room, rushing past additional officers and other people being brought in for one reason or another.

CHAPTER 36

LACI MADE IT back to Riverdale in record time. She wanted nothing more to do with the South Bronx, the SBBs, or the NYPD and started packing her bags to go back to Boston.

"I can't believe this," she said out loud, as the tears she'd already released on her drive back home came pouring down again. Laci began shoving her clothes into her overnight bag. "I can't believe I was so stupid," she said to herself. "I didn't ask for none of this, but they wanna try to get me in trouble with the police? They got me high. They turned me out." She shoved more into her bag. "I'm knocked up by God-knows-who and they can't arrest them?"

"Hey, sweetheart, what are you doing?"

Laci was startled. "Ooh, Uncle Sonny, you scared me."

"I'm sorry, sweetheart," he told her genuinely. "What's wrong? Where are you going?"

"Home." She went to her closet to get a duffel bag. "The South Bronx ain't for me anymore."

"What happened, baby?"

"Those damn bitches!" Laci exclaimed.

"Have you contacted the police at all?"

"Yes, actually I just came from there. I spoke with Officer Jones and his bad-cop partner. He all but told me I had something to do with Crystal's death but when I told them that those girls turned me into a drug addict, they said they can't do anything about it."

Sonny's eyes widened. "What do you mean, can't do anything about it?"

"Yup, that's what they said, claiming they didn't twist my arm to take the drugs."

Sonny was speechless. The police can take crackheads off the streets and throw them in jail, but they can't arrest the person who sold them the drugs. It seemed backward to him.

"Did your mother tell you that one of those girls came here to talk to her?"

Laci stopped and looked at her uncle like he was crazy.

"Who came where?" she said in a hushed voice.

"Some girl named Monique."

Laci became furious. "Now the bitch is coming to my house. If she knows where Mom lives, I'm sure Tonette knows. Naw, this shit ain't happening!"

"Actually, Laci, she told your mother that Tonette was the person behind the drugs."

Laci's anger got the best of her and she grabbed her mother's car keys. She didn't care what would happen. She was going to find those bitches. Laci moved too fast for her uncle to catch up to her, but just as she got outside and marched to the car, she was stopped by someone calling her name.

"Ms. Johnson! Hey, Laci!"

She looked to see who it was. It was Officer Jones, and Laci glared at him evilly. "What?!" she growled.

"Look, I really couldn't talk back in the precinct, but you're Dink's gal, right?"

"Why you wanna know?"

"Look, it's a long story. I want to apologize for my asshole partner," he told her. "He gets a little excited sometimes. But what those girls did to you, that was fucked up—"

"So why can't you arrest them?" Laci began to cry.

"Is that what you want me to do?" he asked her seriously. "With all that they've done to you, you want me to arrest them? Well, if that's what you want, then it shall be done."

"Humph . . ." Laci thought about the unwanted life inside her body, she thought about the accusations the detective made, and most of all, she thought about how the girls treated her like shit, and a deep shade of red covered her face. "You know what, an eye for an eye."

The officer looked at her and nodded his head. "And a blind eye doesn't see."

CHAPTER 37

INSTEAD OF LEAVING as planned, Laci went back inside the house. She changed into a pair of sweats and pulled her hair up into a ponytail. She washed off her makeup. She wanted to be plain and simple, just like she was before her life was turned upside down.

Laci decided to call Dink. He had been on her mind and she wanted to at least start getting things back on track.

She sat down and dialed their number in Boston. "Hey," Laci said once Dink picked up the phone. "It's me."

"Hey you," he replied. There was a long, uncomfortable pause before Dink spoke again. "How are you?"

"Missing you," she told him truthfully. There was silence on the line. "Um . . . Dink, I need to really talk to you about something."

"Anything, baby, you can talk to me about anything."

"You know," Laci paused momentarily, "I came back home to get away and think about things with us. Dink, I know you're not trying to hurt me and your friendship with Simone could be platonic—"

"It is, Laci. I've never touched her and I won't."

"But a lot has gone on and we're going to have to start trusting each other again."

"I agree," Dink confirmed, "but I'm sure we'll get back on track."

"Dink, I'm angry now. Not only am I angry at myself, I'm angry at Tonette, Crystal, Monique, and Shaunna, and they can't get away with what they did to me."

"Laci, I'm not going to stand in your way. You have to do what you have to do, but make sure you have the right people watching you." He read between the lines.

"I do, but just promise me you'll stay in Boston."

Dink got quiet. He inhaled, then exhaled deeply. "Alright baby, I'll stay in Boston, but if I don't hear from you on the day it goes down, I'm coming to town."

"I promise, I'll call you on Friday."

The doorbell rang, forcing her to cut her conversation short, but they'd said all they needed to say and promised to speak again soon.

Just as Laci hung up the phone, she opened her front door.

"Ms. Johnson, I—" Monique spoke, then her eyes opened wide. "Laci, it's you!" Monique was shocked to see her, but equally shocked that even in lounging clothes, she was still radiant. There were no signs of her being a former drug addict, and she was relieved.

"Monique? Is that you?" Laci asked, squinting her eyes, almost not recognizing her. She used to be ghetto-girl thick, but she had lost a lot of weight since she had seen her last.

"Yeah, it's me." She turned around in a circle donning designer clothes that fit her properly, proud of her weight loss.

"What are you doing here?" Laci asked.

"Well, I actually stopped by to see your mother a while ago. I was just . . . I don't know, just coming by to check on her and see if you were around."

Laci did her best to hide her anger. She didn't need anyone checking on her mother. She looked around her. "Where's the girls? Tonette and Crystal? Did Shaunna have her baby?"

Laci had to play her role carefully from here on out. She knew Crystal was dead from meeting with the police and knew Shaunna had had her baby when she saw her in the streets the first time she came back to the South Bronx, but she didn't want to let on that she knew anything. She still wanted them to believe she was naïve Laci Johnson.

Monique hung her head. "Um . . . Crystal's dead, Laci."

"Dead?"

"Yeah, police shot her."

"Damn!" Laci ran her fingers through her hair. "What about Tonette and Shaunna?"

"They still around, doing that SBB shit."

"SBB shit? You mean you ain't one of them anymore?"

"Yes and no."

"What is that supposed to mean?"

"Actually, I told both of them they were wrong for what we did to you and I left the group." Laci couldn't believe what she heard.

"You left because of me?" *Maybe one of them did really like me,* she thought to herself.

"No, I left because what they did was wrong, but I came back, because leaving put my grandmother in danger."

"Oh," was all Laci could say. She was hoping Monique would say that she'd left because of her.

"Sometimes you did act stuck up, Laci," Monique confirmed,

"but just like I told your mother, I apologize for my part in it and I hope that you can forgive me one day."

Laci's stomach tightened up into knots before she spoke. "Actually, I do forgive you. I forgive all of you."

"What?" Monique said, surprised.

"Life is too short to hold grudges, Monique. I've moved on." She got closer to Monique and put her hand on her shoulder and smiled. "You know what I think would be cool?"

"What?"

"If we could all get together tomorrow afternoon or something and hang out, you know, SBB style." Laci beamed with pride. "Y'all will finally be able to see that I'm not stuck up. I'm just one of the girls."

Monique looked at Laci as if the crack she'd smoked had done something to her brain, but agreed. "You know Tonette still don't like you. Actually when I came to see your mother, I was looking for you to tell you that."

"I don't understand, Monique." Laci looked at her with wonder. "If you thought I was stuck up too, why are you here try'na warn me?"

"Because like I said earlier, it was wrong to do that shit to you." Monique paused momentarily. "I just wanted you to know you need to watch your back because she's out there, but I'm outta here on Friday anyway."

"Where you going?" Laci asked.

"Away from the South Bronx. It's time to start my life now."

"That's good," Laci managed to say.

"Actually, Laci, you're not the first person who Tonette did some fucked-up shit to."

"I'm not?" Laci's eyes got big. She wondered what else that

scandalous bitch could have done. "It can't be as bad as turning me out, is it?"

Monique's face twisted in a "don't go there" expression. "Actually, you remember Angel?"

"Yeah."

"Tonette had people in the same house using the same needles. It was rumored that a lot of them were HIV-positive, but there were some who weren't who shared the same needle. I think Angel was one of them."

"What?" Laci's eyes got wide. Her mind went back to when she got high with Angel. She remembered her shooting. "Ump ump ump." Laci shook her head.

"You know Quita used to be a SBB too, right?" Laci nodded her head. "Well you know she was fucking Dame, but when Tonette went after her to jump on her, Dame stopped that shit with a quickness."

"What he do?"

"He kept Quita close to him, but he also kept a close eye on Tonette. As long as she the top ho, she don't care. But Dame put Quita before her and she didn't like that."

"Figures," Laci told her.

"Then there were some other girls, you know, just local junkies she fucked with. A girl owed her twenty dollars for a rock and came back to her for another. Tonette thought the girl was trying to play her, so she told the girl to meet her at the subway. Tonette had the girl's rock, and she threw it on the tracks and pushed the girl off the platform. The train crushed her."

"Ooh," Laci cringed at the thought. "Where's Angel now?"

"She got caught stealing so she locked up, I think. Actually, everyone she fucked with except the dead girl are locked up."

"So what is she doing now? She don't have anyone to mess with?"

"Well, besides looking for you, she's thinkin' 'bout pushin' for Smurf."

This bitch try'na leave with a clean conscience, Laci thought to herself.

"Monique, why doesn't she like me?" Laci asked, seriously. She never really understood why the girls hated her so much.

Monique studied Laci's face. "You really don't know, do you?"

"No, that's why I asked you."

"Laci, the girl is jealous of you. Everything about you, she's jealous of."

"Girl, please," Laci said, ignoring Monique's claim, "she ain't got no reason to be jealous of me."

"Whatever," Monique said in a disgusted tone. "What can't you see? Look at all of this, Laci." Monique pointed to the immediate surroundings. "This is how you live. You got a fly-ass crib, you probably got maids up in this bitch, you stay fly in all of the latest shit, you got cake without having to hustle for it." She looked around again. "And you wonder why she's jealous? This is something that none of us will ever have."

Laci could tell Monique needed to get that off her chest.

"I didn't look at it like that," she told Monique. "You know, I can't help where I came from, but I'm still as down as the rest of you. Actually, I'm going to be leaving soon, but I'd like to see all of y'all before I leave. I don't know when I'll be back here again. You know, let bygones be bygones."

"Are you sure you want to do that?" Monique asked, looking at Laci, not believing she'd said that to her.

"Yes, I don't have any animosity toward anyone," Laci lied

through her teeth. "So do you think you'll be able to hook that up? I really wanna see all of y'all."

"Let me see what I can do to make that happen. I can't make any promises, but I'll call you and let you know what she says." Right before Monique walked off the front porch, she turned to Laci and spoke. "You know what? You're not so bad after all. I'm glad you're okay and again, I'm sorry for everything that happened."

She left so she could see if she could get the girls together on short notice. Monique didn't have a lot of time left. She was leaving the South Bronx on Friday, so she had only five days to honor Laci's request.

Laci watched as Monique drove away. Her plan was already in motion. She grabbed her keys and headed to the mall. Buying a pair of Jordache jeans, different-colored Reebok sneakers, and a couple of oversized sweatshirts, she couldn't believe how tacky she would need to be to fit in with her former crew, but she had to do what she had to do. Making a few more stops, she finally got what she needed to help with her plan. While she shopped, Laci thought about all that Monique told her. Even though Monique was trying to clear her conscience, she had to go down with them, and Laci needed to move quickly. Friday wasn't that far away.

CHAPTER 38

Back at Tonette's, Monique sprawled across the couch and called Shaunna. She had to tell someone what had just gone down.

"Girl, you got to be kidding me," Shaunna said to Monique. "You actually saw Laci and talked to her?"

"Yeah girl," Monique said, amped up.

"Crackhead Laci?"

"Yeah girl," Monique laughed, "but she's changed though."

"What you mean she's changed?"

"I can't describe it. Maybe more like one of us now. More laid back and less—"

"Stuck up?" Shaunna laughed.

"Yeah girl," Monique chimed in.

"Damn, you gonna tell Tonette?"

"Yup. Laci said she wanted to see all of us and kick it SBB style again."

"Bitch, you lyin'!" Shaunna jibed.

"No I'm not."

"Wow. Even after what happened? All I know is she better

watch her ass, because Tonette is one step away from making her Crystal's roommate."

"Tell me about it," Monique interjected. "Oh, she asked about you and your baby."

"Really?" Shaunna said, surprised but excited. "You know, she was the only one who ever cared to ask me about my baby."

Monique felt bad because she hadn't asked how Shaunna was doing, even after she had her son.

"But you just let me know when and where," Shaunna said, "and we can do our shit, SBB style. Well, I guess all we can do is sit back and watch the fireworks."

Once Monique got off the phone with Shaunna, she paged Tonette. Within minutes she called her back.

"What's up?" Tonette said hastily. "Talk fast. The spot is hoppin' tonight."

"You'll never guess who I saw today."

"Who?"

"Laci."

Tonette became quiet and her tone changed. "Um . . . where?"

"Her momma's, but check this out: she wants to see all of us."

"What?" Tonette laughed. "Straight up?"

"Yeah girl. So what you wanna do?"

"You know how we do it: invite her ass over and let's see what pops off from there." Tonette began laughing. "I can't wait to see my dear friend, Laci Johnson."

Monique laughed right along with her. "A'ight, cool."

SMURF LAY BACK in his bed while Quannie rode him like a bull. He still didn't take broads to his real crib; just like Dame and Dink, he had another place for ass only. Smurf had begun to sex Quannie often. For being only fifteen years old, her sex game was tight and she knew what to do to keep a nigga coming back. Even though he usually didn't like fucking young girls because they fell in love quickly, Quannie was different. She kept her ear to the street, alerting him to anything she felt he should know. She truly looked out for young Smurf, without asking for anything in return, and that impressed him.

Smurf grabbed her hips tightly as he watched her go up and down on his dick like a pogo stick. Her small breasts bounced and Smurf liked the fuck faces she made when he dove deep into her. Just as he broke off another nut, Quannie collapsed on his chest. Both of their bodies were worn and well used. She looked over at the clock that sat on his nightstand. "Oh shit," she said, sitting up fast.

"What's up?" Smurf said tiredly. He had dozed off for a minute.

"It's getting late and I gotta go to school in the morning."

Smurf took a deep breath and let it out. That was another thing he liked about Quannie. She had some idea of what she wanted to do with her life and regardless of how well he sexed her, she wasn't going to miss school for anybody. When Quannie saw that Smurf was trying to go back to sleep, she playfully kissed his neck.

"Come on boy, quit playin'. We can finish this up tomorrow."

Yawning, he got up and threw his clothes on so he could take her home.

An hour later, at 3:30 A.M., Smurf arrived back at his crib. He opened his safe and put in another stack of money that he had collected after dropping Quannie off.

Smurf's riches had grown almost fourfold since Dink left. The ice that Dirty brought to town, along with pure cocaine, heroin, and crack, instantly took Smurf and everyone in his crew to another level in the drug game. Because of his reputation of being more deadly than cancer, cats didn't fuck with young Smurf. Many of his rivals felt it was best to work with him instead of against him. It's better to be fed than be dead, many rationalized. With the support of Dink, who still had him under his wing, Smurf rid his circle of the dead weight. Now everyone was benefiting, and he was gaining new territory as quickly as the product came through.

Dirty was around more often, schooling young Smurf. They began to forge a father-and-son type of relationship in just a short amount of time. Dirty took Smurf under his wing and taught him the business side of street dealings—from weight to cake. A man in Smurf's position always needed to know everything he could about running a fine-tuned operation and just like the economy, it changed often.

One particular day, Dirty holla'd at Smurf seriously.

"Yo, Smurf," he called out. "I need ta holla at cha for a minute." Dirty sounded serious. There was obviously something on his mind.

"What's up, man?"

Dirty sat down on Smurf's couch while Smurf walked into the kitchen and grabbed two beers. Handing Dirty one, he sat down on the armchair directly across from his mentor.

"I think it's time to get you off the streets." Smurf remained quiet, listening to Dirty.

"I think you'd be more useful in travel."

"You know I'll do what I can to help you out, but man, you know I ain't no damn runner," Smurf said forcefully.

"You wouldn't be running, son," Dirty said seriously. "You'd be working with me to get weight in." He leaned forward and pointed at Smurf. "You already see what's on the street. We need to make sure we keep getting top-notch shit. You need to look at your areas and see where your slowest spots are and shut them down."

"Shut 'em down? Why?"

"That's too much unproductive time, man." Dirty took a swig of his beer. "We can get more business in areas where it's already high volume. You already got the shit on lock, you just need to tighten it up now."

Smurf sat back and stroked his imaginary chin hair and sighed. "A'ight, man. I gotcha. I'ma call a meeting with my crew."

"Oh, also, you need to switch up yo' houses. Shut down a couple, then open 'em up again." Smurf gave him a confused look. "You always wanna switch up because you never know who's watching you. Remember what I told you before. Never be predictable. You fall into a routine and then boom," he motioned his finger like he was shooting, "that's when you get popped."

SMURF CALLED A meeting with his top execs at the corner store and told them of the plan. Dirty watched as Smurf handled his business.

"Yo, there's been a change in operations here."

"What's up, boss," Drake, Chunky, and Lil' Rob asked.

"We need to shut down and move our operations." The three of them listened intently to Smurf, who continued. He was surprised that he wasn't met with resistance. "We're getting rid of the empty buildings and we're going to start occupying tenement buildings in Southview. Do y'all know someone who could use a lil' cake?"

They nodded their heads in unison.

"Good, so this won't be hard. Make whatever deal you have to with them, and those will be the spots from now on."

"When we doin' this?" Drake asked.

"Yesterday," Smurf confirmed.

Before they left the corner store, Lil' Rob asked, "Hey Smurf, what you wanna do about Tonette?"

"What about her?"

"You shuttin' down buildings. You know she posted by one all the time."

Smurf knew that Lil' Rob wanted a piece of the young meat, so he didn't answer like Lil' Rob wanted. "I'll deal with her. Just leave her there for the time being."

CHAPTER 39

Later that afternoon, as promised, Laci showed up at Tonette's apartment. She was glad that Tonette had agreed to see her.

Nervously, Laci stood outside the apartment in a pair of skin-tight black l.e.i. jeans, a purple turtleneck, and a pair of black riding boots. She also had on a necklace with her name spelled out and a fierce leather jacket. Laci's trademark diamond earrings were replaced by gold hoops and her Movado watch was replaced by ghetto-girl gold bangles.

Butterflies fluttered in Laci's stomach as she knocked on the door and waited for it to open. She smiled when she saw Tonette standing before her very eyes.

"Look at this shit right here!" Tonette slipped, saying what she was thinking when she saw Laci. She was itching to kick Laci square in her proper ass but she'd promised her girls she'd behave, though she didn't tell them for how long.

"SBBs!" Laci said excitedly. Monique, Shaunna, and Tonette couldn't believe their eyes. "What up, tricks?" Laci was getting into true form, and fast.

The three girls looked at each other and then back at Laci. Laci didn't know what took over her, but she hugged each of the girls.

"Hey, y'all want something to eat?" Shaunna said, breaking the obvious tension in the air by cooing at her newborn baby and trying to get her two-year-old to stay still.

"Y'all know what's up," Tonette said and retreated to the kitchen. Shaunna followed behind her with her wobbly toddler. Monique and Laci looked at each other.

"Just be cool and don't overdo it," Monique whispered and walked into the kitchen.

"Y'all want any?" Shaunna asked as she fried up some bologna sandwiches.

"Not right now," Tonette said, grabbing a bowl and a box of Cap'n Crunch cereal.

"Me neither," Monique said as she made a cheese and Miracle Whip sandwich.

"I'll make the Kool-Aid," Laci volunteered, opening Tonette's silverware drawer and looking for the packets. "What kind y'all want?"

"Um ... purple," Monique said.

"That cool?" Laci asked everyone else.

"Yeah, it's cool," Shaunna and Tonette responded.

Shaunna kept her son in the kitchen and turned on a *Garbage Pail Kids* video to keep him occupied. The rest of the girls retreated to the living room and waited for the Kool-Aid.

Laci made the drink with extra sugar, just the way the girls liked it. She grabbed four colored plastic cups out of dish drainer and went in the freezer to get ice. Laci pulled out an ice tray and pulled the silver handle back.

Crack.

She heard it separate the cubes. Not enough ice was available for four cups, so she went to the next tray. It looked funny. She looked closely at the ice and saw that there were little packages of something in the cubes. *Oh shit, did I find where she keeps her shit?* Laci looked at the other cubes and sure enough, there were little packages of something frozen in each ice cube. Quickly, she put the tray back in the freezer and dumped the ice out that was already in their cups and ran hot water on the cubes to melt them. She didn't want Tonette to know she'd found anything.

She returned with the pitcher of warm Kool-Aid and four cups. They all sat around not knowing what to say next. Laci looked like she had changed, but none of the girls really knew how much.

Shaunna reached over and handed Laci her plate of fried bologna sandwiches. Instantly, Laci removed the bread to see if anything was sprinkled on it.

"What the fuck you doing?" Shaunna said sharply, watching Laci inspect her food.

"Looking for the mustard," Laci said quickly. "What you think I'm doing?" She looked at Shaunna as if she should know, then hopped up and went into the kitchen to retrieve the yellow bottle of mustard in the fridge. Laci came back and squirted a nice-sized dollop of mustard in the center of her sandwich. She eagerly picked it up and bit into it. Laci hated mustard, but she wasn't about to fall for that bullshit again.

"So Laci," Tonette said, cutting to the chase, digging into her bowl of cereal, "what happened to you?" She shoveled two spoonfuls into her mouth and milk trickled down her chin. "I looked all over for you. It seemed like you were a ghost."

Laci took a nice-sized bite out of her sandwich, chewed and swallowed it, then she drank out of her cup. "My momma was trippin' and kicked my ass out."

"What?" Tonette couldn't believe her ears. "Miss Prissy got kicked out? What the fuck you do?" She shoveled more cereal in her mouth, but this time, chased it down with Kool-Aid.

Ignoring the "Miss Prissy" remark, Laci continued. "She accused me of stealing something." She took another bite of her sandwich. "You know, bullshit like that," Laci continued with her mouth full of food. She pursed her lips and rolled her eyes as if she were irritated. "Wasn't nothing but a thing. I had to go down to Jackson. That's where the corner store was."

"Stole something?" Tonette said. All of the girls looked at Laci in shock because she was true to the junkie form with theft. "You?"

Tonette looked at Laci and noticed she didn't have on her Movado watch, nor her diamond earrings. "Where your watch, your earrings, and shit like that?" she asked.

"Pawnshop," Laci told them without batting an eye. "Then I tried to get hers." All of the girls broke out in laughter. "When the police came to—"

"Police?" the girls exclaimed, interrupting her. "Hell naw! The po-pos came to your crib?"

"Yeah, she called them on me, talking about she can't control me anymore and she wanted me out of the house." Laci mocked her mother's tone in a sarcastic way, twisting her head back and forth, and reached for another sandwich. "Can you believe that?"

"Damn!" the girls sang, giving each other high-fives.

"Girl, you know you be making the shit outta Kool-Aid,"

Shaunna said to Laci, drinking the rest of hers. "Re-up girl, re-up." She held her cup out. Laci gave her a refill.

"Monique, you want more?" Laci asked.

"Hell yeah!" she handed her empty cup to Laci, who poured, happily.

"She was straight buggin'," Laci continued with her story, "so she called herself kicking me out and I just kept on steppin'."

"Damn, girl, I know she ain't kick yo' ass out just for some earrings. Come on, Laci, fess up . . . what you take that had her so pissed off?" Tonette finished her drink and poured more for herself.

"Shit, I don't remember," Laci said, trying to find something good to tell her. It seemed like the girls were letting their guards down with her, but she continued to make sure. "Money, clothes, jewelry," Laci said nonchalantly. "When it's stuff at your crib, you ain't stealing. It's yours, right?" The girls nodded their approval. "But she didn't think so." She laughed.

"So how she find you?" Monique questioned because when she went to Margaret's house the first time, Laci wasn't there, but when she went yesterday, she was.

"Well, she looked in the best places she could in the hood and she eventually found me. It took her a while, though. When I saw her, she didn't see me." Laci did the bob and weave, like she was hiding from someone. All the girls cracked up.

"How long you been back at the crib?" Tonette asked. She thought it was strange that Laci said she was in the hood, because she'd searched high and low for her there but never once did she come across her.

"Girl, on Thursday," she told her truthfully. "She couldn't have me gone too long because she wouldn't keep getting that money my daddy left her when he died. You know they cut off dependent Social Security benefits if a kid ain't home, right?" They didn't know because none of them knew their fathers, or even knew if they were dead or alive, but they nodded their heads.

Tonette grinned. "I heard that, girl. So you was in the hood, huh? You still fuckin' 'round with Dink?" Tonette was trying to find out exactly what happened with him. When Laci became a ghost, he did too.

"Yeah girl, I was just in the hood," Laci answered Tonette's first question. "I wanted to come to y'all to tell y'all what was happening, but I couldn't do that."

"Why?" Tonette asked. She would have loved to have seen Laci out there. On crack was one thing, but on crack *and* homeless? She would have killed for that.

"Because y'all hated me," Laci said softly with tears in her eyes as she looked among Tonette, Monique, and Shaunna. "I didn't think I could come to y'all." Everyone got quiet. Laci willed the tears back before she spoke again. "You know that was some fucked-up shit y'all did, because I really did consider us to be friends."

"And what exactly did *we* do, Laci?" Tonette asked, getting defensive.

"Giving me that laced weed," Laci told her. "That wasn't cool." Laci scratched her arms thinking of the memory. "What did I do to y'all anyway?"

The air finally became thick.

"Where should I start?" Tonette barked. "Yo' ass was stuck up. Acting like you was better than us." She didn't hold back.

"I just wish y'all would have said something about how y'all felt instead of tricking me the way you did."

"We did say something to you," Tonette said, the other girls nodded in agreement. "You just didn't listen."

"No, you didn't say anything," Laci barked. "Y'all picked on everything I said. Everything I said was wrong and y'all just turned that shit back around on me."

"Well you were still stuck up," Tonette said, with her lips pursed.

"That was not my intention," Laci said truthfully. "I didn't have any real friends here until I met y'all, so I guess I didn't know how to act."

"What about that bougie school you went to?"

"Girl, you really trippin'," Laci laughed along with the girls. "Those spoiled-ass kids at my school...nah, I couldn't deal wit'em. I was on the lower end of things there. Just because you have a little more or less than the average person, you would be judged. Just like y'all judged me without getting to know me." She looked at the girls, one by one. "I wanted to go to another school, but my mother felt like she was giving me what she thought was best." Laci reached for her cup, but it was empty by now. Monique quickly got up and refilled it and the other girls' glasses as well. "Actually, I can't blame her for what she did, I just wish she would have allowed me to experience life a little more. That's why I was glad I was with y'all. You all were real and I appreciated that."

Laci looked around and saw that the girls were finished with their food, so she started gathering empty dishes. "Y'all, I'm really sorry if I made you feel like I thought I was better than you." She looked at each of the girls. Laci noticed that Monique had tears in her eyes. Shaunna looked away, and Tonette made herself look busy by brushing imaginary lint off her jeans. "I know it wasn't personal," she told them, "and I forgive you." She paused to give the girls the chance to say something. They didn't.

While Laci was in the kitchen, the girls spoke quietly among themselves.

"You believe this shit?" Shaunna said to Tonette and Monique. "What you think is up?"

"I don't know," Tonette said, watching Laci fumble around in the kitchen. "I don't trust her."

Laci made her way out of the kitchen and darted off to the bathroom. She turned on the faucet to cover up any noise she might make. With the help of a washcloth, she pried the masking tape away from the unfinished porcelain under the toilet tank top and took all the packets of drugs that Tonette had taped there. *That stupid heifa need to get more creative*, Laci thought. She wrapped the stash up in the washcloth and slid it inside her purse.

"Well, what you gonna do?" Monique asked.

"I'll show you," Tonette whispered as Laci made her way out of the bathroom.

Laci noticed that the girls were mumbling when she returned. She hoped they weren't on to her.

"Um, Laci," Tonette spoke. "That shit that went down … it wasn't our idea." Tonette looked at the other girls. "Crystal came up with the idea." Laci said nothing. She figured Crystal would have had something to do with it because she knew that Dink was feeling her, but she remembered what Uncle Sonny told her.

"Still," Laci said, "it was fucked up, y'all."

"Speaking of Crystal," Tonette said, changing the subject, "you still hollering at Dink?" She noticed that Laci had avoided the question earlier. "We saw how he was peepin' you, plus people saw you with him."

"Did them same people tell you that I was getting my shit from him? I know he was try'na hook up with me, but hell naw, I ain't with him, I don't want no second-hand nigga. That's Crystal's man. Where she at anyway?" Laci looked around.

"Um . . . you ain't heard?"

"Heard what? Girl, I told you I ain't been around."

"She's dead, Laci," Tonette told her.

Laci eyeballed Monique, who looked uneasy. She didn't want Laci to let on that she knew, because she was certain that Tonette would think that she'd told her more.

"What you mean dead?"

"Dead like in shot, six-feet-in-the-ground, ain't-never-coming-back dead."

"Girl, you bullshittin'." Laci played the game so well that even Monique had to question if she'd truly told her or not. Laci's expression told Tonette this was the first time she'd heard of it. Laci didn't want to ask too many questions, because she and Crystal hadn't been all that cool.

"Naw I ain't," Tonette told her seriously. "I'm a lot of things, but one thing I'm not is a liar."

"Damn," Laci said. She sat down for a minute to gather her composure. "That's really fucked up."

"Yeah it is," all three girls mumbled in unison.

"Um . . . what y'all got going on for tonight?" Laci attempted to change the subject and looked at the girls. "You wanna hang?"

"Shit, I gotta page Smurf," Tonette said. "Gotta tell him I'll work wit'em." She went to the bedroom and closed the door.

"Damn, I must've ate too much," Shaunna admitted. "Shit, I need to head home and take a nap."

"Yeah, I think I'm gonna crash for a bit, too. Laci. But maybe later?" Monique responded.

"That's cool. You girls got my number." Laci stood up as Tonette came back into the living room. "That yo' man or some-thin', Nette?"

"Nah . . . but I gotta head out real quick," Tonette said. "Maybe we can hang later?"

"A'ight, cool."

Tonette walked out of the apartment. Laci said her good-byes to Shaunna and Monique, and followed behind her.

CHAPTER 40

As TONETTE DROVE to the corner store, she thought about Smurf's proposition to join his crew and realized it wasn't such a bad idea. Ice was the newest drug to hit the street and she was sure to make a killing with it.

She knew that ice gave a more potent and longer high than the brief high with cocaine, so she would have to push more than just ice to keep her money flowing right. What Tonette liked most was that it was odorless and undetectable, and it was more easily transportable, in penny-sized plastic bags, than crack, which she carried in the plastic vials. Pulling up at the spot, she waited.

"Aye, yo Lil' Rob," Smurf called out, "go around the corner, and you should see a blue Camaro. A bitch in it," he described. "Tell me if she's by herself."

Rob did as he was told and came back within two minutes. "Yeah, she's by herself. Whatchu fuckin' with Tonette for?"

"Damn, man, just be cool. Just cover me, okay?" Smurf didn't trust her one bit, but he was gonna tame her.

Within minutes he had pulled his car up next to hers. She got out of the Camaro and walked over to his car and climbed in.

"Cool, so you also down for payin' off Dame's debt?"

"Yeah, but I wanna make a deal with you."

"A deal? Girl, this ain't no fuckin' game show," Smurf said, irritated.

"No, hear me out. This will benefit everybody."

"Make it good," he told her as he took his gun out of the holster and shined the chrome with his shirt.

"What if I pay off Dame's debt with this?" She pointed to the small v in between her legs.

Smurf looked over at her. Her winning smile, smooth skin, and smoky eyes did something to him. Smurf felt an erection growing in his pants.

"And what makes you think that's gonna replace what he owed me?"

"Because my shit is that good," she told him seriously.

"That was a lot of shit you got from him," Smurf reminded her.

"And I got a lot," she said teasingly.

"Is that so?" Smurf unbuckled and unzipped his pants. "Well you know I gotta test the product. Take your clothes off," he ordered.

Tonette didn't object. The opportunity to fuck Smurf was what she wanted, since she'd heard of his reputation. This was also an opportunity for her to shine, because she was tired of sexing the niggas who worked for another muthafucka. Smurf was the big nigga in charge and she wasn't going to fuck up this opportunity.

Tonette slipped her blue and white Reebok sneakers off, then slid out of her Jordache jeans. Her black cotton bikinis covered her perfectly shaped bottom and Smurf could see the tender puff of pubic hair that was hidden by the black fabric.

"Take your shirt off, too," he ordered.

She did as she was told and removed her sweatshirt. Smurf saw that her bra matched her panties. He pulled the lever to recline the passenger seat so he could have better access. Tonette attempted to lie on her back, but Smurf didn't want that.

"Turn over and get on your knees. I wanna hit it from the back." Smurf reached on the side door, grabbed the small bottle of lotion he always kept there, and greased up his dick real good.

Tonette got on all fours, arched her back, and tooted her ass up high in the air. It was something that Dame taught her and each time he hit it from the back, she would have an orgasm so strong that she'd fall asleep within minutes after it was over.

Putting her right hand on the seat and the other hand against the door, Tonette braced herself for the big dick that Smurf was rumored to have. Actually, she wasn't too worried about the size because Dame had also been big. She just hadn't had none in months, and it would be a little difficult for her.

Smurf appreciated the sight of Tonette's perfect round bottom in front of him and he lotioned it eagerly.

Smurf took his dick and ran it up and down the slit of her pussy. The wetness of her snatch teased the sensitive nerve endings at the head of his penis. The visual of him behind her reminded him of the tape of Dame fucking Laci. He got angry thinking about it, but it also got him turned on. In one swift motion, Smurf shoved into Tonette. She attempted to scream, but he pushed her head down into the seat to quiet the noise. He grabbed her hips and thrusted inside her again. Pulled out and pushed again, ignoring Tonette's muffled whimpers.

Smurf looked down and saw the width and length of his dick in Tonette's tight asshole. Besides the obvious smell of sex in the air, he smelled the faint scent of blood. *Guess I didn't use enough lotion,* he told himself. Smurf didn't care, because he began to move his dick in and out of her until she moved to his rhythm.

Tonette was pissed that Smurf fucked her in her ass without saying something first. She never let Dame get it back there, but the more Smurf dug into her, the better it was starting to feel and the more aroused she became. Reaching back to remove his right hand, she felt his pistol on her waist. Tonette smiled because the rumor was true that he fucked with his piece on, so she grabbed his left hand and pulled him forward so he could grab her titties while he banged her. Smurf pulled and twisted her hard, brown nipples, which caused Tonette to moan in pleasure and pain.

Tonette held her ass cheeks open to let Smurf watch himself drill into her under the flickering lights, and she threw it back on him like it was just a thang. He looked to his left and saw his boys across the street high-fiving each other while they watched Smurf handle his business. With a small audience, Smurf decided to go all the way and stroked her deeply, causing Tonette to thrash around wildly.

He couldn't hold back too much longer before he came. The vice-like grip that Tonette's ass had on his dick was too tight and too good. Letting go of her titties, Smurf grabbed Tonette's hips tightly and bucked one last time, filling her tight hole with his cum. Once he was done, he sat back down in his seat and fixed himself up.

Tonette got off all fours, turned around, and sat down gingerly in the seat in an attempt to put her clothes on.

"Don't get that shit on my seat," he told her, making reference to the nut that was in her ass and the blood. She was exhausted by what had just happened and didn't want to argue with him, so she quickly pulled her panties up and put the rest of her clothes on.

"So we're cool?" she asked Smurf before she got out.

"Just like you said, you're trading in your shit for Dame's debt, right?"

"Right."

"And it'll benefit everybody, right?"

"Yup." She beamed, high from the good dick she had just gotten. "We cool on the money tip too, right?" she asked.

"Yup, we're cool," Smurf told her. The loss he would take on the money was worth what he was going to do with her. Little did Tonette know that Dame sold his shit on different corners. The corners now had new lieutenants, and each would have his turn collecting on his debt.

WALKING BACK INTO her apartment, Tonette was relieved to see that Shaunna, her kids, and Laci were gone. She was worn out and a little sore, but had to get back out on the streets to make money. After she showered and changed clothes, she saw Monique.

"You going back out?" Monique asked when she returned from the kitchen.

"Yeah. But girl, let me tell you what happened." She filled Monique in on all the dirty details. "Girl, I was pissed that he fucked me in my ass, but—"

"He ain't even try to get the pussy?" Monique asked.

"Naw, girl."

"You think he kinda . . . you know."

"Smurf? Hell naw!" she spat back. "You know niggas. They

always try'na get the bootyhole, like they really think our pussy is up that high."

"Right!" Monique agreed.

"But that's cool," she told Monique, "it's over and done with, but I tell you what, if he fucks my pussy the way he did my ass tonight, he can have me selling anything anywhere without no kickback."

"Get the fuck outta here," Monique said out loud. "You'd give up the money for some dick? It was that good?"

"I'm sure he'll break me off some money, but just like you know, a nigga with deep pockets is good, but a nigga with a deep stroke is priceless."

The two girls giggled and high-fived each other.

CHAPTER 41

THE NEXT DAY, bright and early, Laci and Shaunna were back at Tonette's. Coming in from a late night, Tonette had more energy than usual. "So damn, what we getting into?" she asked. "I know we ain't gonna sit around this bitch all day."

"I wanna hit The Hub. I was up there earlier and saw some earrings I wanna pick up," Laci told her.

"There you go with that rich-girl shit again, flashing your fuckin' money around," Tonette barked.

Laci twisted her face. Tonette was always jumping to conclusions and heard what she wanted to hear. "I said 'pick up,'" Laci told her, making a swiping move with her hand. "Who said anything about money? Y'all wanna roll with me?" She looked at the girls and dug in her Dooney and Bourke purse for her keys.

"What you rollin' in?" Tonette asked.

"I got my momma's car but she don't know it," Laci said sneakily. "I don't know if she's gonna report it stolen, but we'll handle that if it happens." She dangled the keys in the air. "Y'all game?"

"Hell yeah!" Tonette announced, shaking her head at Laci's crazy ass.

Just as the girls were getting ready to leave, Laci turned to her. "Tonette, I'm really glad to see you." Laci embraced her. "I really hope we can put the past behind us and be friends."

She turned and walked out of the apartment with Tonette following closely behind her. Tonette had one test for Laci to see if she was genuine about what she was saying.

As they all rode, Laci cranked up "How Ya Like Me Now" by Kool Moe Dee and headed to Fordham.

Enjoying the smooth ride of the Mercedes, Tonette pulled out a bag of weed and started rolling a blunt. "Y'all want some blow?" she said, concentrating on picking out the seeds and not spilling anything.

Monique and Shaunna agreed, but Laci didn't know if she should or shouldn't. True enough, she smoked a little at school, but her friends there were nothing like the South Bronx Bitches. One thing she would make sure of: the girls would hit it before she did. Laci kept a sly eye on Tonette, making sure the shit was kosher.

Tonette lit the blunt and handed it toward Laci and smiled. "You want the first hit?"

"Nah, y'all hit that shit first, then I'll do it," she said seriously, and the girls laughed. The girls passed the bud between each other like it was no big deal. Laci noticed that nobody said anything about Shaunna's kids being in the car. She didn't agree with kids being around drugs of any kind, but if their own momma didn't care, hell, she didn't either.

When the girls arrived in the business district it was packed. They found a parking spot and Laci squeezed her way into it. "Damn, shit poppin' down here," Shaunna said, getting out of the car and hoisting her two-year-old on her hip. She closed the door and grabbed the stroller out of the trunk for her baby. Laci went to her and helped unfold the stroller, but neither Tonette nor Monique offered to help.

Plopping the carrier into the stroller, all four girls walked down the strip. Not only were they checking out the niggas, but the niggas were checking them out, too. Laci saw a couple of faces from her past, but the memories were vague. She couldn't remember if they'd fucked her or supplied her with what she needed, or both. It didn't matter though. She had something for them too if they approached her.

The strip was the hot spot for hustlers. They hung out there not only for quick and easy trade, but to get first dibs on a honey that nobody in the Bronx had been up in.

The girls walked into Zales and looked around. They let Laci do her thing, because diamonds didn't mean anything to them.

"Come here, girls," Laci said after the clerk put a row of earrings on the counter. "Look at this."

The girls came over and ogled the perfect stones, and they nodded with approval.

"Would you like to fill out a credit app?" the clerk asked happily. She was looking for commission and was doing everything she could to secure it.

"Sure," Laci told her and began filling out the paperwork.

The girls looked at her like *yeah, we knew you were gonna pull this shit.* Within minutes, Laci spoke loudly, "That's fine. I didn't want your funky-ass earrings anyway." She stormed out of the store. The girls looked on and mouthed to each other, *what the fuck just happened?*

"Fuck that heifer," Laci mumbled angrily as she stomped away. "Said my credit ain't been approved."

They made their way to Pandora's Fashions and browsed until Tonette saw a store she liked.

"Yo, let me stop here," she announced once she saw the Gold Palace jewelry store. They all walked in, and Tonette's gray eyes lit up as she looked at the new styles of name-plate necklaces. After careful deliberation, she chose the style she wanted and ordered one.

"Make that two," Laci said to the man behind the counter. "One for me and one for her. We'll be back in an hour. They'll be ready then, right?"

"Yes ma'am," he told them.

The girls went to Kentucky Fried Chicken to grab a bite to eat. They ran into some guys who wanted to holla, so they bummed around with them to pass the time.

As promised, the girls returned to the Gold Palace to pick up their orders. Tonette took her name-plate out of the small plastic bag and admired her name, spelled out in small gold letters. She already had a big one, but the small one was perfect. Laci put hers in her bag and the girls headed out of the store.

They window-shopped a little more and left around eight P.M. They all piled in Laci's mother's car and as they rode, none of the girls, especially Tonette, could believe the change in Laci. She had gone from stuck-up to hood rich, and Tonette liked the new Laci. *If she was like this when I first met her, hell, I wouldn't have turned her out,* she thought to herself.

"Y'all wanna get into something else tonight?" Laci asked once they got back to Tonette's and got settled. She helped Shaunna change her son's diaper and went into the bathroom to wash her hands. "Y'all wanna hit the clubs or something?" she asked once she'd returned, wiping her hands on her jeans.

"Damn, girl, you off the chain," Tonette remarked, seeing just how down Laci was now.

"Nah, I'm cool," Monique said truthfully. "I gotta work tomorrow."

"Me too," Shaunna replied.

"What?" Monique looked at her like she was crazy. "Bitch, you ain't got no damn job."

"That's right, and I don't want none either," Shaunna snapped back. "This check I get every month does me just fine!"

Laci looked at her girls and laughed. "That's cool," she told them all. "I'll just holla at y'all tomorrow." She walked toward the door. "Oh, I forgot, I have a little present for you." Laci reached into her bag and pulled out three small burgundy boxes and handed them to each of her friends. "Don't ever say I ain't never give you nothing," she laughed.

The girls were amazed when they saw one-carat diamond studs.

"Laci, how did you—"

"Girl, please." Laci smacked her lips. "That was a piece of cake. They fell right into my purse. Oops," Laci joked. "I'll see y'all tomorrow." She burned out.

When Tonette got back to her apartment, she sat back on her living room couch, with one leg over the arm. She thought the new Laci was cool, but it was all too coincidental. *I know this shit can't be real,* she thought to herself. *I know this bitch ain't go from a prissy heifa, to a crackhead, to this shit overnight. I'ma put her to the test and see if this is real.*

BEFORE SHE GOT home, Laci paged Officer Jones.

"Yo, who dis?" he yelled into the receiver.

"This is Laci."

"Oh yeah. How's it going?"

"Officer Jones, can you meet me at the park on 159th? I need to talk to you." Within twenty minutes, Laci was sitting inside Officer Jones's car.

She told him, "I overheard Dink and Smurf talking about a dossier before. What was in it? If it can incriminate Dink, I gotta do something about it."

He knew she could do nothing about the street shit, but he remembered one piece of paper that he'd seen. Dink's account numbers.

"Before Dink left, what did he do with his money?"

"Um," Laci had to think back, "he closed his accounts. Why?"

"Damn." He rubbed his chin.

"What's wrong?"

"Even though they're closed, it's traceable."

"Can you get me some money?" Laci asked.

"What? How?"

"You a cop. When ya'll apprehend drug dealers, don't you get money from them?"

"Well, yeah," Officer Jones smiled.

"Can you get me some? How much unaccountable money can get someone in trouble?"

"Um, about five to ten G's."

Laci thought about it. "Well, can you get me ten G's? You'll get it back on Friday, I promise."

Officer Jones thought about her request. "Let me see what I can do. Hit me up in the morning."

Back at home, Laci's nerves got the better of her. She even threw up a few times. It disgusted her to be near those heifas. *Keep going*, she told herself. *You can't stop now.*

CHAPTER 42

THE NEXT MORNING, Laci awakened, still throwing up. She didn't know if it was the pregnancy or the fact that she would have to see the girls again. In the bathroom, she looked at herself in the mirror. "What are you doing?" she asked herself, looking at who she had become. Laci splashed cold water on her face.

Just as she turned to go out of the bathroom, her phone rang. She answered with a groggy, "Hello?"

"Hey Laci, what you doing, girl?" Laci knew it was Shaunna, because she heard a baby crying in the background.

"Shit, nothing right now." Laci yawned. "What's up? The kids okay?"

"Um...do you think you can swing by and pick me up? I don't wanna drag the baby on the damn bus. He's sick."

Laci looked at the clock. It was eight-thirty in the morning and she had somewhere to be at nine. "A'ight," she told Shaunna. "I'll be there in about an hour."

Margaret walked into Laci's room. She wanted to hang out today, but she thought she'd heard Laci come in very early that morning. She had been keeping strange hours and Margaret was concerned. Seeing that she wasn't in her bedroom, Margaret walked to the bathroom door and tried to open it. It was locked.

"Laci, Laci!" Margaret called out.

"Yes, Mom?"

"Sweetheart, you okay?"

"Yes, Mom, I'm fine," Laci told her.

"Come out here. I want to see you."

"Mom!" Laci yelled.

"Now!" Margaret responded forcefully.

Laci opened the bathroom door and looked at her mother. "Yes, Mom." Laci had straightened her hair, but she decided not to say anything about it.

"Sweetheart, are you okay? Were you throwing up?"

"I was just a little sick earlier, that's all."

Margaret looked at her daughter. "Laci, I have to ask."

"No, Mom, I'm not." Laci was hurt that her mother would think that she was back on drugs, but she couldn't blame her. Laci knew that her behavior had been different lately, but rightfully so. She just couldn't tell her mother what she was doing. Laci now knew what Dink meant when he said the less she knew, the better off she was, and he was right.

"You wanna do something today? I haven't really spent any time with you over the last couple of days."

"Um . . . Mom," Laci stuttered, "I'm meeting some friends, but I promise, we'll do something." She pulled up her Jordache jeans, put on a pink sweatshirt, and laced up her pink Reeboks.

"Why are you dressed like that, Laci?" Margaret asked.

Laci didn't respond. She just grabbed her purse and kissed her mother on the way out of the house. "I'll see you later, Mom."

• • •

AFTER MEETING WITH Officer Jones, Laci pulled up to the parking lot of the First Bank of New York, where Dink used to bank. First Bank was well known as the place where hustlers kept their stash and nobody asked questions.

Dink was smart, though. Unlike most hustlers, he deposited money weekly into his accounts, as if he had a real job. Most cats got busted when they made hefty deposits without a traceable source of income.

She waited in line until she was called.

"Next!" the teller yelled.

Laci walked up to the window.

"Um . . . yeah," Laci spoke, in true ghetto-girl fashion. "I need to reopen my man's account but I need my name on it."

The teller looked on in disgust, wondering how she'd pulled a hustler. "Here," she snapped, handing her two half-sheets of paper, "fill this out, and I need to copy your ID or driver's license."

Laci handed the teller her photo ID along with the two completed sheets. Moments later, the teller handed Laci the cashier's check she'd requested in addition to a key to the safety deposit box she had just rented.

"Thank you, Ms. Thomas, and come again," the teller said.

"Thank you," Laci said, "and I'll be back."

It was colder than normal for a November day and Laci was glad she'd dressed appropriately. After she left the bank, she gave Officer Jones the updated account information, then arrived at Shaunna's four hours after she'd told her she would be there, making it a point to be late only to see what Shaunna was going to do or say. Surprisingly, she said nothing.

Laci helped Shaunna get her baby in the car.

"Where's the lil' man?" Laci asked of her two-year-old son.

"At the babysitter, girl. She just lives a few blocks over. I need a break."

"I understand." Laci helped put the stroller in the trunk and helped secure the baby in the car seat. "So where we rollin'?" She asked after Shaunna got in the car. She looked at her quizzically. "You alright?"

Shaunna looked at Laci. "I don't know. I feel like I'm about to fuckin' lose it," she told Laci truthfully.

"What's wrong?"

"Girl, look at me," she said sharply. "I'm eighteen years old, got two kids in diapers, and neither one of my baby daddies are around." Shaunna looked like she was going to cry. "I ain't got a damn job, no real transportation, but I was ridin' dirty anyway when them niggas was stickin' they dick in me, try'na knock my ass up. Shit, my life is fucked up, Laci, that's what's wrong."

"No it's not, Shaunna, it could be a lot worse."

"A lot worse, how?"

"Shit, you could be homeless, strung out on drugs, or being beaten."

"Yeah, but that might be better than me being stuck with kids and can't provide for them."

Laci began to feel sorry for her, and reached over and hugged her. Shaunna was grateful, because she felt the sincerity come through Laci's hug.

"Why, Laci?"

"Why what?"

"You know what we did to you, so why are you so nice?" Shaunna said, breaking the embrace.

"What do you mean, why am I so nice?"

"I mean, I called Tonette earlier to see if she could run me around. She told me flat-out no. You know Monique is at the post office but when I call you, you come. You even ask about my kids. The other girls never do. With the shit we did to you, why would you still fuck with us?"

Laci paused momentarily to gather the right words. "Y'all had a problem with me," she pointed to herself, "but I never had a problem with y'all." Laci was serious in her admission. "I considered you my friends back then and regardless of what happened, I consider you my friends now, and friends help each other out, right?" Shaunna nodded her head. "As far as your kids go, they're kids. They've never done anything to me."

"I guess you're right," Shaunna said. She couldn't hold back her tears any longer. Laci forced out a few droplets of her own. She did care about Shaunna's children. She felt bad for them because her kids were given a bad start at life by having Shaunna as a mother. They didn't know their fathers, and unfortunately, Shaunna's choices would dictate how they lived.

Shaunna gained her composure and wiped her face. "Um . . . okay, can you run me down to Southview? I know someone in Housing and they supposed to hook me up with a two-bedroom. Right now that one-bedroom ain't workin' no more."

"A'ight, we on our way." Laci took off, hoping to show Shaunna her new home but canvassing the spot for herself, too.

An hour later, they were leaving Southview and Shaunna looked over at Laci. "Well, what did you think?"

"Think about what?"

"The apartment."

"It's fine."

"Really? Do you think so?"

Laci knew what she was getting at. Shaunna wanted her approval. She really didn't give a fuck where Shaunna lived. Most snakes lived under rocks, but she couldn't tell her that.

"Yeah, it's fine. The kids will share a room and you got that big room with the huge-ass walk-in closet."

"I guess," Shaunna said apathetically.

"You peep those mirrors on the closet door?" Laci tried to lighten up the mood. "They face your bed and you can . . . well, you know."

Shaunna giggled.

"You need to go anywhere else?" Laci asked. She was tired of driving, but she had to keep up appearances.

"No, but I really don't want to go home. I been cooped up in the house too long as it is."

"Okay, well, let's call Tonette and see if she wants to hang out with us too. Monique can catch up with us when she gets off."

"No," Shaunna said abruptly.

"Why?" Shaunna's reaction startled Laci.

"I dunno. I guess I ain't never hung out with you by myself, you know. This is pretty cool."

Laci shrugged her shoulders. "A'ight girl, let's hit The Hub and see what we can get into there."

The two went to the heart of the Bronx and scoped out stores. Laci boosted some items from The Gap. Although nervous every time and out of her character, she couldn't believe how easy it had become. Plus, carrying a diaper bag was the perfect disguise. Nobody would ever suspect anything.

Almost two hours later, Laci looked at her watch. "Um, it's getting close to five o'clock. Don't you have to pick up lil' man from the sitter?"

"Oh shit, it's that late?"

"Yeah."

"We need to get back there. Do you mind taking me over there?"

"Nope, not at all."

Just as the girls were walking to Laci's car, Shaunna stopped. "Oh shit!"

"What?" Laci asked, looking around. She didn't know if she needed to run or what.

"Over there, girl," she pointed slyly, "it's Play."

"Play? Who the fuck is Play?" Laci asked, trying to see where Shaunna was pointing.

"Girl, I been wantin' to get at that for a minute."

Laci looked at the man and he looked familiar. She wondered if she'd tried to get at him when she was high. Everything was a blur to her. She had done a lot in such a short amount of time.

"Shaunna," Laci spoke in a tone to get her attention again. "Don't you need to go pick up lil' man?"

The smile on Shaunna's face disappeared as she thought about it. "A'ight. Come on."

CHAPTER 43

OVER THE NEXT couple of days, Laci made it a point to spend time with each of the girls alone. She noticed something that she'd never noticed before. When the girls were all together, they were cool, but when they were alone, Monique and Shaunna talked about Tonette, and Tonette dogged them too.

Thursday night, Laci was riding shotgun with Tonette in Dame's car.

"You don't wanna get the girls?" Laci asked, holding onto the door handle as Tonette drove wildly.

"For what?" she answered.

"'Cuz, we the SBBs, Tonette, we roll together."

"Fuck them. They can't roll with me no more."

"Why not? They your girls, ain't they?"

"Shit, look at it. Shaunna got them goddamn kids. I ain't try'na hear all that goddamn crying and shit. Then you got Monique with her ole scary ass."

"Well, I'm here," Laci told her, trying to calm her mood. "Damn, what's up with this?" she asked as she looked around.

"Nothing. Just another day at the office for me," Tonette told her. "Come on."

Tonette got out of the car and began to walk. Laci's heart beat fast, because she was back in the Jackson Projects, on St. Nicholas Street to be exact. It was a place Laci knew all too well. She looked at her nemesis, who was waiting for her outside the corner store with a sly smirk on her face.

Laci looked at her and wanted to kill her with the rage that was inside her heart. She finally got out of the car and walked toward Tonette.

"Sorry it took me a minute," Laci told her. "Let's do this."

Laci hung tight with Tonette throughout the night. She noticed that mostly women copped from Tonette. There were no female dealers just months ago.

"Nette?" Laci called out. "Is it just my imagination or are there more female junkies out here now?"

"Nope, it's not your imagination." Another person came up to Tonette and they exchanged product for money. "It's easier to have a woman dealer. You pay your money, you get your shit, and then you go get high. Niggas always want something."

"You got that right," Laci said to her.

"Damn, I ran outta shit." Tonette looked at her watch. "I need to run back to the crib."

The two rode back to Tonette's apartment and went inside. Laci waited in the living room for Tonette to return from the bathroom.

"What's up, girl?" Laci said when she returned.

"Shit, I gotta re-up. I ain't got jack!" She patted her pockets and dug her hands inside them. Nothing. "I thought I had more, but I guess I sold it all. Guess it's been busy, huh?"

She picked up the phone and paged Smurf.

Within moments, he called her back.

"Um, hey Laci," she said when she got off the phone with him, "you go ahead and leave. I got some shit I need to take care of."

"A'ight, cool. I'll see you tomorrow."

Laci left, knowing some shit was about to kick off. Just as she had heard nasty rumors about herself, Laci heard rumors on the street that Tonette was giving up ass when her shit came up short. She wasn't sure if it was true, but she would find out.

THERE WAS A knock at Tonette's door.

"Hey Smurf," she said when she swung it open.

"Nah, it ain't him." It was Lil' Rob.

"What the fuck you doing here?" Tonette asked.

"Came to collect on boss man's shit. You got his money?"

"Yeah, here." She let him in the house and closed the door. She counted out her money.

"It's short," he told her.

"What the fuck you mean it's short?"

"You get fifty packets of ice alone every time you re-up. I ain't even including the crack you get. You sell ice for twenty dollars, that's one G, ma, and right here," he counted out, "is only eight hundred dollars, so where's the other two?"

Tonette began to get pissed. *What the fuck is going on?* she asked herself.

"Look, I can make that shit up; just give me my shit and I'll work just as hard to make that money up and bring back the right amount. I don't know what the hell is going on, but I'm gonna find out what's up."

"That's cool and all, but boss man said to collect before I give you anything else."

"Well, what the fuck am I supposed to do?"

"Gotta pay the piper, ma. You got debt now and so does that nigga Dame."

"What the fuck you mean, 'and Dame'? That shit already worked off."

"No it ain't," he told her. "I didn't get my payment yet."

"What fuckin' payment you talkin' 'bout?"

"That nigga owed me too, so you know what's up. Drop dem drawers." Tonette looked down and saw an erection growing in his pants.

"Nuh uh," she smarted off.

Lil' Rob pulled out his gun and cocked the trigger. Tonette stopped in her tracks. "Now, drop 'em," Rob ordered. Becoming scared, Tonette did as she was told.

BACK AT THE spot, Laci walked the street and held it down with niggas who weren't on Smurf's payroll. She had her backup, though. Terrance wasn't that far away.

Feeling comfortable, she mingled with the fiends and the hustlers.

"Hey," a crackhead said to Laci. "What'cha got for me?"

Laci looked at the man. He was skinny, had pimples on his face and missing teeth, and smelled of urine. Laci had to turn her nose up to deal with him.

"Hey, I got a job for ya."

"A job? I don't want no fuckin' job! What you think I am?"

"I ain't talking about that kinda job, damn. I need you to do me a favor."

"How much you payin'?"

"If you got about four friends, they'll get two rocks each and I'll give you three."

"You know where I be at. Just tell me where to be and what to do." He grinned a snaggle-toothed grin.

"You got it!"

CHAPTER 44

LACI WAS AWAKENED by a gentle knock on the front door. She had fallen asleep on the couch after she got home the night before.

She stumbled to the front door and opened it.

"Oh hey, Monique," Laci said, sleepily.

Monique looked at Laci and couldn't believe how she still looked pretty even when she first woke up.

"You said you had a package for me you wanted me to take to the post office."

Laci blinked, trying to get her into focus.

"Oh yeah," she said, remembering what she had told her the night before. "I got a couple of packages. Do you mind sending them off for me?"

"No, it's not like I'm going out of my way."

"Cool, let me go get them."

Laci left and within minutes, she came back with two perfectly wrapped boxes, one in brown paper, which she handed to Monique while she kept the other one, wrapped in decorative paper, in her hands.

"So, you still planning on leaving?" Laci asked, handing the packages to her.

"Yup. Friday morning, me and my granny are outta here. I can't wait, girl."

"I bet. It's nothing like starting your life over," Laci confirmed.

"Actually, we're moving to Jersey and from there, I dunno."

"So you really going through with it, huh?"

"Yep. After my shift tonight, I'm outta here." Monique looked down at the package in her hand. "Oh, you need to address this."

"Oh shit," Laci exclaimed, looking at the box. "I need to get the address from my moms. It's a pair of shoes she's sending to my aunt. She's been busy with housework and stuff and keeps forgetting to mail it. Guess she forgot to address it too, huh?"

Both girls laughed. Monique looked at the clock. She had to get going so she wouldn't be late. "Oh, and this right here," Laci handed Monique the box wrapped in decorative paper, with a card attached to it. "This is for you."

"What is it?" Monique said happily, putting it down to tear into it immediately.

"Girl, don't open that now," Laci urged. "It's kind of a housewarming gift, so you have to wait until you get to your new home to see what it is. I don't like good-byes, so . . ."

"Thank you, Laci," Monique said genuinely. "You didn't have to."

"I know, but you really helped me out by coming clean with everything and I really appreciate that."

"It's the least I could do." Monique smiled at her and looked at the clock once again. "I gotta get going, but hey, call down to the post office and ask for me when you get the address. I'll address it for you."

"Alright, cool." Before Monique could walk out the door, Laci stopped her. "Oh, and Monique?"

"Yeah?"

"Good luck with your move."

"Thanks," Monique acknowledged and left.

LATER THAT DAY, Laci rode over to Tonette's to see what was up with her.

"Hey girl, what's up in here?" she asked while walking into Tonette's place.

"Everything's all fucked up," Tonette growled, looking down the hallway to see if anyone was outside. She was still sore from the assault that Lil' Rob put on her the other day, but she was making it.

"What's wrong, Tonette?"

"I think Monique is stealing from me."

"Stealing? Stealing what?"

Tonette looked at her as if she should know.

"Oh," Laci sighed. "So is that the reason she's leaving town?"

"Leaving town?" Tonette screeched. "When?"

"She said tomorrow, but—" Laci looked at Tonette. Her nostrils flared. She looked like a red bull on the run. "You didn't know?" Laci asked with shock on her face. "I thought y'all were tight. I mean, she *is* living in your apartment."

"What else she tell you?"

"Girl, it don't matter," Laci assured her.

"Yes it does."

"Nothing much, other than how you played Quita and the other SBBs."

"She told you that?"

"Yeah. If she is selling yo' shit, I don't know if she's really selling it or giving it away. Monique doesn't strike me as someone who could be as smart on their feet as you are. I can see her givin' yo' shit as payback for the beatings."

"She told you that?" Tonette raised her voice.

"Tonette, she told me everything," Laci said, in the most convincing tone she could muster. "How you giving up booty to all these niggas."

"I'm gon' kill her!"

"Tonette, don't even trip. It ain't even worth it. You my girl, and you know I got your back."

"Laci, I need to be alone for a minute," Tonette said somberly. "Please go, and I'll talk to you later."

"Did I say something wrong?"

"No, it's not you. I just need to be by myself."

"Well, she said she'll be at yo' spot, if you wanna talk to her." Laci hesitantly got up. "Um, okay girl, if you need me, let me know."

Tonette realized that Laci was true blue. Even after all she had done to her, Laci still had her back. Tonette picked up her keys and switchblade. She hadn't used it in years, but today, it was going to come in handy. "I'ma cut this bitch's tongue out."

She headed to her spot to find Monique.

Laci waited a few minutes, then got in her car and tailed Tonette. She pulled up to the spot, making sure to park out of Tonette's sight, just as Tonette jumped out of her car. Running into the building, Laci waited until she heard the sound she was waiting for.

The screams that echoed through the air were music to Laci's ears. *And it only cost me ten rocks*, she thought to herself.

Although she hated to poison other people's bodies with the drugs, ten rocks were well worth Tonette getting gang-raped and beaten by crackheads.

Laci left and drove to Southview. Knowing that Shaunna's new apartment building was a known crack spot, Laci called her from the pay phone.

"Hello?" Shaunna spoke into the phone.

"Girl, you won't believe this shit!" Laci yelled, all hyped. "Play is down here."

"Where you at?"

"Girl, the arcade, and guess what . . ."

"What?"

"He lookin' good and he askin' about you."

Shaunna smiled momentarily, then said, "Um, Laci, I can't come down there."

"Girl, why not? He waitin' for you."

"I don't have anybody to watch my kids."

"Ain't it time for them to be in bed anyway?" she looked at her watch and saw it was about eleven o'clock at night.

"Yeah, but—"

"Yeah but nothing. Just come on down here for an hour. The kids will be okay."

Shaunna paused for a moment. Her mind was racing a mile a minute. She'd left the kids at home alone before to get some milk, and they were fine when she got back. *What the hell*, she thought.

"Tell his ass I'm on my way. Don't let him leave, Laci."

"A'ight, I won't. I'll see you in a minute."

After Laci hung up the phone, she once again stood in the shadows and watched as Shaunna propositioned one of the hustlers who was standing by his car, jaw-jacking with his boys.

"Hey which one of y'all wanna take me to the arcade tonight? I got some business down there, but if you do, I can treat y'all really good later on."

Laci couldn't believe her ears. Shaunna was propositioning a man to take her to meet another man. She shook her head in disgust.

Seeing Shaunna drive away with the unknown man, Laci went to the nearest pay phone and dialed an 800 number.

"DFS hotline," the lady on the other end said. "How may I help you?"

"Um, yes, there are two children alone in an apartment in Southview. It's a known crack house and people are in there."

"Do you have the exact address, ma'am?"

"Yes, I do." Laci gave them Shaunna's address and got off the phone with the worker. She hated to hotline anyone, but she felt that Shaunna's kids would be better off without her.

Laci had already tipped off Officer Jones about Monique's money laundering and selling drugs.

Hearing the sirens fill the air, Laci took off in her car to make her visit to one last SBB—Crystal. Laci wasn't one for going to a cemetery at night, but this special visit was well worth it.

On this cold November night, the grass crunched under her feet as she made her way to the headstone. Laci shined the flashlight on it and engraved was the name "Crystal Moore." Laci didn't wish death on anyone, but the way the girls had played her, resting peacefully in a grave was too good for Crystal.

Laci thought back to Crystal's immense jealousy and how it had changed her life. Her temperature began to rise and she shook with anger. Screaming at the top of her lungs, Laci doused the gravesite and tombstone with two cans of lighter fluid, then she dug in her purse and took out the plastic bag that she'd received when she and the girls went to the Gold Palace jewelry store. She took out the name-plate necklace that she'd bought, glad that the clerk understood that she meant to make another "Tonette" necklace.

Standing away from the combustible liquid, Laci lit a match. "You may be dead, bitch, but I hope you burn in hell," she said as she threw the match on the gravesite.

Instantly, a glow warmed Laci's body. The plot went up in flames and she walked away.

Laci drove to the police station and sat inside her car, waiting to see how long it would take before they brought everybody in. Within the hour, and within minutes of each other, each of the girls arrived. Officer Jones got out of his car with a battered and bruised Tonette in tow. Within seconds, two additional officers drove up with Shaunna and Monique.

"My kids, my kids!" Shaunna said repeatedly as she was pulled out of the car. "I gotta get my kids."

Laci watched as they dragged Monique out of the police car as well. She was crying profusely, as if there'd been a death in her family.

As all three girls were being led into the precinct, Laci walked away from her car. "SBBs!" she yelled. Tonette, Monique, and Shaunna looked at her.

Their faces showed a sign of hope. "We'll be out of here in a minute," Tonette barked to Officer Jones, "that's my girl right there!" She doubled over in pain from her assault.

"Damn, what happened to y'all?" Laci asked, looking at each of her so-called friends. "Ya'll look like shit."

Each of the girls began to plead her case, but Laci started laughing, and it surprised them.

"What's so funny?" Tonette growled.

"Y'all are so goddamn stupid, look at y'all. How does it feel to be played now, ladies?"

The girls looked at her in bewilderment. "Played? What the hell you mean, played?"

"You all tricked me and changed my life, but now, the joke's on you." She walked up to Tonette and spit in her face. "I hope y'all rot in jail."

Laci turned and walked to her car and drove away.

As promised, Laci called Dink and gave him the rundown.

Laci's mother was angry with her for not letting her in on her plans, but as Laci explained to her, the fewer people who knew, the better off she was. She was already under pressure and didn't need any more.

Leaving the South Bronx late Friday afternoon, Laci anticipated seeing Dink again. She had only been gone a week, but it was the longest week of her life.

CHAPTER 45

S MURF FRANTICALLY KNOCKED at his mother's door. He thought about using his key, but he didn't just in case she'd changed the locks, which in Smurf's eyes would have meant she truly wanted him gone.

Within seconds, the door flung open.

"Wayne!" she screamed. "What's wrong, baby?"

He walked in.

"Momma, I know what you doin'."

"What?" she asked.

"You fuckin' 'round with a hustler. Mama, I never thought you would stoop that low."

She shook her head and sighed. "Wayne, you don't know what you're talking about."

"I know more than what you think. You resort to this just for money?"

"Look, boy," Wayne's mother said, "You my baby and I love you and will always love you until I leave this earth, but I'm a grown woman, not a little bitch off the street. I've sacrificed a lot and I've seen a lot. I know what's up with Demond and it's not as simple as you think. I'm not leaving him alone."

"Demond? Who the fuck is Demond?"

Just then, the front door opened and there stood Dirty.

"Smurf!" Dirty said with a confused look on his face. "What are you doing here?"

"Man, what are *you* doing here?" Smurf looked at him with obvious hurt in his eyes. Dirty looked between Gloria and Smurf and his eyes became wide.

"Yes, Demond, he is," Gloria said softly. "You've been working with your son all this time."

"Son?" Smurf said as he looked at Dirty. "Momma? Wha—" Smurf was at a loss for words.

"Wayne, the Feds busted him seventeen years ago when he was sixteen. D was taken away from me and I had to track him down. Once I did find him, he refused to see me, read my letters, or allow me to visit him. Then when you were old enough to start asking questions about your dad, I tried to contact him again, but I couldn't find him. I didn't want to keep getting your hopes up, so I just tried being the best mother I could to you."

"Momma, you *are* the best momma. You don't need this nigga right here." Smurf's anger got the better of him.

"Nigga, do you know how we lived because of you? Do you know what my momma has been through because of you? Momma, you don't need this nigga!" He pointed toward Dirty. "I can give you what you need."

"Wayne, this is your father."

"Why now, man?" he looked at Dirty.

"Because I fucked up. I was a fuck-up then and I'm still one now. I loved your mother. I wanted her to move on with her life and not wait for my sorry ass. She was supposed to be with me the night I got knocked, but I'm thankful that she wasn't. The Feds were trying to take any and everybody down with me, so I promised myself that I would stay away from her for her sake. Nothing good would come to Gloria as long as she was around me. But think about what you and I have built. Don't let your temper get the best of you. I'm back now, man. Let me make it up to you. We work well together, son. The whole fuckin' state of New York is ours."

CHAPTER 46

WHEN LACI RETURNED to Boston, she knew that she would have to address everything with Dink, and she was now ready. He picked her up at the airport and immediately, upon seeing his face, she ran into his arms and cried.

"There, there," he told her, holding her close and kissing her hair. "It's all over, sweetheart." He held Laci until she calmed down and they left the airport.

Driving in silence, they made it back to their apartment. Once inside, Laci looked at Dink and walked over to him. Taking in his masculine smell, she craved him.

Without speaking, they undressed each other and made love on the living room floor, bringing about the closeness they each longed for.

Afterward, as they lay on the couch, Laci wrapped herself in Dink's arms.

"Baby, what happened between us?" Dink asked. "Everything was so perfect. I'm sorry about everything that has happened. A lot of this has to do with me."

"Everything that happened over the summer, I never really

got over it. Yes, I went to counseling, and yes, you stood by me every step of the way, but there were things that were going on with me that only I could deal with in my own time."

"Do you regret me coming here with you?"

"No, not at all. I'm glad you're here. You are too smart to be on the streets, Dink. I just wanted my space and I felt you were crowding me."

"When you told me that, I gave you your space, Laci."

"Yes, you did, but then you started up with Simone."

"Baby, there was nothing going on there."

"I know that, Dink."

He touched her chin and turned her face to look at his. "Do you really know that?"

"Yes, I know where your heart is." Laci kissed Dink.

"So why did you go off the way you did?"

"No woman wants to see her man with another woman, but Dink, I had to go back to the Bronx to take care of those girls. If I told you what I wanted to do, you would have either tried to talk me out of it or gone with me, and I had to do it on my own."

"You're right."

"But Dink, there are some things that I think you need to know."

"What's that?" he ran his fingers through her hair.

"Um, T.J. First of all, I have never slept with him. I wouldn't do that, but there's a tape that—"

"A tape of what?" Dink asked, getting angry.

"A tape of me when I was strung out. I don't know how it was made, but I'm on there, along with Dame and Quita."

"How did T.J. get the tape?"

"I don't know, but he has it. He wanted me to sleep with him or he was going to show you."

"Why didn't you tell me about this when it happened?"

"I couldn't, Dink. When I saw the tape, I was horrified. It was rape and it was on tape. You and I were trying to build a relationship, and a tape of me being raped is out there for anyone to see. You wouldn't look at me the same, Dink, trust me. I didn't look at myself the same." Laci had tears welling up in her eyes. "It was degrading and I didn't want to embarrass you. Even though you and Simone were just friends, it would have driven you right into her arms."

She looked at Dink with tears in her eyes. "But there's something else you should know, too."

Dink sighed, "What's that?"

"That I'm pregnant."

"What? How?"

"Obviously sometime when I was tweakin'."

"Who's baby is it, Laci?"

"Dink, I don't know. I really don't know," Laci answered honestly.

"Damn." Dink moved his arms from around Laci and got up off the sofa. "You can't have that baby, Laci," Dink demanded.

"Dink, I know there are a hundred reasons why I should get rid of this child, but deep down I just don't think that I can."

"You want it? Laci, it's a fuckin' crack baby!"

"True, but I was a crackhead and I'm able to face my demons and suffer the consequences of my actions."

"Man," Dink said and rubbed his hand across his forehead.

"Dink, I'll make this easy for you." Laci got off of the couch and stood up. "I don't expect you to stay around and I'll understand if you don't; I don't want you to stay around out of obligation. I'm a big girl now."

"So, are you trying to break up with me, Laci?"

"I don't know, Dink. Everything is just so confusing right now. Just time apart and a fresh start, I guess. Drugs brought us together, Dink, but we don't have anything keeping us together now. We tried to make it work, but it just got too hard."

"If that's what you need, Laci, I can't do anything but honor your request." He knew what that meant—they were over. "But I promise to be around if you ever need me."

"I know you will."

EPILOGUE

TONETTE WAS BOOKED on multiple charges ranging from possession of controlled substances to theft. On their many shopping sprees, Laci had filled out credit applications in Tonette's name and every time she was denied, she stole the merchandise. She was also charged with the intent to sell narcotics. Monique turned the tables on Tonette as well, when she learned what was in the packages that she took to the post office. Tonette was also charged with abuse.

Shaunna was booked on possession, child abandonment, child endangerment, and neglect, and as a result, her children were placed in protective custody and she lost parental rights.

Monique was charged with intent to distribute drugs through the postal service and receiving stolen merchandise. When they raided the post office, they found packets of ice and crack rock in a box wrapped in brown paper, unlabeled. In the other box, with her name on it, was $5,000 in cash.

In prison, each of the girls ran into someone they had done wrong either on the streets or as South Bronx Bitches. Trying to be cool with them, the girls quickly learned that payback was a bitch and they would receive their just rewards.

Tonette was raped and beaten every night by the male wardens. Monique ran into girls who she dogged because Tonette hated them. The all-female clique now preferred pussy over dick and made Monique their bitch every chance they could.

Shaunna, already feeling like a failure as a mother, learned of the underground drugs that floated freely in the system. Having never done anything harder than weed, Shaunna got her hands on the first thing she could, but the dosing proved to be lethal.

With Laci's part in bringing down the girls who'd played her, the dossier that would have been used as evidence against Dink now had information pertaining to the South Bronx Bitches. The bank accounts and all street activity registered back to Tonette. When the girls went down, Officer Jones replaced the dossier that his colleague had with one of his own. The original dossier was burned, and no trace of drug activity would be traced back to Dink, Smurf, or Dirty.

Wayne and Dirty pledged to strengthen their bond as father and son on the streets. Dirty wanted to make up the seventeen years of time that he'd lost with his only son and the woman he loved.

Laci enrolled in counseling, because she'd never fully healed from ending up on the streets trading sex for a hit. She was still angry and hurt by her so-called friends and she needed more time to recover from the trauma of addiction. She took a semester off from school, and with every day that passed, her emotional life came closer to getting back on track.

Laci decided to carry her unborn child to term. It was something she had to do. Tonette and the South Bronx Bitches had changed Laci's life by making the decision to take her life away, her innocence, but who was she to make that decision for the innocent life inside her?

ACKNOWLEDGMENTS

First and foremost to Vickie Stringer for believing in me. Without your help in bringing the reality of addiction to literature, the story would never have been told. Because of you, people were able to identify with the harsh and nasty reality of addictions and seek help. Let's reach more with this one.

Mia McPherson and the Triple Crown staff. Danielle Ferneau and Raegan Johnson for editorial guidance and support. Without your vision and ability to push me that extra mile, I don't know where I would be.

My boys, Marlon McCaulsky, Quentin Carter, and Leo Sullivan. You three truly inspire me.

A special thank you goes out to Shirell Watson, who read every draft, never got tired of talking about Laci, and gave me serious constructive criticism and support. You encouraged me when I wanted to give up and for that, I truly thank you.

A special thank you goes out to my dear friend James Jones. Thank you for all of your support, input, and enthusiasm to finally see this work come to fruition. You have no idea of how much it means to me.

Last but not least...to all of my readers. Without you, I would be nothing.

Printed in the United States
By Bookmasters